Don't Blame Me

The Convict Chronicles

To Melissia,

Stay Blessed,

Jonathan Queen

By
Jonathan Z. Queen

ASKARI
Publishing

Don't Blame Me; The Convict Chronicles

Copyright © 2005, 2007 Jonathan Z. Queen. All rights reserved

First printed by Authorhouse 5/27/2007

ISBN:
0-9773347-0-8

For information address:

Asikari Publishing
P.O. Box 478
Lexington, VA 24450
1-888-438-4860

WWW.ASIKARIPUBLISHING.COM

WWW.MYSPACE.COM/ASIKARI_PUBLISHING

DEDICATION

For my children, who are my proof that even in my era of ignorance and self-destruction, God blessed me. I love you all so much and I appreciate your patience. Daddy will be home soon.

And for Lenia, who I call Forever …because that is my promise to you. Thank you for always believing in me. Quitting is not an option!

Note from the Author

First and foremost, I thank you for purchasing my book. I am not one of those writers who write simply for the art of it; I write because I have something I want to share and I value every single person who takes the time to read my work.

This book is a compilation of short stories that I wrote during the last 3 years of my prison term. It was written during a time when I was extremely focused on doing the right things to prepare myself to return to society as a benefit and a blessing instead of the menace I was prior to going in.

With that said, I write this note to warn you that, although, each story in here has a sincere message of hope and redemption some of the stories are written from the point of view of America's lost generation.

In particular, **By the Sword** uses the obscene and vulgar language most prevalent behind prison walls. The story illustrates the desensitized and callous mentality of a young man raised by the streets who has no regard for human life, including his own. It is the most difficult story I've ever written not because I no longer curse or use the N-word myself, but because everyday, I saw and heard hundreds of young black males to model this character after.

Yes, the language is offensive and I wrote it so that you as the reader can share in the same outrage I felt daily. I offer you a peak into the mind of preventable madness while introducing the possibility of hope through the other protagonist, Malik, who, now reformed, spent his youth as "an animal with a hardened heart" as well.

So, I invite you to read **By the Sword** as well as the other stories and if you find yourself offended, outraged, and angry... Good! Now do something about it.

Peace, Hope and Love,

Jonathan Z. Queen

Table of Contents

Suffer the Little Ones...
(A Father's Pain)

A piece of me is dying inside.
Butterflies with clipped wings
Crawl across my heart slowly
Like the caterpillars they once were.
Lightening bugs fly around my conscience,
No longer flashing in illuminated splendor,
But winking an opaque dimness reminding me that,
A piece of me is dying inside.
I miss my children.

I'm a 6-foot Rose growing from the sand of my homeland
It hasn't rained in seven years and
I'm struggling to still stand.
I look towards the horizon, pass the heavy gray clouds that promise
the long awaited showers.
I'm looking for my children,
'cause a piece of me is dying inside.
I cry unheard whispers into apathetic oceans.
They wash up on deserted memories where they grow, confused,
clinging to the hope of tomorrow.
I miss my children.

In my pursuit to provide perfection for my peoples,
I turned off the path of righteousness and ended up on a lonely road
littered with potholes and lost souls, who ... miss their children too.
I live around the corner from misery and one floor up from hell
And it's hard to keep my head up being a 6-foot rose in a 5-foot cell.
A piece of me is dying inside.

So I place in your care this open-heart plea, this sincere soliloquy.
My warmest respect to you, the Woman, the Mother.

I won't even pretend that I can relate to the 9-month epic you
endured or the infinite bond you've made that gives you the strength
and dedication to give up without hesitation, your life for theirs.
I mean you go through the worst, give birth and then nurse, just so
they can look like me and say 'Da-Da' first.
But, you're the lucky one.
They will always run to you.
I just want them to know they can run to me, too.
Can you understand why a piece of me is dying inside?
I miss my children.

And I dedicate this half-written half-cried psalm to you, my most
beautiful creations.
You carry the best part of my soul.
Your laughter sounds like rainbows exploding and though
I must apologize to you a thousand times, your smiles let me know
that you'll forgive me a thousand and one.
If I could,
I'd put y'all on my shoulders and carry you until hurt and pain were
just words in a book of days long gone.
You are my reason for walking away from a fight and my rationale for
preparing for war.
A piece of me is dying inside, slowly withering this 6-foot rose and I
can only become whole again when we become whole again.
I miss you!

My Eve

She was even more beautiful in person. I had been looking at this woman in paintings and pencil sketches for three years. To see her in the flesh was enough to make me hold my breath and confirm my belief in miracles.

Her name was Evelyn Barnes. Her father called her Eve. Rodney Barnes, who everyone called Mr. Slim, was my cellmate. He was an artist, a teacher, and the closest thing to a father I've ever had. He was also a convicted murderer; serving a life sentence without the possibility of parole.

A bank robbery that went bad, and *I didn't shoot first,* was all he would say about his case.

It didn't matter to me. It happened 20 years ago and I don't know what kind of man he was back then, but it was obvious he had changed for the better.

I was 19 years old when I came in. It was my first bid and I was a little scared. I was sentenced to five years for gun possession. To me that was a lot of time; however, throughout transit I kept hearing that I was a 'short timer.' The other convicts said my sentence was sweet, and I guess it was, compared to the 15, 20, and 30 year stretches most of them had to do.

I was in transit for three months. I experienced six different holdover jails, each one worse than the one before. I shared two-man cells with five and six men, watched rats congregate less than 12 inches away from my face and saw a man get stabbed in his throat over a cigarette.

When I finally got here, I was exhausted. I hadn't slept well, showered with real soap, nor eaten a decent meal the whole time. I walked into this cell and barely noticed Mr. Slim sitting at the desk drawing. I gave him a half-hearted hello, climbed on the top bunk and fell into a dead sleep.

I woke up six hours later to the sounds of soft jazz filling the room. I rubbed the sleep from my eyes and noticed all of the pictures and paintings. To say they were only beautiful would not be fair. They were extraordinary. For a while, I sat there, staring at life-like sunsets, African children dancing, clocks with numbers falling into a boiling sea, and naked couples entwined into one. I was amazed. There was no way you could have convinced me I was in an eight-by-twelve-foot jail cell.

I climbed down to get a closer look at the pencil sketch leaning against the desk. It was a picture of a little girl, about four years old, swinging on a playground swing. As the swing went higher, it showed the little girl growing older and then jumping from the swing as a beautiful young woman. She seemed to be smiling directly at me or whoever was lucky enough to witness such magic created by a simple pencil.

Mr. Slim walked in carrying two bowls of food that smelled like heaven dipped in curry powder.

"I see you done 'rose from the dead," he said with a big smile. He set the bowls down and shook my hand. "Rodney Barnes, but everyone calls me Slim."

"I'm Rashad. Rashad Green," I replied, trying to match his firm grip. "It's nice to meet you, Mr. Slim." I looked around, about to comment on all the beautiful artwork, when I noticed how clean and orderly everything was compared to my messy bunk. "Aw, man, my bad. Let me get up here and make this bed."

"Don't sweat it, youngen. I know you just went through hell on a slow boat. You can take care of that later." He pointed to my locker, where there was a new pair of shower shoes, a bar of Dove soap, lotion, shampoo, deodorant, toothpaste and a toothbrush. "Your property won't be here until the end of the week and these people here will probably wait until next week to give it to you," he said with a 'you know how it is' sigh. "Go 'head and get yourself together. If you need anything else, just let me know and I got you."

"I appreciate it," I said with sincere gratitude. "I feel like a serious viking and I'm going to introduce myself to the shower right now."

"Do your thing, youngen, the shower is right down the hall. When you come back, this bowl is for you," he set the bowl on my locker. "I let you sleep through dinner, but one of my homies hooked us up some curried-chicken and rice."

I could only nod as I felt the butterflies that had been living in my stomach ever since Judge Goldman banged his gavel and said, "60 months in a Federal Correctional Institution," slowly fly away. For some reason the kindness of this old man made me feel like everything was going to be all right.

"Thanks a lot, Mr. Slim."

"It's nothing," he shrugged it off and then started to leave. He opened the door, turned back around and looked at me earnestly. "I noticed you looking at my Eve when I came in," he glanced over at the little girl on the swing. "That's my daughter. I haven't seen her in over 14 years. Today, right after you came in, the officer passed out the mail and I got a letter from her."

Mr. Slim smiled like a little boy and some of the sadness disappeared from his eyes. He pulled the small envelope from his back pocket and held it up like a Bible. "She hasn't wrote me in six years youngen," he pulled the letter out like a child opening his first Christmas present.

"Listen to what it says," he said and then began reading. "I'm sorry it's been awhile since I wrote to you Dad. I really do miss you," he looked at me to make sure I understood, then continued reading. "I'm only two hours away from you and I'm off on the weekends. I was thinking I could come see you one of these Saturdays."

He folded the letter and put it back in his pocket. Then he laughed. It was one of those musical laughs that start way down deep in the stomach.

"So you see, youngen, I should be thanking you," he said through his laughter. "Even though you came in here looking like a wet food stamp, you brought a rainbow in behind you." He laughed again and I couldn't help but laugh with him.

"Take care of your business and we'll talk later," he said as he stepped out.

I glanced at his *Eve*, jumping off the swing and smiling like the world was her playground. I smiled back at her and headed for the shower.

That was over three years ago. Mr. Slim and I have developed an incredibly close bond. We've won three straight basketball championships with him coaching and me playing the point. He helped me get my G.E.D and a job in the barber-shop. I, in turn, started helping him sell his artwork out on the streets, promoting his paintings through my family and friends. He introduced me to jazz music and old-school R&B and I put him down with the latest hip-hop.

One night, during a food strike lock-down, he opened up and told me about the bank robbery that cost him his freedom and took the life of a 25-year-old security guard.

"Me and my crew were professionals," Mr. Slim began in a monotone voice that hid his emotion. "Thirteen banks in nine months. Three minutes, in and out. We were good. The Feds had been called in after the fifth bank and they were clueless," he shook his head as he thought back.

"It was a small independent Bank & Trust that sat on the corner of a one-way street and had only one security guard. It was basically a piece of cake for us, but for some reason, the job didn't feel right to me from the beginning."

"My Eve was only six at the time and she had the chicken-pox. My wife begged me to stay home. But I did what I usually did back then; I snorted some heroin, disregarded my intuition and went to handle my business."

Mr. Slim stared through me with glassy eyes. The vein in his temple jumped, he closed his eyes and breathed deep. When he opened his eyes, he wasn't the same Mr. Slim.

"Everybody get the fuck down and don't move!" he shouted as if reliving the experience. "My cousin Smokey came in behind me and hit the guard with the butt of his 12-gauge, knocking him to the floor unconscious. What none of us knew was the guard he had knocked out was a rookie being trained by Smitty— the regular guard, who was in the back with his gun drawn, ready. He had just been accepted into the Police Academy and couldn't think of a better way to end his security guard career than as a hero."

"Two minutes!" Mr. Slim shouted again, spittle flying from his mouth. He stared at the ceiling and sighed heavily. "I saw him, Rashad. Out of the corner of my eye, I saw him, sliding in slowly; he had his gun aimed at Bart, who was bent over the counter scooping money into the bag.

"Bart! I yelled and the world went silent. I didn't hear a thing. I saw the flash of fire and felt the blood splash on my face," Mr. Slim spoke with his jaw clenched. "It felt like ... like fire, burning me from the inside out. Half my body went numb as I slid down the wall. I tried to call—"

"You got shot?" I interrupted him, my voice a higher octave than usual. We'd been cellies for over a year and that was the first time he ever mentioned being shot.

He nodded slowly and pulled down the collar of his tee shirt, revealing a quarter sized bullet wound that stained the crease of his collarbone.

"I tried to call Bart," he continued. I heard a tremble in his tone that captivated and scared me at the same time. "I looked up and Smitty was still aiming his gun at me. Call it reflex or self-preservation, but I shot before he could shoot again. He died right there in front of me. Looking into my eyes as he coughed out his last breath."

Mr. Slim stood up and looked out the window. He stood there for a few minutes watching a bird search for crumbs in the empty courtyard. He turned to me and said, "Some people say I did what I had to do. No. I didn't do what I should have done. I should have stayed home with my wife and my sick little girl." He shook his head and sighed, "Yeah, if I would've done that, Smitty would still be alive. And in so many ways, so would I."

In the 20 years Mr. Slim has been incarcerated, he has grown from rebellion and defiance, to repentance and benevolence. He is a kind, caring, and very respected man. But after spending two decades behind walls and barbed-wire fences, he is also very institutionalized.

For the past three years, Mr. Slim has faithfully spent every Saturday morning getting ready for a visit with his daughter. He wakes up at five a.m. and has a cup of coffee. He works out in the gym from six until seven. He then showers, shaves, and pulls out his visit uniform; freshly pressed the night before.

By the time I wake up to get ready for work, Mr. Slim is fully dressed, sitting at the desk reading, and occasionally looking out the window, which looks down onto the visiting room courtyard. Every

Saturday for the last three years, Mr. Slim has followed that same routine, and not once has his daughter shown up.

I can't help but blame myself. The letter from his daughter came minutes after me and it's like I gave him some type of false hope. There's even a quiet joke around the compound, where instead of saying something will never happen, a person will say, 'Yeah, that'll happen when Mr. Slim gets that visit.'

Nobody says that in front of him. Mr. Slim is a humble man now, but his reputation from his days at Lewisburg Penitentiary still gives chills. He also has a lot of men who would go to war for him, myself being one of them.

Today started out like every Saturday before it. I woke up to the sounds of little kids laughing and running around the outside patio of the visiting room. The late August humidity was on full blast. Mr. Slim was sitting at the desk in his creased khakis and tee shirt. His khaki shirt was draped over the back of the chair.

"Good morning, old timer," I said as I climbed out of bed. "You're looking like a million dollars."

"You know me, so fresh and so clean," he smiled faintly as he quoted from his favorite Outkast song.

I headed to the shower, knowing that was all we'd say to each other until after three p.m. when visits were terminated. Until then, Mr. Slim would be at that window, watching, waiting, every now and then a tear trying desperately to escape his sad eyes. I'd be in the barber shop silently praying for the crackle of the intercom to be followed by, 'Inmate Rodney Barnes. You have a visit.'

As usual, there was no such luck. After lunch, I saw Mr. Slim on his way to the Rec yard. The A-league softball championship was at one o'clock and Mr. Slim was the only man both teams trusted to umpire home plate. Mr. Slim rarely broke his visit vigil. Last year, the Recreation Department actually rescheduled a basketball championship from day to evening due to his Saturday-seclusion.

I suspected someone either begged him to come out and call the game, or even worse, he had given up on his daughter coming to see him. He gave me thumbs up as he strolled past the barbershop window and headed down the walkway with a crowd of eager softball fans behind him.

I got off work at 12:30 p.m. I took a quick shower and was getting ready to go to the game. I had just tied my sneakers when I heard someone from the courtyard calling in a loud whisper, "Mr. Slim! Mr. Slim!"

I looked down and scanned the crowded patio, my eyes finally landing on Bo-Bo, a young cat from Ohio who stayed down the hall from us. It was against the rules to talk with inmates inside while you were on your visit, so Bo-Bo was staring straight ahead while sitting at a table directly beneath my window.

"Mr. Slim," he called a little louder.

"He's not up here Bo-Bo," I answered him. "He's out calling the game. What's up?"

"Hey, Green," he spoke low and fast. "I think I just saw Mr. Slim's daughter come in. She looked like she was crying and went straight to the bathroom."

"You sure?" I asked doubtfully, "I didn't hear them call him."

"I'm not a hundred percent, but she looks just like the girl in his paintings."

"You said she was crying? For what?" I questioned.

"Man, look out here," he said impatiently. "It's packed, and they're having problems with the metal detector again. My wife said they actually made her take the bobby pins out of her hair. It took her two hours to get processed and she was hot. My wife is used to the drama, but imagine someone having to deal with this madness for the first time."

Before I could answer him, the world around me ground to a dream-like, slow-motion-kind of moment.

The intercom beeped and just as C.O. Stephens announced, "Rodney Barnes, visit!" Evelyn Barnes strolled through the visiting room door into the courtyard. The sun pushed through the clouds and bathed the entire patio in a warm and brilliant light. Eve brushed a strand of hair from in front of her eye and searched for an empty seat.

"It is her," I whispered to myself. Then it dawned on me that Mr. Slim wouldn't be able to hear them calling him. Only one of the yard speakers worked and the game would surely drown it out.

I sprinted down the hall and took the corridor steps two at a time. I raced past the kitchen, barely noticing the greasy smell of French fries filling the air. I turned down the west end hallway that leads to the yard, only to be greeted by Correctional Officer Diggs and Lieutenant Fulton closing the gate.

"Report back to your unit Green," C.O. Diggs was out of breath, having just run himself. "We're closing the compound."

"But why? I have to tell my cellie that he—"

"You heard the officer," Lt. Fulton spoke harshly. "Compound's closed. Now report back to your housing area."

Lieutenant Fulton was one of those by-the-book officers, so I knew it'd be fruitless to argue with him. Over his shoulder, I could see a few inmates coming up from the yard. Mr. Slim's pinochle partner, Patrick Thomas was among them.

"Yo, Pat!" I yelled, "Go tell Mr. Slim he has a visit."

Pat looked at me with a smile of disbelief and waved me off as if to say, "stop playing." The look on my face must have convinced him it wasn't a game. "Are you serious?" he asked me and took off before I could answer him.

"Was that Barnes they called a minute ago?" Lt. Fulton asked C.O. Diggs, who shrugged his shoulders.

"It was," I interjected. "And Lieutenant you know how long he's been waiting for this visit."

"Green, why are you still here? I'm giving you a direct order to go back to your room. You gentlemen there," he addressed the crew that was with Pat. "You'll have to return to the yard until the lockdown is lifted."

"Lieutenant Fulton," I persisted. "Can't you radio the yard and get Mr. Slim—"

"You must not hear well," C.O. Diggs said forcefully. "Either that, or you must want me to write you up."

"I don't care if you write me up!" I screamed at him. "Just get my cellie to his visit!"

C.O. Diggs started to unlock the gate, clearly determined to lock me up. Lt. Fulton put a restraining hand on his arm.

"Get to your room, Green. I'll see what I can do," he said evenly.

I rushed back to my room and went straight to the window. My eyes combed the courtyard anxiously, but I didn't see Eve anywhere. I looked down to ask Bo-Bo where she went and that's when I saw her, sitting at the table where Bo-Bo had been earlier.

She was wearing a pair of loose jeans and a tee shirt with Tweety Bird on the front. She wore her hair in a stylish bob that framed her heart-shaped face. She had on little or no make up and was absolutely gorgeous.

I felt my heart skip when I saw her smile at a little boy who approached her and offered some of his potato chips. It was the smile from the pictures; intense and inviting at the same time. But when the child walked away, her smile faded and her expression became despondent. She checked her watch and shook her head in frustration.

My alarm clock read one fifteen. There was no telling how long she'd been waiting. From the way she was looking around, it didn't seem like she'd wait much longer.

"Eve," I whispered out the window, not really knowing what to say, but sensing I had to say something.

She lifted her head and said, "Yes?" Her expression was a mix of curiosity and sadness.

"Uh," I stammered. "Your father, uh, he should be on his way."

"Who is that?" She turned all the way around in her seat and asked with an attitude.

"No. Don't look up here," I responded quickly. "You can't let the guards see you talking to me."

She turned back around and let out a sarcastic laugh, "My God. This place is horrible. So many rules, how do you stand it?"

"Uh, I guess we get used to it," I answered lamely.

"Well, I could never get used to this," she waved her hands to include everything. She looked at her watch again. "Actually, I don't think I can go through with this." She stood up.

"Eve, wait. Please, don't leave. Your father would love to see you. It would mean—"

"How do you know," she interrupted. "You still haven't told me who you are."

"I'm his cellie and I can tell you—"

"Oh, so you're Rashad," she said knowingly and sat back down. She must have been able to hear my mouth hanging open. "No, I'm not psychic," she laughed. "Rodney talks about you in some of his letters. He cares about you a lot."

Rodney? It took a second for me to register she was calling her father by his first name.

"He cares about you, too. I mean, he talks about you all the time."

"Does he know I'm here, Rashad? I've been here for a few hours and if he doesn't want to see me, then I can—"

"Doesn't want to see you?" I almost laughed out loud. "Eve, you are probably the only reason Mr. Slim still knows how to smile. And he would already be out there, but the jail is locked down and he's stuck outside. He should be coming any minute now."

"Well, I'm going to give him a few more minutes, then I'm out of here." She crossed her arms, closed her eyes and chewed on her bottom lip. It was a sexy look, but her attitude made me too upset to see it as such.

"What's wrong with you?" I countered; my attitude just as obvious.

"What's wrong with me?!" She shook her head the same way Mr. Slim does when he's trying to explain something he considers simple. "I'll tell you what's wrong with me. For the last two years, I've received letters from Rodney. I don't write him back, yet every Wednesday, like clock work, I get a letter from him. Letters about when I was a baby, letters about how him and my mom fell in love, letters about this place, letters about you, and all of them end the same way; 'I hope to see you Saturday,' like he's trying to make me feel guilty or something.

"When I finally get up the nerve to come see him, I have to wait 45 minutes in line just to get turned away at the door because the sundress I was wearing didn't have sleeves. I go to the store down the road and buy something else to wear, only to come back and wait an hour while they count the inmates. Then, another 45 minutes to get through the metal detector. I finally make it inside and lo and behold, he has me waiting as well." She took a deep breath and went on. "That's the story of my life; waiting for a father who is never going to come." She sucked her teeth, stood up, and grabbed her little change purse. "I'm getting the hell out of here."

"Go 'head then," I said over the lump in my throat. She had every right to walk away, but I didn't want to admit that, to her, or to myself. "You came all this way just to walk away without accomplishing anything. You're giving up before you even start, and you couldn't have gotten that from your father, 'cause Mr. Slim doesn't give up on anything or anyone."

"He gave up on me!" she shouted while looking up at the window, no longer concerned if the guards could see her or not. "You don't know anything about me. I don't know why I'm even arguing with you about it." She turned and started away.

"That's right, run away, Eve," I was shouting now myself. "When I first saw you, I could tell you were just a spoiled little girl."

She turned back around and squinted her eyes up at the window, trying her best to see me through the glare. "Spoiled?" she hissed. "Spoiled how? By who?" she asked as she walked back towards the table. Bo-Bo, his wife, and just about everyone out there halted their conversations. They tried to seem indifferent, but it was obvious her outburst had captured their full attention.

"Spoiled by who Rashad?" She stared up at my window with her hands on her hips. "After Rodney went to jail, it was just me, my mom, welfare, efficiency apartments, and food stamps. And, oh yeah, the visits. Visits to see Rodney in different jails everywhere. Do you realize how many things I had to go without so we could use the money to visit him?

"Then, a divorce I knew nothing about. All of a sudden no more visits. When I turned 13, my mom was so caught up with her new boyfriend she didn't have time for me. And how could I be mad? After watching her give seven years to a man who was never coming home. Seven years of disappointing appeals, seven years of forcing herself to stay optimistic, wearing a smile so phony it hurt her face; seven years of crying herself to sleep. How could I be mad at her? She deserved some happiness!" Eve screamed as tears streamed down her face.

"That boyfriend became my stepfather. He never liked me because he knew I couldn't stand him. Tell me Rashad, who spoiled me?" She was breathing hard and looked drained. I didn't know what to say or do. I honestly considered walking away from the window and pretending none of this was happening.

Stan, the visiting room photographer, came outside and announced; "Last call for photos!"

I glanced over at the clock, it was almost two. Before I turned back to the window, I noticed the portrait of Stevie Wonder that Mr. Slim had been working on the night before. I felt a chill run through my entire body.

The song! The thought struck like lightning. There was a Stevie Wonder song that Mr. Slim used to sing to her when she was little. But what was it?

I looked at Eve and mentally scanned all the Stevie Wonder songs I knew. She wiped her face with some napkins a little girl gave to her. I watched her nod her head and smile as the little girl implored her to stop crying.

"Eve," I called to her. "Your father loves you, He didn't come to jail on purpose and he really does regret what happened." I was telling the truth, but the panic in my voice probably betrayed the fact that I was stalling.

Ribbon in the Sky? No. *I Just Called to Say I Love You?* No. *These Three Words?* No. Damn! It has a baby crying in the beginning.

"Rashad," Eve spoke in a defeated, but calm voice. "I appreciate what you're trying to do and I see why Rodney loves you."

That Girl? No. *You and I?* No.

"Please tell Rodney," she swallowed hard and closed her eyes to hold off the tears. "Tell my father I love him too, but I can't do this."

Overjoyed? No. *Lately?* No. *Isn't She Lovely?* No. Yes! *Isn't She Lovely*, that's it!

I saw her walking away and even though I don't consider myself a singer, I do know how to hold a note, and so I sang. My eyes closed, head back, I sang like I was in concert.

"Isn't she love–lee, isn't she won–der–ful," I could tell she had stopped even without looking, "Isn't she prec-ious, mmm, mmmm, mmm, mmmm, hmm."

I heard her giggle as I forgot some of the words.

"I never thought, through love we'd be, making one as lovely as she. Isn't she love-lee, made from love."

I wasn't sure if all the words were right, but I was blowing like it didn't matter.

"Isn't she love–lee" Bo-Bo sang with me, his voice a smooth baritone.

"Isn't she won-der-ful," his wife and about four others joined in.

"Isn't she prec-ious?" Almost everyone in the courtyard was singing now. "Less than one min-ute old."

Eve stood there with her hands covering her mouth, laughing and crying at the same time. A few inmates were standing at their seats as they sang. Children ran around yelling, trying to join in the excitement.

C.O. Daniels came to the door to see what all the commotion was and after waving her hands to signal those standing to sit back down, she shook her head and returned to her desk.

"But isn't she love-lee, made from LOVE!" we all screamed as we tried to hold the last note longer than our talent would allow.

I don't know if she was overwhelmed or embarrassed, but when everyone stopped singing, Eve's smile faded. She gave a final look towards my window, turned around and opened the door to leave.

Mr. Slim was there. He stood in the doorway with a hesitant smile, staring into the tear-filled eyes of his only child. He had a bit of infield dust on his shoes and pant cuffs, but other than that, he looked good.

"Look at my Eve," he said more to himself than to her. He reached forward and brushed away one of her tears with the heel of his thumb.

It was a small reflex to him, but for Eve it brought back the clearest memories she had of him. She recalled the visits they had shared when she was a child; that no matter how hard she tried not to, she always ended up crying at the end of them. She remembered her father holding her face in his big, strong hands and using only the side of his thumbs to wipe all the tears from her face.

That gesture, added to hearing their song sung to her by a bunch of strangers was too much for Eve. She collapsed into Mr. Slim's arms and cried hard. She cried like a lost child who had finally made it home.

Mr. Slim guided her to a table where they sat together, talking and staring at each other. They only had an hour together, but somehow that hour showed them enough respect to crawl by in seconds.

At three o'clock, when C.O. Daniels told them visiting hours were over, they were the only ones still outside. They stood up and held hands as they walked to the door.

"I'm sorry you had to wait so long," Mr. Slim apologized.

"I'm sorry for making you wait so long, too," Eve replied as they approached the door. "I saw a hotel down the road," she went on. "I was thinking that maybe I could get a room for the night and come back tomorrow."

Mr. Slim nodded his head and smiled brightly, "I would love that Eve, and I promise I'll be ready."

"You better be," she punched his arm lightly.

Mr. Slim held the door open for her and before she walked through, she looked over her shoulder and yelled, "Goodbye, Rashad!"

Mr. Slim looked up to the window, his eyebrows bent in curiosity. "Youngen, you see my Eve?" he shouted proudly.

I gave them a slight wave and watched them go inside. I offered a quick prayer that she'd make it back and that maybe, one day, with Mr. Slim's blessing, I too, would have a chance to call her … My Eve!

Next

(A spoken word performance piece)

Setting -   (Center Stage is set up as a hospital waiting area in a
            Correctional Institution.
            Five men wearing prison uniforms sit in a row of chairs
            facing the audience. A young, black nurse stands behind
            them in the doorway of an office/exam room holding a
            clipboard while speaking on the phone.)

MEN -   (Speaking all together) Five inmates enter. Nervous, scared
            and unsure.
            On a call-out to receive our test results from the week
            before.
            An overworked nurse who believes she's still alone, her
            office door wide open, she speaks loudly on the phone.
            Sitting there waiting we all here her say,

NURSE-   I need someone from Psychology to come right away.
            One of these men has tested positive for HIV.

MEN-   We locked eyes with one another, all thinking the same
            thing;
            DAMN! It could be me.

(Lights out, Spotlight on first man. He stands up and steps forward. As each man speaks, the spotlight changes colors to match their moods.

Optional- Music and/or still pictures flash on a big screen behind the Men as they recite their pieces. i.e. behind the junkie we see slides of Marines in action, a medal, a chapel, a crack house, etc. Behind the rapper we see shots of cheering crowds, project buildings, new cars, champagne, VIP rooms, hotel suites, etc ...

The Junkie- Sssssss! Water, baking soda and cocaine congregate in a metal spoon, Seven matches struck at once. Liquid becomes solid, a tiny rock forms, more beautiful than a baby being born. Sssss! My favorite sound, similar to the strings of a symphony or the angelic voices of a mass choir, but it's the sizzling sound of a crack rock met with fire. Ssssssss! The pungent odor alone gives me a hint of heaven, that rock is my God, getting high is my religion and I'm a devoted disciple who worships daily. Even now, knowing that I might have AIDS, I got a 20 piece stashed in my sock and can't wait to give praise, cause even though it could be me, I'm not afraid. I was a Marine at 18. I've traveled the world and slow-danced with death often. I've tasted opium in Okinawa, took turns with ten- dollar-tricks in Thailand, prostitutes in the Philippines, had a close call in Kosovo, four tours through Desert Storm. I got my leg and lower back seared with shrapnel, sent home with a limp and an unnamed medal. I served my country well and came back to a hell where my mental was more miserable than my physical until I met and fell in love with an Angel. Her touch, softer than the wings of a butterfly, her kiss, like a granted wish, her smile became my high. A small wedding, a steady nine- to-five, a used car, a one-bedroom flat that eventually felt like four walls closing in on my insufficient existence. My war wounds throbbing with persistence, I popped painkillers like candy, but my tolerance outgrew my resistance. I slept in cold sweats and would get feverish chills. I snorted cocaine through rolled up dollar bills and still felt empty, inadequate, unsatisfied with life. I was looking for that hard-core, heart-stopping hype, a rush that can only come from a rock and a pipe. Sssssss! Crack became my mistress and when my Mrs. complained that she missed 'us', I convinced her to meet me and my other lover in a demeaning ménage à trois. Ssssss! The sticky smoke stung her virgin lungs and sent scintillating shock waves to the synapses of her cerebrum, she knew after only one pull that she was in love too. She looked at me through new eyes, wide, silver-dollar-sized, I told her she was now baptized. We became a team, missionary fiends, determined to get high by any means. Our cravings eradicated our savings and our jobs were sacrificed on the alter of our addiction. Crack-rock-religion. Sssss! We went from smoking on the weekends all by ourselves to frequenting the corner crack- house and then roaming the streets when our money ran out. We sold the car. The phone and cable were cut off, the rent was neglected. We smoked a half ounce to celebrate my wife being pregnant. We both made an oath to quit once the baby was born. In the meantime I'd be the man and make sure we maintained our habit; I approached heavy-set hustlers, asked to see a bag and grabbed it, ran like a rabbit, raced home, fell into my wife's arms out of breath. She hugged me like she was proud, teased me, called me Speedy. When she caught me holding out on extra rocks, she cried and called me greedy. Sssssss! We went from bad to worse. Friends and family forsook us, tired of being our victims. Whatever we borrowed we sold, what they wouldn't give, we stole. Our desire became desperation, our self-respect turned numb, crawling on our hands and knees searching the carpet for one crumb. No income, it was hard to get by. Some days we sat in silence, wishing we were high. We cooked up plots that would lead to us cooking up rocks. At night we walked, waiting for a way to give worship. A dark alley ... a dealer no older than seventeen, his baggy jeans down to his knees, his eyes closed in ecstasy … my wife … her face buried in his crotch … bobbing up and down … slurping sounds … I stood and kept watch. My beautiful angel selling sex to get us set, she became a "crack whore" and I, the reluctant pimp. Sssssss! Sssss! We had to stay hyped to keep from facing the reality of our lives. My soul had already died; I watched it drift away on a wisp of smoke. I couldn't cope and I'd forgotten the feeling of hope … until my wife's water broke. An eight-hour labor, a baby born premature, his tiny heart barely beating, his top lip missing, just … a hole beneath his nose. His under-developed lungs let out a shallow cry, an urgent call for the drug his mother and I loved. My first son … a 'crack baby.' I hung my head and cried, the doctors said he had a 50/50 chance to survive, my wife kept a vigil at his side. For three months we prayed that our innocent baby would be saved. And by God's grace … he was. His pre-natal addiction was curbed and his cleft closed into a sickle-shaped scar. He gained five pounds and started holding his head on his own, trying to act grown. My wife spent 30 days in a Rehab and they allowed us to take him home. I became a father. My baby boy, my pride and joy. His crooked smile, his baby smell, his small patch of hair and his soul-searching stare somehow reawakened my spirit and sparked my inner-man, made me whole again, helped me recognize my responsibility, providing for my family— my number one priority. I worked hard all day and held my two babies at night. My wife laid in my left arm, my son laid in my right. Everything was all right, and then … Sssss! I started stressing, regressing, I went back to the corner for confession and spent my entire paycheck on a few bagged-up blessings, that I shared with my wife, who with tears in her eyes, renewed her vows with the pipe. We gave up our fight and fell back into the abyss of crack bliss. Just like old times only now we were sicker, everything was lost quicker, that flame of hope no longer a flicker. The future, a faint image, ugly and out of focus, the love for our son, still there but now hopeless, hard to notice, unlike the flies that hovered above his crib like locusts and the sickening scent of spoiled meat and decay or the absence of his cries for, I don't know how many days. NOOOO! My wife screamed until her throat went raw. I held her against my chest, my heart stopped and I stared ... at my precious son lying stiff, blue with no breath, his face contorted in pain ... he starved to death. While we were feeding our demons and ignoring his screaming, he suffered severely until finally falling into that fatal sleep ... I pray the Lord his soul to keep ... and as you can see ... my sins run deep.

The nurse said one of us has tested positive for HIV ... Sssss! It could be me ...

NURSE-   Next!

RAPPER-   Stages, Mics and spotlights, money and fame,
thousands of fans screaming my name. A dream that came true; a soul that was sold to a game that is cold.
I wanted to be a rapper since I was 10 years old.
Lunch room battles, banging beats on the table,
I was a Hip-Hop prodigy; I rhymed parables and fables,
focused on finding a future with a major label
so I'd be able to have a future that was stable,
steady, no more misery. I'd have money instead of food stamps,
Nikes instead of Pro Champs, a whole fam' instead of just Gramps.
I'd get my mom off drugs and I'd free my dad.
I wished for this with every word I wrote in my pad,
'cause all I had was the hope that someone would notice me,
a poor lil' nigga in the projects spittin' poetry,
blowin' up block parties, droppin' flows at talent shows,
sneaking out after dark for ciphers in the park.
Hip-Hop was my heartbeat and I was good.
I was the hottest kid in my hood
and I kept at it, made demos in my homeboy's attic

filled with street sounds and static.
My chance came and I grabbed it,
held it tight like a cordless mic.
I caught my big break after spittin' great on a local mix-tape.
Finally, somebody willing to sign me, willing to give me a chance
along with a platinum chain and a six-figure advance.
I bought my gramps her own home, a four-bedroom Brownstone.
I got a Caddy Escalade with 20-inch rims, all chrome.
Now I'm known, my first single is certified gold,
I got A-list producers on hold, beats from Dre and Kanye,
shout-outs from Flex and Kay Slay, offers from JD and Jay Z,
calls to do collabos with Lil' Kim, Common and Lil Jon,
songs with Beanie Siegel, Trick Daddy and Game that I'm wanted on.
Interviews with The Source, Vibe and XXL,
positive predictions of how well I'm gonna sell.
I'm shining; I can't stop smilin', on the radio freestylin'
at night clubs wildin'. My song is in the top ten,
my video is requested again and again.
I'm doin' it big and now my old block is acting strange.
Them kids I used to cipher with claim that I changed.
They mean-mugging when I come through in my 4-dot Range,
looking hard like they counting the diamonds in my chain.
I throw them lames some change and tell 'em ain't nothing changed
and if they stay patient I will get 'em in the game.
It's my world, the consensus is my flow is the phattest.
I'm thug-pretty and my body's toned, so I'm on sex-symbol status.
In the VIP with actresses and models, Dom P. and Crystal bottles.
I'm touring in different states every night.
I'm scoring with a different date every night.
I'm in a hotel room with 3 groupies calling me Lover,
one riding me the other two pleasuring each other.
Some nights I make sure my whole squad gets blow jobs,
my suite filled with weed smoke and chicks who deep-throat.
I hit hood-rats and high-siditties, country girls
and freaks from the city as long as they're pretty.
I'm big pimpin', Baby! Trying to ball 'til I fall
and I don't like condoms so I'm hittin' everything raw.

Lifestyles of the rich and shameless. Different places,
new faces most of them nameless. And I believed I was blameless,
just a young nigga having fun, then one
night the Hennessey and Hydro weed had me numb.
I had this sexy shorty in the bed with her knees spread
trying to get up inside her when I noticed the sheets red.
The blood made me thrust deeper, wanting to make that whore scream.
She winced and then whispered that she was only fourteen,
yet proud to call me her first, proud to let me tape her,
proud to take me to court, proud to say I raped her.
Another rapper arrested, front page story.
I was dropped from my label, indicted by the grand jury.
I ended up pleading guilty to statutory,
a five-year sentence, but most of my fans still for me.
The women still adore me, the freaks still come through.
I get a visit every weekend and I love when the room is full.
Last Sunday I was visited by my youngest son's mom,
she wore the wrap around skirt with a butterfly thong.
She kissed me on my ear while I fingered her wetness,
she stuck her had in my pants and stroked my erection.
We got hot and restless, both ready to bust,
I gave a signal to my homie who I knew I could trust,
letting him know I was about to go hard.
We slipped in the bathroom while he distracted the guard.
Raised skirt ... unbuttoned pants ... quick kisses ... trembling hands,
doggy-style in the last stall, my hands gripping her hips,
she fights not to scream, biting her lip,
looking over her shoulder wanting to see my face,
I hear someone coming so I pick up the pace.
In and out ... while I pull on her hair.
Harder, faster, I'm almost there.
we came together and she started crying. She said
she loved me, I didn't say it back 'cause I know she was lying.
I'm a star. She loves my name and my image.
Next week another freak will come visit
and I'll be all up in it.
So, if I am sick, no one will ever know

I'll just take that cocktail and still keep my glow,
and you better know I'm still sexin', I'm just being honest.
I will try to be careful, but that's not a promise.

The nurse said one of us is positive for HIV.
I really don't care, but it could be me ...

NURSE: Next!

THE AFRICAN:

I remember ... my village. Peaceful. Clean. United.
One family formed by many families. I remember ...
ceremonies. Festivals. Drums. Dancing. Beautiful songs
sung by many voices. I remember my mother. Smiling.
Clapping. Prettier than a clear night sky filled with
many stars. And my father. Strong. Proud. Tall like the
Baobab tree. His dark, smooth skin and his smile, brighter
than the break of day. It was the harvest celebration, I
remember. I was 12 years old. Tall like my father, but
still thin. My sister, two years older than me. Almost a
woman. Sharing sugar-cane with me. Laughing. Playing.
I remember ... joy. Lying down to rest, my belly full with
yams, beans, and cassavas. Sleeping. I remember ... the
night was still. Quiet. Like death. I remember ... Rebels
creeping through darkness. Armed with guns. Knives.
Anger. Hatred. I remember ... FIRE! Screams. Shrieks.
Moaning. Crying. Women and children running and
hiding. My father ... fearlessly fighting. I remember ...
BOOM! BOOM! They shot him. He laid there dying.
Bleeding ... blood dark like oil. I seized the sword from his
hand. His eyes shined pride. He cried, be a man! I stood
ready. Skinny arms holding a heavy, sharp machete ... I
remember. Laughter. My enemies mocking me. Taunting
me. Their guns aimed at my chest. I remember ... a blow
from behind from the butt of a rifle. I fell to the ground.
A piercing scream from the back, my mother and sister

were found. Arms bound. Abandoned by our Gods. I remember the shame. Witnessing my mother and my sister ... Beaten. Raped. Again and again. I remember ... their nude bodies ravished, bloody, drenched in urine and flooded with the semen of murderers. I remember a knife held to my mother's throat. Her eyes closed, craving death. Yearning. Longing for escape from such heinous humiliation. NO! Please don't! I cried like a child. I will do anything. I begged for her life. So they forced me to lie down and make my sister ... my wife. I remember ... that abominable scene. My mother seeing the seeds of her womb, flesh and blood of her being, joined ... incestuously. When she fainted they slit her throat anyway, I remember. They laughed loudly as they left me and my sister locked in an immoral embrace. Yes, I remember ... Sadness. Shock. Sorrow. Sin. Still alive, but no spirit within. I remember the sickening scent of charred skin, the bodies of those burnt alive. Our village, destroyed. Filled with fear. Guilt. Shame . Unburied remains. Widows. Orphans. Most ran away. Fallen men, who refused to rise up, but I remembered and I plotted revenge. I aspired to atone for my cowardice. Be a man. My father's final command. I learned to fight, learned to kill with my bare hands. I learned to lead and at age 13, commanded my own faction. We fought the rebels, the militia, each other. We fought to survive. I remember war parties wrought with rage and wrath. I, now the murderer, the rapist, the one who laughed. Battles. Lost. Won. Enemies. Hunted. Hung. We were starving. Not only for food, but for songs. And for joy. Peace. Love. I remember ... how quickly the new enemy came. The curse. The disease with no name. That invading illness. Death from an unseen hand. Woman, child, or man. Blind eyes. Legs paralyzed. Body sores. Elders sleeping with virgins, believing innocent blood to be a cure. A plague worse than war. I remember ... my sister, her beauty buried behind her disgrace. She dreamed of becoming a teacher. A wife. A mother. Instead she became a Bar-girl. Bringing men home to her hut, sharing a straw mat behind a tattered curtain. Selling sex for money or food. And I could do nothing to stop her. I remember ... when the Americans came. They build churches, schools, and clinics. Gave us condoms we will never use. Test our blood. Take our picture. Put us on their news. Their offer to help is sincere, but maybe it is too little, too late. I remember ... the young doctor. His face solemn. Sad. He said my sister is sick from sex. HIV positive. He said he could help her live. Offered us a life in the United States. A life with school instead of war. A life in the American village where no one is poor. I told my sister to go. Get medicine. Get education. Get love. Get treated. I chose to stay at home where I was needed. I remember ... a sad farewell. My sister held on to me for a very long time. Trembling. Afraid. She clutched my arms and would not stop crying. I lifted her chin. Remember, Sister. Mother said we fail only when we stop trying. A tiny smile. Her lips fixed with courage. She waved goodbye. One year later. A letter. My sister was about to die. I remember ... A plane ride over wide water. A handsome couple who called my sister, daughter. Buses. Trains. Bridges. A building made from steel and glass that rose into the sky, filled with enough doctors to save my entire country. A room. Cold. Grey. A bed surrounded by machines. My sister, the size of a branch on a tiny tree. I remember ... her mouth would not open. Dried blood crusted over her split lips. Her body shriveled. Drained of all she once was. Her eyes. Yellow. Blinked slow when I said her name. A single tear trekked down her bony face. Her hand in mine. I spoke stories of old times. Remember, Sister, remember ... IVs were removed. Plugs were pulled. The strangers, her second parents cried hard and then left. I wrapped my sister in my arms, and she ... shivered to death. I remember ... the anguish of Africa reflected in the dying eyes of my sister. I never went back. Too ashamed. Too afraid. I stayed. Discovered urban jungles. Concrete villages with different natives and different languages, but that same warrior mentality that guides me daily. The hood calls me Shaka. The girls love my accent, the thick scar on my chin. They all see the savagery evident even in my grin. I remember ... and it has made me ruthless. Fierce. Cold. Unforgiving. Death has been my companion, hope is for the living. I am held in this prison awaiting deportation. The prodigal son returns to his infested nation. I remember ... most of all the numerous graves. And I have loved at least three women who died of this AIDS. AIDS ... Such a sweet, gentle name for a deadly foe. Maybe it should mean; Africa is dying slow ... or ... Africa is dying! So! Do you think if it is me, maybe I won't have to go?

The nurse said one of us has tested positive for the HIV. No one will remember, but it could be me ...

NURSE   Next!

THE BROKER

     I have a secret, I will tell you soon.
     It has nothing to do with why I'm here.
     I was a rich man, you're right to assume
     and I'm innocent of my crime, I swear.
     My world was filled with Mutual Funds,
     corporate boardrooms, investment returns,
     trading in commodities, stocks and bonds,
     keeping track of revenue lost and earned.

     I built picture-perfect-portfolios
     and managed a profit producing team
     that quadrupled price-earning ratios
     and warned that Atkins would kill Krispy Kreme.
     Every quarter I guaranteed gains
     for day-traders or single-share holders
     and yes, the slightest whisper of my name
     could influence mergers and takeovers.

Not one company who did not want me.
I'm the man who made millions for many.
The number one broker in the country,
I could build equity from a penny.
I'm not boasting or tooting my own horn,
but I must admit to being the best.
I had to accept jealousy and scorn
as a result of my major success.

So proud of the future I was building
for my two children and beautiful wife.
All of my holdings made me worth millions.
I'm the 'American Dream' come to life.
Houses in Hilton Head, Cape Hatteras,
The Hamptons, Martha's Vineyard, and Key West.
Vacations to the Great Barrier Reef,
trips to Aspen, Fiji, Rome, and Paris.

I owned two Porsches and the first Maybach,
a '56 Gullwing Mercedes Coupe,
an Astor Martin, a Lear jet, a yacht
and my own tailor who hand-made my suits.
Silk ties from Talbot's, Church's English shoes
and cufflinks that matched my Paték Philippe.
Smoked Cuban Cohibas and drank the best booze;
Dom Perignon and Louis the Fourteenth.
Spoiled my family, dinners at Ruth'sChris,
bought my son and daughter each their own horse.
Gave Tiffany trinkets to my mistress.
My wife got diamonds from Wellendorf.

High-stakes black jack in Bellagio suites.
 I once blew a mil in Monte Carlo.
Consoled my loss by snorting cocaine treats
off of the soft breasts of high-priced call-girls.
But drugs and whores were just some of the perks,
a small way to avoid the 'crash and burn.'

My partners and I were rich, snobbish jerks,
still, that's not the secret I said you'd learn.

I worked hard twelve years, my rep was solid,
then started a small firm to open doors.
Hired ten brokers straight out of college,
my two partners and I still worked the floors.
We built up an exclusive clientele,
from first to fourth quarter, money was made.
Management protocol was 'buy and sell,'
high-margin investments, we all got paid.

I was on the board of several councils,
wrote a column for Fortune for six months,
helped break IPO's, which amounted to
splits and dividends and net profit jumps.
Meanwhile, my partners had formed a new team,
off-shore accounts on the Cayman Islands.
Money laundered through a 'pyramid scheme,'
'tax-shelters', and irregular filings.

Caught in the middle, I had no idea.
The subpoena came, I refused to sing.
The SEC were prepared for the kill
and I ended up losing everything.
My license, my reputation, my friends,
assets were seized, houses put up for sale,
lost my jet, my yacht, and my classic Benz,
and then sentenced to eighty months in jail.
Surrounded by thieves and thugs who might snap
tired of living lives so neglected,
their anger rubbed off, I learned to fight back
and vowed to keep my secret protected.
For if it was known, I'd probably die.
My sickness is much worse than having AIDS.
My secret is the most disgusting crime;
I have a passion for boys young of age.

Their innocence, high-voices, and soft skin,
their scent alone makes me weak in the knees.
I gave runaways cash to touch them,
I tried to stop, but it's like a disease.
My computer was filled with 'Kiddie Porn,'
images that I miss more than my wife.
Tears fall slow; I wish I never was born
and contemplate ways of taking my life.

No way to make it right, I'll make it end,
No more make-believe, no more play-pretend.
They say Karma is a circle of fate,
I either die of AIDS or from self-hate.

The nurse said one of us has HIV.
A righteous punishment … it could be me.

NURSE   Next!

THE DOWN LOW BRO

There's this silent fear coursing through my body at the exact same speed of the sweat drops that race down my back. It could be me. I mean look at me. I'm sure you've noticed that my appearance is above average and like a soft shade of blue I'm easy on the eye. I'm fly and my conversation is at all times intriguing. My voice is light, soft like silk, almost feminine, but … I am not gay. I'm just smooth, candy-cane sweet. You would think I sweated honey the way the Honies swarm over me, buzzing like bumble-bees in heat. On the streets, I was the Casanova of my city, the Valentino of the valley, the Don Juan of 'getting it on.' My style was either copied or envied. I wore ascot ties and alligator sandals. I kept my nails meticulously manicured and I even had a diamond stud pierced through my tongue. But … I'm not gay. I was a playa' with pimp potential and I usually got my way. Of course, I wasn't always so fortunate. My childhood memories are a medley of me playing make-believe, my pissy-drunk step-father always mocking me, the sad Saturdays when I was called a sissy 'cause I'd rather jump rope with the pretty girls than play ball with the boys, but ... I am not gay. I remember chasing fireflies on sultry summer evenings, when games of 'It Tag' and 'Red-light Green-light' turned into 'Spin-the-Bottle' and 'Find and Grind.' I learned to french-kiss when I was nine and I lost my virginity at the early age of eleven. See my mother worked nights and my step-dad stumbled around in a constant stupor. My adolescence was an unadulterated, after-school-orgy, crowded with over-developed teenage girls and acne-scarred hoodlums, all of us haunted by the high of our hormones. We had blue-light basement parties where we yelled, "SWITCH" and changed partners while in the middle of intercourse. Or played my favorite game; 'The Choo-Choo Train.' That's five or six boys and one wild and willing female. I used to feel the most exhilarating thrill while standing with four of my homies, all of us naked, measuring our 'Johnsons' while waiting our turn, but ... I'm not gay. You see, I was sexing way back when I was only shooting blanks, but eventually I busted off my seed and sent my little soldiers on a search for some eggs. I became a father at the age of fifteen, two sons born four months apart. At sixteen, I was blessed with twin daughters and another son. What can I say, my seed runneth over. By the time I turned twenty-one I had eight children to six different women, who all love me devotedly, but not one of them lost any sleep after taking me to court for child support. Every payday I was the victim of an unarmed stick-up. My wallet was filled with wishes, baby pictures, and unpaid bills, but there were always a few friends willing to lend and yeah, some of them were men, but ... I'm not gay. I grew tired of walking the straight line. The influence of my environment exposed me to a life of petty crime that led to some not so petty time. My consequences, bad food and barbed-wire fences.

Yet, I have discovered that prison is simply a scaled-down version of the outside world, only without the false illusion of freedom and well, there are a lot less girls. But I'm a survivor and I'm still the sexiest, six-footer you'll ever meet. Even in a sea of multi-cultural men, I stand out like a gold coin in green manure. I'm sure. So, if some of these men who want to pretend like they're women, find me attractive that certainly doesn't mean I'm gay. I let them lace me with new sneakers and sweat-suits and my distinct dialogue keeps my locker on full. I lost a few friends who believe hanging with Homos isn't cool, but hey, I'm not gay. And to be honest, my one friend used to take those hormone pills and he has long, curly hair, a flawless complexion, and nice full breasts that bounce when he runs the track. The fake thugs be shootin' ball and sneaking peeks out of their peripheral, whispering under their breaths that my friend does look a lot like Beyonce. Me? I've played with those soft melons and sucked on those chocolate nipples while he beat me off ... uh ... but I'm not gay. I still get visits from some of my children's mothers, old flames who sport tattoos of my name on their upper-arms or lower-backs, beautiful, head-turning women who stop traffic with their tantalizing looks. I got them hooked, each one hoping they will have the privilege of welcoming me home, helping me settle in to the role of husband and daddy. And no matter what I'm doing now, one of them will have me. I'm ready and I know my kids need me, a strong male to mold them into men. Two of my sons play Little League, three of my daughters cheerlead and when they call me, Dad, I get a surge of pride that convinces me I can conquer the world. In their bright, adoring eyes I can do no wrong. They are my joy and my reason for staying strong. That is why I take their pictures down when I'm in my cell, because sometimes it gets lonely and I hunger for constant companionship, and my friend ... well, he, uh takes care of me and my need to release some of this pressure, passion and pain that has run through my veins ever since I was six years old. So when the lights are off and the keys are silent, and the sweat from my chest drips on his back and he moans that he loves me, I know it's true, they all do. I was born to be loved, born to bring joy, so when I tongue-kiss his ear and softly say, "I love you, too," I almost mean it. But ... I am not gay.

The nurse said one of us has tested positive for HIV.
I'm telling you, I'm not gay ... but it could be me.

NURSE- They say confession cleanses the soul and I don't know, it just might. Unfortunately, it does nothing for the fight of deficient leukocytes, and the loss of T-cells or the way the thymus gland swells when your immune system fails ... to fend off antigens and when the tiniest virus could easily lead to death. Do you know who it is? Have you fathomed a guess? Try not to be influenced by who they are or were or where they come from, or by the unvirtuous deeds they may have done. AIDS does not discriminate nor discern who is or isn't worthy, it attacks ... anyone. Can you imagine being afraid every time you hear someone sneeze, or feeling so nauseous that it buckles your knees and you kneel over the toilet only to dry-heave? Imagine the despair of knowing your body is unable to fight off infection and having to take over 10 pills a day to provide a synthetic protection. Imagine inspecting your reflection every morning and praying that a pimple isn't really an early lesion. And imagine watching your weight fluctuate, losing every aspect of your appetite, and wearing a phony smile so people will stop asking if you are all right. Tell me who it is. Go ahead and guess. There's no win or lose because whoever you choose the answer is ... Yes. And it's a shame something so serious isn't easier to see, because actually there are two people here who are positive with HIV. Two lives that can no longer be lived care-free, one of these five men and the other is ... me. Please do not be shocked, it really shouldn't come as a surprise. I'm an

African American female— age 29, and I know by just looking at me it's hard to believe, but I'm the number one target of this horrific disease. And no, I've never shared needles or done illegal drugs, and I've had only two sexual partners my entire life. My first was a barely-remembered prom date, my second made me his wife. Our marriage was monogamous, magical, two young lovers in love not only with each other, but with the beauty of being in love ... but my husband had been in a car wreck a few years before we met. It was touch-and-go. His temporal lobe had minor bruising. He suffered internal bleeding and had to have an emergency transfusion. By grace, chance or circumstance he pulled through and he made it, but his second lease on life was granted by blood that was tainted, blood that would mix with mine and leave our lives twisted. See, for me, HIV was a threat I never knew existed, but I became the victim of a victim, another statistic. Now, let me ask you, am I no longer beautiful? Am I no longer gifted? Must I forsake my faith, should I not have friends, have I lost the ability to laugh, must I never smile again? LOOK AT ME! Could you love me? Or should I be condemned? Should these men? Do you believe HIV is a penalty for past sins? Well, it's not. It isn't a punishment; it's not a gay disease or an African curse. NO! It is a problem, that when ignored, only gets worse. It is a piercingly, painful struggle, but it's not a dead-end. It's not an automatic death sentence, not an excuse to give up. It's not a stigma, not something you keep a secret. It is a wake-up call for all to know who you sleep with. Do you know who it is? Do you know if it's ... you? Look at me and learn. I didn't know it was me. I was ignorant and naive. Think about it and tell me, do you know. Do you know the facts? Do you practice safe sex? Do you know if it's you? Have you taken the test? DO YOU KNOW WHO IT IS!? ... Are you willing to guess? Do you want to know or not? Fine. I understand and it's cool. You want that peace of being able to say, you never knew. Yeah, you know it's true.

You want to selfishly live your life not caring what you do. Well, beware, because the next name I call ... could be you. (Spotlight goes off. Stage lights shine bright on men.)

MEN-   (All together.) YOU WANT TO SELFISHLY LIVE YOUR LIFE NOT CARING WHAT YOU DO. WELL, BEWARE, BECAUSE THE NEXT NAME SHE CALLS ... (Whisper low.) Could ... be ... you ... (Light's out.)

NURSE-   NEXT!!!

Daddy's Favorite Girl

I was 13 years old when my mother died after a short bout with cancer. A year later, my father fell in love with my best friend. Most people believe I killed my father, but I didn't. Even if I did, it wouldn't have been because of his affair with Kristen.

I was born and raised in a small country town on the coast of South Carolina. My mother was a slender, pleasant, and very pretty woman. She adored my father and me and spoiled us both. She loved to cook and always had a smile for everyone. She was a true Southern belle and the sweetest woman you could ever know.

I remember riding with her when heavy storms were expected—or when the weather turned unnaturally cold—to pass out blankets, water, and food not only to our neighbors, but also to the blacks who lived on the 'other side' of town. Throughout my childhood, I've often heard people say: 'That Mrs. Jennings is a true saint.'

My father owned the only merchandise store in town. Whereas my mother was well loved, my father was equally respected.

He was a weatherworn, ruggedly handsome man, one of those country boys the South is famous for. However, he was no bumpkin. He was a no-nonsense businessman who kept his mouth pursed in a perpetual frown as if he was always calculating figures.

My father would extend a line of credit to anyone and during the rough times he would even allow a missed payment or two, but if he thought someone was welshing him or trying to get over, well everybody knew that A.J. Jennings did not play.

My parents had one of those traditional loves. They were high school sweethearts—star quarterback and head cheerleader—who got married right after graduation. My father then took over the store so my grandparents could retire and move to Myrtle Beach. I was born two years after they were married and we were living your typical 'American dream.'

When I was 12 years old, my mother became ill. The dream began to fade away.

In the movies, when they want to show time flying, they'll show a sky with the clouds speeding by and changing from day to night over and over again. That's how it felt for the year my mother was dying.

One minute, she was in the kitchen laughing cheerfully while she made me and Kristen some fudge brownies. The next minute she was bedridden, frail and delicate, looking the part of a porcelain doll with closed eyes that would never open again.

My mother passed away three days after my birthday and I was completely distraught. If it weren't for Kristen, I probably wouldn't have made it through the wake or the funeral.

Kristen has been my best friend ever since the second grade. She's like the sister I always wanted and my mother treated her as such. But my father didn't like Kristen. He said it wasn't her personally, he just didn't like where she came from, but that was ridiculous since my father, like everyone else, had no idea where Kristen actually came from.

She was an orphan. She was loud, outspoken, adventurous, and sometimes violent. In other words, she was the exact opposite of me. I loved her from the very first time we met.

It was in elementary school, during recess. Eddie Tasker and Sam Burton were teasing me, pulling on my pigtails and calling me names. I ran over to the sliding board. They followed and kept at me until I covered my face and cried.

They chanted, "Carol Ann, cry baby whaaann! Carol Ann, cry—"

"Why don't you leave her alone?" Kristen snapped. She held her balled up hands on her little waist.

"Ah, she's just a spoiled little rich girl," Eddie said with perfect child-like meanness.

I remember peeking through my hands and seeing the triumphant smirks on both of their faces and then hearing Kristen laugh. Even though we were the same age, her laugh, like everything else about her was more mature.

"Well, both of you bastards should kiss her spoiled, little, rich ass," Kristen emphasized every word.

I was shocked to hear a seven–year–old swear like that but when I saw the wounded and comic expressions that Eddie and Sam made, I couldn't hold in my laughter.

Their eyes and mouths made perfect O's and Eddie looked as if he might actually break down and cry. They ran off as Sam called over his shoulder, "You said a bad word and we're telling."

From that moment on, Kristen and I formed an inseparable bond. She came to play with me often. I let her dress up in my clothes and play with my dolls and she taught me how to jump rope and play jacks. Most of all, she kept me from getting hurt.

Kristen wasn't much prettier than me, but she was so sassy and bold that, standing next to my shyness, she stood out like a Queen and I was a simple lady in waiting.

We were both early bloomers and our bodies began to fill out by the time we were eleven. I covered up with big tee shirts and loose overalls while Kristen wore tube-tops that accented her budding breasts and little shorts that exposed her long legs. She walked so naughty, well; sometimes it was just outright embarrassing. By the time we were twelve, she was turning the heads of grown men.

I didn't know it at the time, but my father was one of those men. He must have been fighting his urges valiantly, because in the beginning he was just plain old mean to Kristen.

He used to come home from work and after kissing my mother he'd come looking for me.

"Where's Daddy's favorite girl?" He'd yell up the stairs.

Sometimes Kristen would be with me and she'd answer playfully, "I'm right here."

When my father reached my room he'd cut his eyes at her, "I was talking to Carol Ann." Kristen would look up at him with a challenging gaze. I would race into his arms and hug him tight. I'd tell him about my day and ask him all kinds of silly questions to distract him from Kristen being there.

My affections would usually calm him and he'd give my cheek a light pinch before going off to get ready for dinner. Though, sometimes he'd turn around with a stern look and say, "Make sure your friend leaves before it gets too late."

It helped that Kristen and my mother were very close. Kristen was raised without a mom and she had a neediness; an emotional indigence I never felt. It stirred my mother's instincts to nurture her.

My mother taught Kristen how to cook—something I never could or would get the hang of—and there were times when I would walk into the kitchen and find my mother holding her close as Kristen cried angry and bitter tears of despair; her misery chased away the pangs of jealousy that clawed at me.

The bond between my mother and I also grew stronger as we stood side by side defending our relationship with Kristen to my father.

"She's here too much," my father would exclaim. "It's like she lives here with us."

"She needs us," my mother would counter.

"She doesn't have anyone else," I would add.

"Well, I ... I don't trust her and I don't think she should spend so much time here."

When he realized my mother and I were standing our ground, he shook his head, "Well, keep her away from me!" Then he stormed off to smoke a cigarette out back.

Kristen was not blameless for the hostility that existed between her and my father. She did little things she knew would irk him; like calling him "Daddy" instead of Mr. Jennings or talking to him as if they were of equal age and social standing.

One evening, during dinner my father announced he had to make a trip to Charleston to pick up some supplies for the store. My mother and I gave the appropriate and encouraging smiles, but Kristen stabbed her fork into the plate and in an icy tone declared, "You need to spend more time with your family!"

We stared at her in silent consternation, neither of us accustomed to hearing that tone used with my father.

Kristen gave us a watery smile and added, "I just thought the family might want to go with you for a change."

To my surprise, my father took us with him, even Kristen. I guess that was the turning point for us as a family. Unfortunately, two months later my mother was diagnosed with cervical cancer, which finally explained why she could never have any more children. The cancer spread to her heart and lungs. It was irreversible.

While my father and I immersed ourselves in a premature mourning—crying at the kitchen table and giving my bedridden mother phony smiles of confidence—Kristen ran our household with an efficient know-how.

She cooked, cleaned and catered to all three of us until one day, without any formal request or announcement, she moved in.

At my mother's wake, while my father chain-smoked and sulked on the back porch and I laid down weeping, Kristen welcomed the guests and thanked them for the food and condolences

Some of the visitors eyed Kristen with barely concealed disdain or arched a curious brow, but most of them knew she wasn't a stranger and she belonged there as much as I did.

Kristen stopped going to school. She spent her days doing chores around the house and maintaining my mother's garden. She cooked delicious meals each evening and although dinner was usually a quiet and somber event, there was no trace of the tension and animosity that used to exist between her and my father. That should have been my first sign something ominous was forth coming.

The second sign was the change in my relationship with Kristen. We were no longer chatty schoolgirls under a blanket with a flashlight, teasing each other about which one of us thought Jeremiah Albright was cute.

Kristen's protective nature had turned maternal and even though I could never see her in a motherly way, I recognized how happy she was. Her life now had a purpose and I went with the flow.

When Jeremiah wrote me a love letter, it was Kristen who told me I was too young for someone with such obvious intentions. She even convinced my father to forbid me to see him. When I snuck out to Mills Lane to see him anyway and he pushed me away because I wouldn't kiss him, it was Kristen who comforted me and wiped away my tears.

A few months before my fourteenth birthday my first period came. It was Kristen who smiled away my fearful cries and explained the entire process of a woman's nature and why it should be celebrated rather than shunned.

My birthday came around. It was the first without my mother and so painfully close to the anniversary of her death. Kristen and my father went out of their way to throw me a small birthday party. My father bought me a beautiful dress from Charleston and Kristen baked a red-velvet cake almost as delicious as my mother's.

The three of us tried our best to stay cheerful, but eventually the balloons and music failed to distract us. Our laughter turned hollow and our smiles became forced as we silently admitted my mother's presence was sorely missed at times like these.

My father opened a bottle of wine he saved from my parents' last anniversary together. He allowed me and Kristen to drink with him, and after toasting one glass to my birthday and a second to the memory of my mother, we were both a little tipsy and senseless.

I remember laughing and crying at the same time and finally falling asleep on the living room sofa.

I woke up in the middle of the night, my bladder screaming for release. My head was throbbing and I felt nauseous. I rose up slowly and tried to get my bearings in the dark and shadowy room.

I heard them before I saw them.

I held my breath and laid still as I listened to the guttural sounds emanating from my father mixing with Kristen's feathery gasping.

The full moon cast a thin light through the open window and in the faint illumination I saw them. My father and my best friend on the floor, their limbs entwined, rocking in unison.

A sense of outrage flooded me as I watched my father kissing, caressing, sucking, and sometimes biting on Kristen's perky breasts and erect nipples.

Their intercourse was fast and hard like some primal act of contrition. When my father arched his back and released himself inside of her, his face became an ugly mask of pleasure and pain.

He collapsed on top of her, exhausted and afraid to look at her. Kristen turned her head so he could nestle his face in her long, wavy hair. She looked directly at me and our eyes locked. I saw a few tears, but also a glazed look of acceptance.

I shut my eyes quickly and resumed breathing. My chest burned. I didn't know if it was from holding my breath so long or if my heart was exploding. I laid there pretending to sleep as I listened to my father

42

sobbing, saying he was sorry over and over again, while Kristen rubbed her hands up and down his back and whispered it was okay.

I spent the entire next day in my bedroom brooding. My father crept off to work at the crack of dawn. Kristen and I did an excellent job of avoiding each other. Later that evening I felt Kristen gently shaking me awake. The sun was almost gone and the sky was a soft blend of orange and indigo. The temperature had turned cool and I could smell the Atlantic Ocean wafting on the early night air.

"Dinner's ready," Kristen said as I eased out of bed. "Your father isn't home yet, but I figured we could start without him since you haven't eaten all day and I—"

"I saw you Kristen," I cut her off.

She didn't say anything. She stared at the floor and wiped imaginary lint from her lap. She looked at me with downcast eyes and said, "I'm sorry, Carol Ann. I don't know what to say. He's lonely, and this has been building up for some time now. He needed me—"

"You slept with my father, Kristen!" I shook my head angrily, trying to shake off the uninvited tears. "I can't believe you ... you had sex with my father."

"Carol Ann, please listen, try to—"

"You're a whore, Kristen! A god-damn whore!"

Kristen flushed red and her eyes narrowed in anger. "A.J. is the only man I've been with," she snapped.

"A.J.? Oh, so now he's A.J.?"

"He's ..."

"He's my father!" I shouted. "He's 'Mr. Jennings' to you!"

"I love him, Carol Ann! And he loves me. Please ... try to understand."

"Understand what, Kristen? Understand how you could betray my mother after everything she did for you. How could you do that to her?"

"I don't know," she whined. "I didn't know what else to do. You see him, Carol Ann. He barely smiles anymore. He's always sad," she paused. "I didn't think about ... I didn't think about your mom."

Kristen covered her face with trembling hands and began crying uncontrollably.

I stared at her, trying hard to hold on to my fury, but the longer I stood there the more my anger subsided, sympathy easing into its place.

I pulled her hands from in front of her face and held them in my own, oblivious to the tears and snot that accompanied them.

"It can't happen again, Kristen. You have to promise me it will never happen again."

Kristen brightened when she saw the forgiveness in my eyes. "It doesn't change anything, Carol Ann," she urged. "We're still best friends. We're still like sisters, right?"

"Yes, but you have to promise, Kristen."

"Everything can stay the same and I won't have to leave, because he loves us both—"

"You have to promise!" I persisted.

Kristen looked at me with pleading eyes and bit her bottom lip. "I can't, Carol Ann. He's going to come to me again and I ... I can't turn him away." She took a deep breath and her eyes implored understanding. "How can I deny him what is rightfully his?"

I dropped her hands in disgust, like I had just realized I was holding snakes. My heartbeat quickened and I looked at her with all of the loathing I could muster.

"I hate you!" I shrieked at her.

"Please don't say that, Carol Ann. I love you and I know—"

"Get away from me, Kristen. Just get away ..."

"We're family, Carol Ann. Don't you see?" She spoke slowly as if explaining the obvious to an impatient child. "We will always be family."

The tears streamed down my face and my head was pounding again. "This doesn't make us a family!" I screamed. "This makes us nasty! Now leave me alone, Kristen. Just go!"

I flung myself on the bed and buried my head between my folded arms. She slipped out as quietly as she came and I stayed in my room and cried myself to sleep.

I woke up in the middle of the night and saw my father standing in my bedroom doorway staring at me. His face was drawn and haggard and his eyes were red from crying. He looked old, like he had aged ten years overnight.

He saw my eyes open and gave me a tiny smile. "You know you're still Daddy's favorite girl." he whispered to me.

I blinked back my tears and nodded yes.

His smile lasted a little longer, but it was obvious he didn't know what else to say. He looked down at his feet then back at me. His smile was replaced by a countenance of despair. My heart ached for him. He shook his head slowly and pushed the door shut behind him. I heard him call for Kristen.

Weeks turned into months and I developed a look-the-other-way tolerance for my father and Kristen's relationship. They never showed any affection towards each other in my presence and as long as I went to sleep early I didn't have to suffer through their passionate moanings.

My father and I never discussed his affair with Kristen. To me it felt almost taboo to even talk about his shamefulness. But I found ways to express my anger—I began to talk back and lash out. I was rude and disrespectful. I started smoking my father's cigarettes and staying out late. I would only go a few miles up the road to the tire swing at Gillespie's Pond, but they didn't know that, and the worried look on my father's face when I came dragging in at two or three in the morning was bitter-sweet revenge.

My father brought me gifts almost every week; dresses, expensive shoes, candy, and even a television for my room. I knew the presents were intended apologies, but I refused to acknowledge them. I gave most of them to Kristen since he never bought her anything and she was the one earning them.

I tried hard, but for some reason, I couldn't stay mad at Kristen. She waited patiently as my temperament shifted from silence, to cursing, to cordial conversations, and finally returned to where we started as seven year olds—best friends for life.

Early one morning in May, Sheriff Bundy knocked on the door.

"Hey, Uncle Bud," I exclaimed and gave him a warm hug.

"Hey there, yourself," he replied with a genuine smile.

Sheriff Roy Allen Bundy was my godfather and I'd been calling him Uncle Bud from the time I learned how to talk.

He stood on the porch with his hat in his hands and a toothpick clinging to the corner of his mouth.

"Come on in, Uncle Bud," I stepped aside so he could enter. "My father is at the store, but I could fix you some ice tea or lemonade."

"No, no," he protested. "Don't trouble yourself, sweetie. I was in the area and just dropped in to check on you."

"Well, that's mighty kind of you, Uncle Bud."

He nodded his head slowly and glanced around the living room. "So, is everything okay?"

"Sure. Why do you ask?"

"Well, I ain't seen ya much and," he paused and switched his toothpick to the other side of his mouth. "Actually, no one has seen ya much since your ma passed. Lot of folks in town are asking 'bout ya."

"Ah, Uncle Bud," I sighed and gave his arm a reassuring pat. "I'm alright, I'm not much of a socialite like my mother was, but you tell everyone I sure do appreciate their concern."

Uncle Bud stared at me and nodded his head again. "You sure are growing up, Carol Ann. You look just like your ma," he smiled. "What are you, about 16 now?"

"Almost 15, but Daddy says I'm more mature than most girls my age."

"I reckon you have to be now that it's just you and your father out here."

"Oh, no, Uncle Bud. Kristen's here too. She's sleeping right now, but she helps out a lot."

He stared at me again, his eyes twinkling as if I was a little girl asking him to give me a piggyback ride. "Wow, I ain't heard that name in a while."

He looked up at the ceiling for a few seconds, almost like he was waiting to hear her moving around so he could call her down and speak to her. I couldn't help but feel a twinge of jealousy.

"So Kristen's still around, eh?" he asked more to himself than to me. When I didn't answer he did that head nod thing again. He then removed his toothpick to kiss me on the forehead.

"Well, I'm going to mosey on back into town," he said as he started towards the door. "Listen, Carol Ann, you look a little tired. I don't want you wearing yourself out. If you need anything; any help out here or anything at all, you just give me a holler, okay?"

"Sure thing," I agreed. With that he put on his hat and strode to his car. I gave him a final wave as I watched him pull off, then I went back inside.

"Who was that?" Kristen asked from behind me.

"Just Uncle Bud."

"And what did the good Sheriff want?" she asked sarcastically.

"He was just ..." I started to answer, but when I turned around and saw her I couldn't believe my eyes. "What's wrong, Kristen? You look sick."

"It's nothing," she shrugged. "Just a little bug I've been trying to shake since last night. I've been throwing up all morning and I have the worst cramps ever."

"That's terrible. Here sit down. You want me to make you some soup or some tea?"

"No, no. But could you call your father and ask him to pick up a pizza or something from Sarah's Place. I don't think I'll be up for any cooking tonight."

"Sure, I'll do that. Why don't you go back to bed until you feel better?"

"I think you're right. I am tired and I keep getting these dizzy spells." Kristen stood up slowly and after a few steps she had to brace herself against the staircase. She gave me a weak 'thumbs up' and said, "I'm okay. I betcha by tomorrow I'll be all blaaaaah—"

She threw up all over herself and the floor. She didn't have much on her stomach so there wasn't a big mess, but she was dry heaving and it sounded painful. She finished retching and stood up straight to catch her breath.

She unbuttoned her soiled blouse and slid her arms out of her sleeves. She must have heard me gasp, because she looked at me and her eyes followed mine. We both stared at her small protruding stomach with a mixture of fear and fascination. Kristen was pregnant.

By our calculations she was close to three months. It was hard to tell since we both had irregular periods.

"You can't keep it," my father was saying as he and Kristen sat at the kitchen table. I had excused myself so they could discuss the "situation" as my father called it, but I could still hear pieces of their conversation.

"Why not, A.J.? I don't understand," Kristen asked.

"It's not right," my father stated.

"But we're a family. We can be a bigger family and I—"

"It's not right!" my father shouted, interrupting her plea.

I couldn't make out what they were saying after that, but I could tell Kristen was crying. She was mumbling what sounded like, 'my baby, too …' Then I heard a glass crash against the wall and my father's voice filled the house.

"You are not keeping that baby and that's final!" He stormed out of the house with the door slamming behind him.

Kristen slept in my bed with me that night, but it was not like old times. We cried together and held each other while my father, in a drunken stupor, banged on the locked door, begging for us to open it so we could talk.

He eventually passed out in the hallway, his loud snoring drowning out our weeping. A few days later we weren't as lucky.

It was late and raining so hard I couldn't see anything through my bedroom window. Kristen and I were in bed with the covers pulled up to our necks, jumping each time we heard thunder. I had just started drifting off when we heard a boom that wasn't from the storm.

My father kicked in the door and stood there motionless. The hall light cast his shadow across my bed and a quick flash of lightning revealed a maniacal expression that stained his face and made him look grotesque. He reeked of alcohol and as he slowly approached the bed I felt Kristen freeze. We saw a wire hanger clutched in his right hand and the tremors that racked her body shook me as well.

"What are you doing, Daddy?" I tried to sound calm.

He didn't answer me. He pointed at Kristen with the hanger.

"Don't, Daddy. Please don't hurt her."

"This doesn't concern you, Carol Ann," he slurred.

I rose to my knees on the bed and positioned myself to face him. "I won't let you hurt her." I reached for the hanger and he jerked back so violently a startled scream escaped me.

"Go, Carol Ann!" he roared at me. "Get out of here!"

I reached for him again and grabbed hold of his arm. I was determined to stop him from doing whatever his sick, intoxicated mind was urging him to do.

"I said, get out of here!" he yelled and tried to shrug me off. When I refused to let go, his eyes lit up and his mouth pulled back in a hideous sneer. With his opposite hand he smacked my face so hard I heard bells ringing for an instant and then immediately fell into blackness.

As the darkness lifted, I heard Kristen screaming in agony. Her hands were tied to the bedposts and my father was leaning in between her wide-open legs. I blinked rapidly to clear my vision and saw him, his hand inside of her at an unnatural angle and grinding hard at a rapid pace.

I traced the inside of my mouth with my tongue and tasted blood. I started to rise when Kristen screamed so loud that she lost her voice mid-yell.

A steady string of lightning gave the room a strobe-light effect and in it I witnessed my father pull the hanger from inside of her. A bloody piece of something thick and meaty hung from the end of it.

"No!" I wailed. The blackness called me back and I fainted.

Kristen stayed in bed for three days. She refused to speak and only ate when I fed her. Her gaze became lifeless. She didn't cry anymore, but her sorrow was unmistakable. It was a painful sadness that covered her like the satin blanket she held tightly against her shivering body.

Shuffling gently from the bathroom, Kristen finally spoke. "I'm leaving," she said.

"I'm going with you," I answered back without hesitation.

Kristen didn't ask me if I was sure or tell me I didn't have to. She simply took my hand into hers and gave it a light squeeze. We both knew we needed each other.

We also knew that my father would try to stop us so we began planning our escape carefully. I called my grandfather and told him I wanted to buy my father a gift and I wanted him to call our bank and get me permission to withdraw some money from my trust fund. I told him it was for an expensive fishing rod and my grandfather, being just as passionate about fishing as my father, didn't think twice about it.

We needed somewhere to go, but our options were limited. I had an aunt on my mother's side who lived in Michigan and some distant cousins in North Carolina. After a short discussion we settled on Michigan and the greater distance it would provide us.

The day after I got the $450 from the bank and put it with the $84 I had already saved, we were packed and ready to go.

The plan was to leave late that evening after my father fell asleep. He had been drinking everyday and we were hoping that he'd pass out early as had become his routine.

I don't know how Kristen was able to stay so calm when my anxiety was so high. I was on pins and needles the whole day. I was trying to act normal and I had to force myself to stop looking towards the laundry room that concealed our light luggage.

The clock ticked slowly. It felt like time was teasing me and I jumped every time I heard the hourly chime from the grandfather clock that stood sentinel in the dining room.

My father stumbled in after ten o'clock. He declined my offer to heat up his dinner and sat in his lounge chair in front of the TV. He turned on a baseball game, opened a beer, and began mumbling to himself. I waved goodnight and headed upstairs.

Kristen and I spent the next few hours in my bedroom talking softly about all of the things we were going to do when we got to Michigan. Every half hour or so, we'd take turns tip-toeing to the top of the stairs to peek down at my father, hoping he'd be passed out snoring or on his way up to bed.

Our bus to Charleston was scheduled to leave at 5:30 a.m. and the walk to town would take about an hour. At two o'clock I started to get nervous.

"It's your turn to check," I told Kristen as I paced in front of my window.

"No, I went last time. It's your turn."

"But I went twice in a row so you should go twice, too," I reasoned.

Kristen stared out the window and spoke in an eerie voice, "Let's just go Carol Ann. He has to be asleep by now and if he isn't, I promise you he won't be able to stop us."

"No, Kristen, we agreed to do it like this, with no confrontation. Let's go check together," I suggested.

She nodded her assent and we crept down the hall quietly. At the top of the stairs I laid down on my stomach and peered through the railing. I could see the living room clearly and my father's chair was empty.

"He must have gone to bed and we didn't hear him. Let's go listen outside his bedroom door."

"No!" Kristen countered with wide eyes. "Let's go now," she insisted. Before I could answer she was halfway down the stairs.

I followed close behind and when we reached the bottom I led her to the laundry room to retrieve our bags.

We stood there, panting heavily in the darkened room. I slung the carry-all over my shoulder and Kristen picked up the suitcase. We stepped back in to the hall, exhaled and headed for the front door.

We passed through the dining room and I couldn't help but think about my mother and how much love she had brought into this house. My fondest memories were in this room especially and in a way it felt like I was leaving her, too.

I shook that sentiment off and was on my way to the door when I heard my father's voice.

"I can't let you go." He was sitting at the dining room table and if he was drunk earlier, he sounded completely sober now. "I already lost your mother, I won't lose you too."

I stood there speechless, my heart thumped in my chest.

"Put the bags down, Carol Ann. You're not leaving me."

Sweat beads popped up along my hairline, and a few of them raced down my back. I swallowed the lump in my throat and said, "Kristen wants to leave and … I'm … I want to go with her."

My father shook his head slowly and I noticed how tired he looked. "Let Kristen go then." He stood up and his voice was firm. "Please let her go. For seven years I've been praying you would let her go!"

"Oh, so now you want me to go?" Kristen chimed in. "You didn't want me to go when you were laying up inside of me."

My father hung his head and didn't say a word.

"You … didn't want me to go when you were kissing every inch of my body."

My father remained silent.

"Did you want me to go when you were fucking me and whispering in my ear that I was Daddy's favorite girl?"

My father raised his head and made it over to her in two strides, "Shut your damn mouth, you … evil … bitch!"

Kristen laughed in his face, "Bitch? But, I thought I was your favorite girl." And she kept laughing and laughing until my father reached out and wrapped his hands around her throat and choked her viciously.

I dug my nails into his hands and tried to pry them from around her neck, but his grip was savage and unrelenting. I drew my hands back

51

and saw pieces of skin caught under my nails. Helpless, I screamed and screamed, so loud that I barely heard the gun go off.

It sounded like a sharp clap, not the deafening boom I'd heard in movies. My father fell back and slid down the wall. He was holding his stomach and the look on his face was pain and pure shock. Blood soaked his shirt and gushed between his fingers. He took shallow breaths and stared at the ceiling.

Kristen held the gun with steady hands. It was my father's .38 revolver, the one he kept in his bedroom closet. Kristen had a faraway look in her eyes and as she raised the gun and took aim at my father's crumpled body, I knew she intended to kill him.

"Don't Kristen," I spoke softly. "Please ... please, don't kill him, Kristen."

Her expression held an equal amount of pity and contempt. "Wake up, Carol Ann!" She shook the gun at him as she spoke. "He doesn't deserve to live. After everything he has done to us he deserves to die. To die like the animal he is."

"No!" I urged. "Not like this, not in cold blood."

"Cold blood? There's no such thing as cold blood, Carol Ann." She wiped away a single tear. "Ain't you tired yet? Ain't you sick and tired of the nasty, disgusting—"

"What are you talking about?" I asked her.

"I'm talking about him!" she shouted at me. "I'm talking about us!" She closed her eyes and let out a frustrated moan. "Open your eyes, Carol Ann. Wake up, please!"

"I don't under—"

"You brought me here to help you deal with him, but I can't do it anymore. I can't love him the way you do and still take on all his hurt. And I shouldn't have to ... you shouldn't have to."

"Kristen," I pleaded. "You're talking crazy. Please just put down the—"

"Talking crazy? Talking crazy!" She threw her head back and laughed psychotically. "Crazy is the magic word here, Carol Ann. Don't you get it?"

"No, I don't. I just want you to put away that gun and let me call an ambulance."

"For what? To save this sick bastard? What's wrong with you?"

"What's wrong with you?" I hissed angrily. "I know he hurt you, Kristen, but this isn't—"

"Hurt me?" she scoffed. "Hurt me?" Her tone turned sympathetic. "Carol Ann, don't you see? He was hurting you. "When he laid down with me at night he was laying down with you. When he held my legs in the air and pounded inside of me, he was pounding inside of you. And when he scraped my uterus raw with that cold, metal hangar, it was your baby that he murdered."

I was shaking my head no, but I couldn't find my voice.

"Yes, Carol Ann. It's true. You and I are one! We are one!" she yelled. "And old A.J. here has been screwing us as if we're not his own flesh and blood."

"No!"

"Yes! You created me to protect you, but you also made it easier for him to feel like it wasn't you. You made it so he could pretend like he wasn't having sex with his own daughter."

I looked at my father and tried to match her words with the man, but I couldn't. "Maybe if my mother—"

"Don't you dare," Kristen admonished. She read my thoughts before I could speak them. "Don't you dare make excuses for him. He's sick and perverted."

She sighed deep. "You were going to say he was lonely, that he missed your mother and since you look so much like her, well … No! No! No! He's been hurting you for as long as I've been with you. For as long as you needed me with you."

She saw understanding wash over me and dug even deeper. "That's right, Carol Ann. You've been Daddy's favorite girl since you were seven years old."

She let out another hysterical peal of laughter then cut it off abruptly. She licked her lips … my lips, squinted her eyes … my eyes and leveled the gun at my father. She spoke inside my mind: *He deserves to die.*

"Noooo!" I squealed. It didn't make sense. My head was aching and I couldn't think straight. Kristen was real. She had to be real. I can't be crazy and my father … couldn't have done—

Boom! A crash at the front door interrupted my mixed up emotions. Uncle Bud stepped into the room and after taking in the scene he instinctively drew his gun.

"Put the gun down," he ordered.

Yes! I thought. Please make her put the gun down. We all need some time to think—

"Please put it down," his tone was soft, but official.

"Listen to him, Kristen. Put it down."

"You have to drop the gun, Carol Ann. Just put it down."

Me? No, it's Kristen. Kristen has the gun. It's her, Uncle Bud. She's there. I turned my head a little and caught my reflection in the glass of the grandfather clock. My scream got stuck in my throat. It was me. Alone. Holding a gun on my father.

My father watched me with glassy eyes. His skin was ashen gray and his breathing was unsteady. Our eyes locked and a fleeting image of him kissing me goodnight as a child was quickly replaced with one of him French-kissing me awake.

His eyes gave a silent confession and begged me to end it all. I raised the gun and lined the barrel up with his chest.

"No! Carol Ann!" Uncle Bud yelled.

I closed one eye and felt a tear slide down my face. I held my breath and I ... I couldn't pull the trigger.

So Kristen pulled it for me.

BLACK SOULS UNITING

I see black souls ... struggling, black souls confused,
their mental states altered by special elixirs,
got 'em screaming profanities,
but only whispering scriptures.
If a picture can paint a thousand words,
 then a thousand words should paint a million pictures
of black souls ... searching,
black souls seeking serenity,
finding solace in syringes filled with self-hate and comfort in
the poignant smoke that drifts slowly from a crack pipe.

I see black souls crying from Mount Zion,
sounding like abandoned angels,
giving melody to misery and harmony to hardship
heart-breaking ballads, belted out by bitter, baritone voices,
who made careless choices,
and are caught up in the affliction of their addiction,
while so-called saints fight for jurisdiction of the crucifixion.
I see black souls ... lost,
rejecting religion and refusing redemption,
worshipping worldly ways and walking away from wisdom.

I see Christians hesitant to accept Salaams,
from their second-cousins who carry Qurans.
I hear the Lord's Prayer.
I hear someone calling the Adhan.
I see black souls ... betraying,
phony homies give testimonies almost as ruthless as Judas, only today
30 pieces of silver comes in the form of platinum chains, Bentleys and Escalades,
Idol-worshipping adolescents screaming, "Let's get paid!"

Black souls selling sin in sandwich baggies on scandalous streets,
getting high on their hypocrisy, holding it down with heat.
Hustling illegal goods

with their faces hidden behind hoods.
And I see sisters with no clothes,
dancing seductively on poles,
exposing their ... black souls.

But look right there!
If you squint your eyes you'll see it clear.
I see black souls believing, black souls striving
black souls loving, black souls surviving.
I see black souls uniting.
I see beautiful sisters with fascinating physiques
finding love with broad-shouldered brothers who seek knowledge
even when they sleep.
Pouty lips meet, almond shaped ebony eyes lock.
Vows are recited while cool calloused hands slide rings on
soft manicured fingers turning "baby mamas" into beautiful wives.
I see babies born in truth,
infants with their heads bowed in prayer,
saying, 'God bless Mommy and Daddy and everyone everywhere,'

And look there,
I see black prodigies with the potential to be prophets or powerful pioneers
pouring out of over-populated prisons and preparing their mentality
to confront and conquer their reality.
Rising.
I said Rising!!!
Responding to the universes call for black souls to represent,
Represent black souls ... surviving

I see black souls uniting ... and still surviving.

By the Sword

CARLOS

They kept yelling for me to drop the knife. I could tell they was scared. I could hear it in their voices. They was actin' like they ain't never seen blood before. I only hit him twice, but the one that caught him in his stomach must've did some serious damage 'cause he was leaking all over the place.

I told the first nigga, the one who started everything, to stop playing with me. Everyone in my unit knows that at 12:30 I watch the Soaps. I walked into the TV room and this big, dumb nigga was watching the Spanish channel. Not *Caliente* or something with some bitches in bikinis. No, he was watching the Spanish news.

This nigga is black just like me and I know he didn't understand nothing they were saying so I turned it to CBS and sat down right beside him in the front row.

This nigga got up and turned it back to that, 'Mida-Mida'shit, talking 'bout he was looking at that. Now, I know it ain't nothing but them got-damn weights making these niggas think that they super-heroes. I eyed him down. He was a big boy, too. Ol' fake-ass muscle nigga. But my name is Carlos Demond Briggs and I will fuck a big nigga's whole world up. And that's exactly what I told him when I turned the TV back to, *The Young and the Restless*.

He said fuck me and Victor Newman and turned it again. I was looking at that nigga like he was stupid. He just transferred here a few weeks ago, but he's been here long enough to know how I get down. He stood there at the TV gritting on me like he wanted to war. Someone should've told him that I live for that shit. I walked up to him real cool, like I only wanted to turn it back, like I was going to play the channel-changing game. Yeah right! I reached up towards the button with my left hand and when he went to grab my hand I came from way down deep with my right hand and punched him dead in his temple.

BAM! I almost knocked him out cold, but he hit his head on the TV shelf and bounced back into me. He was half-sleep on his feet when I swung a vicious upper-cut and busted his nose. I was trying to knock his nose bone into his brain so I could see someone die like that, but I didn't connect right. He fell into me and held on like a punch-drunk boxer.

I was laughing at him and there was a crowd so now I was talking shit. *Yeah, niggas! Carlos 'Crazy Los' Briggs! That's me and as you can see I handles my business. What!?*

The big nigga was leaning on me and he was heavy for real. Then I felt a sharp pain in my shoulder that made my legs wanna give out.

Aahhh! This nigga bit me like a bitch. He locked on me and growled like a pit-bull. I had to actually shake myself loose and when I finally pulled free, he had a piece of my flesh in his mouth. Nasty mothafucka'!

I slid over to the air-conditioner, where I kept my TV room-knife. I would've preferred my phone booth-knife 'cause it's made from fiberglass and it's easier to hold, but it was too far away. While I was taking the screen off the AC, the big nigga started hollering, *Let's go!* like we were on *WWE Wrestling* or something. His high-pitched voice made me want to kill him even more.

I gripped the knife by the electrical taped-handle and spun around. You should have seen his face when he saw the shiny six-inch blade. His eyes got big as hell and blood was still gushin' from his nose; the nigga looked sick. He put his hands up and started backing away.

My adrenaline made me feel excited and crazy. It was the same rush I'd felt when I was 13 and used a knife for the first time on this fool at the detention center. I started creeping towards old muscle-head. I was ready to cut his throat. I was only inches away from him and knew I could catch him if he tried to run. Just when I was 'bout to make my move I felt someone grab me.

I turned around to my left and saw Mr. Dave holding my arm in a tight grip. He was holding me like I was his son or his girlfriend or something. Mr. Dave was the unit clerk and he taught some business classes in the school. We were in the same dorm and he might of gave me some extra toilet paper a few times, but that old nigga didn't know me to be grabbing on me while I'm in the middle of a fight.

He was talking all soft and shit, telling me it was over; that the big dude had had enough and it didn't have to go any further.

I could barely hear him. I felt my blood pumping in my ears, I was so mad. Plus, I was feeling the pain in my shoulder getting worse like all wounds do when the fight is over. While Mr. Dave was holding my arm and playing peacekeeper, the big nigga snuck out of the TV room and ran down the hall.

Son of a bitch! He was getting away. I had pulled my knife and not used it. Oh, hell no! Knives are like guns and my motto is: If you pull it out, you better use it. If you don't, then you're a straight sucker.

So, I turned around and stabbed Mr. Dave in his stomach, pushing the knife in as far as it would go.

Fuck that! So what! He should of minded his own business. He got what he deserved.

He fell over sideways holding his stomach. Blood was squirting through his fingers like a fountain. I heard keys jangling and I knew the officers were coming. I bent down and pushed the blade into Mr. Dave's neck. That's when the guards rushed in, screaming for me to drop the knife.

They were 12-deep and strapped with helmets, electric shields and stun batons. They looked ready to whup some ass. I wiped the blade on Mr. Dave's shirt collar and then threw it at their feet. Then I turned around and put my hands behind my back so they could cuff me.

Of course they roughed me up some. They slammed me to the floor and kicked me in my ribs a few times. Then they cuffed my hands to my ankles and carried me hog-style to the infirmary. The Chinese nurse stitched my shoulder up and gave me a Motrin for the road. Then they put me here— in the hole— with you.

MALIK

I had witnessed death up close many times. That is how I knew I'd be able to carry out the order to kill Fat Cat.

I was 18 years old and trying to join the Black Gangster Syndicate. The B.G.S. was the meanest gang in the state and they ruled the Stateville Penitentiary. Ever since I was old enough to pronounce Syndicate—about three years old— I knew it was my destiny to be a Black Gangster.

My reputation was solid. I'd been putting in work since I was 10 and by the time I was 12, I had become a professional car thief. When I was 14, I drove the getaway car after me and some older cats robbed an armored truck.

There was a high-speed chase with eight police cars from three different counties. I was handling that old Plymouth better than a race car driver. I pulled off the highway underneath the exit ramp so my folks could get out and run. Then I evaded the police for another two hours. I finally crashed into a water-barrel barricade after they shot out three of my tires. I was the only one who got caught. Two security guards shot, $147,000 stolen from the newly designed Brinks truck in broad daylight, and all they had was a baby-face, fourteen-year-old with 80 cents, and a melted Hershey bar in his pocket.

This was in the sixties when being a rat wasn't cool. And since the guys who had been with me were Syndicate, being a rat wasn't an option. Once the D.A.'s office realized they weren't going to get anything out of me, they offered a plea that my mother forced me to take—Juvenile life plus 20 years.

I spent almost four years in a violent and notorious juvenile camp and then on my 18th birthday I was shipped to Stateville to start serving my real time.

Fat Cat was a non-affiliate who sold reefer all over the city. On the streets he was loved and respected, but all the love and respect was left at the front door. You had to be willing and able to start from go and earn the two again. Fat Cat may have been willing but he just wasn't able.

He owed the Syndicate some money. I don't know how much and it really didn't matter. The rule was: If you owed, you paid. The Syndicate Chief-of-Security on H block was a tall, light-skinned guy named Du-Drop. He told me Fat Cat would have to be made an example of and I was willing and able, as well as eager to set the example.

We met up in the mess hall. Du-Drop passed the shank under the table. It was made from a black-diamond file and could cut through bone. Fat Cat was sitting three tables away from me. He was laughing with some Neutrons (non-affiliates) and piling half-done peas on top of a tasteless heap of mashed potatoes.

My heart was racing. I had never killed anyone before and this was my chance to prove my loyalty to the Syndicate.

Du-Drop gave me a discreet head nod and I stood up slowly, easing my leg over the long, narrow picnic table bench. I held the shank tightly against my leg as I quick-stepped my way over to Fat Cat's table.

I was in a zone. The loud chow hall chatter became a muffled din and I felt the ridges of the knife burning into my palm. As I closed the short distance, one of Fat Cat's friends saw me approaching and gave him a warning. Fat Cat turned around too slow and by the time he swung his legs from under the table, I was already on top of him. Without hesitation, I plunged the knife deep into his chest.

There was a wet, suctioning noise as I pulled the shank back out. Fat Cat had fallen in between his table and the one behind him. He laid on his back with his mouth half open, sucking for air. I bent over to finish him, but someone came up behind me, wrapped their arms around my waist and started pulling me away.

I couldn't see who it was, but my arms were still free, so I angled the knife towards me and sliced across the forearm of my attacker. He let out an agonizing moan and released me. I spun around and saw the same guy who had warned Fat Cat that I was coming. I pointed the knife at him and ordered him to back up.

Syndicate soldiers came from everywhere to make sure I was alright. The guy held his arm against his chest as blood flowed down the back of his hand. He begged me to let Fat Cat live. He said they were cousins and Fat Cat was the only family he had. He begged me to give them five minutes and he would get whatever money was owed.

His pleading was getting to me, but I couldn't show any signs of weakness. Not in front of my folks. I looked at him like he disgusted me. I shook my head no and told him it was too late. I turned back to Fat Cat, who was using his feet to push himself under the table. Right then the riot alarm sounded and I heard guards screaming into bull horns, telling the inmates to lie down on the floor with their arms extended in front of them.

Du-Drop told me to throw the knife and when I hesitated, he snatched it from me and passed it to someone I couldn't see. I glanced over at Fat Cat's cousin leaning down trying to put pressure on his wound. His bloody arm kept getting in the way and as they squeezed each others' hands for comfort, the blood they shared mixed together as one.

I took two steps towards the man who had delayed me and made me a failure. When he looked up at me I sucker-punched him in his jaw. He fell at my feet and I stomped him five or six times, loving the sound of my boots landing against his head and stomach. Du-Drop and someone else grabbed me and even as they pulled me away I managed to land a gob of hawk-spit on his face.

Of course, I had no idea the man I had just humiliated and disrespected so viciously would one day hold my life in his hands.

That incident happened over 30 years ago and it's not one of my fondest memories. But as I look into the empty eyes of this deadly young man with his cornrows coming loose, looking as wild as he sounds, I can't help but feel I'm being stalked by my past.

CARLOS

I'm sure you can see where I'm corning from, Pops. You don't mind me calling you Pops, do you? I mean, you is kinda old. Anyway, was I wrong? Niggas in the unit looking at me like I'm the one who's crazy. Mr. Dave is the nut. He shouldn't have got involved. He should of stayed in his place.

Plus, I did all them niggas a favor. Now they can stop feeding into all that fantasy shit Mr. Dave was selling them in his classes. Stocks & Bonds, Real Estate, starting their own businesses. Yeah right! How come all these niggas come to jail and all of a sudden want to start learning business plans? Half of them can't even get their G.E.D., but they're gonna go home and start a business. Shiitt! They ain't going to do nothing 'cept go home, get high or get killed.

At least I know what I'm gonna do. I max out in 18 months and I can't wait to get high. The stuff they have in here is garbage. When I get back to them streets and I can get some real 'water', some of that super-wet. Man-oh-man! I'm going to get so high.

You know what I'm saying? I'm gonna get blasted. Have you ever been so high that you breathe out of your eyes and you feel your heart in your big toe? So high, you get stuck in one spot for hours, your mouth is full of slobber and you done pissed on yourself?

I got so high one time, I was on the corner hustling and I forgot where I put my drugs at. Right after I served some crack-head I put my rocks in one of my pockets but I couldn't remember which one. I'm on the corner, stripped down to my boxers, shaking my clothes out and some more shit. A foot-police walked up on me and told me I better put my clothes back on or he'd run me downtown.

Now remember, I'm high as a kite, so while I was looking for my rocks, I had them in my hand the whole time. My dumb-ass gave the rocks to the cop and asked him to hold them while I got dressed. Damn! That was some good shit.

That PCP is my wife, Pops. I love it. I be ready to kill a nigga when I'm on that wet. I'm talking about strangling a mothafucka with a car antenna or beating a nigga's head in with a baseball bat.

Don't look at me like that. I'm just telling you that it's crazy out there and where I'm from, if you want to survive, you gotta be crazy too.

Let's be real. I'm 23 years old. I'm past my prime. I can't go back out there on that rah-rah shit. Them young niggas is blasting their guns if you so much as look at 'em, funny. They're 11 and 12 years old with guns that weigh almost as much as they do and they don't respect nothing. Little bastards is way worser than I was.

But don't get me wrong, Pops. I ain't ducking no rec. I'm just saying they can have that shit. All I want to do is make a few dollars, get high, and fuck a few bitches. That's it. But if one of them wild-ass niggas get out of line, I will lay their whole family down.

See, this generation is on some new shit. Instead of just killing each other they want to kidnap your peoples and demand ransoms. What kind of mob-movie bullshit is that? I wish a nigga would call me up talking 'bout they got my girl and they want X-amount of dollars or they're gonna kill her.

Shiitt! I'd tell 'em quick, you can have her. Kill her, keep her, do whatever you want with her. I wish I would pay a nigga some money for a bitch. I'll send them niggas the rest of her shit and a list of her favorite sexual positions. Fuck her, she shouldn't of been slipping.

Now, if they take my son? Oh well, I'll have to make another one. If they get my mom? Damn, I love my mother, but fuck it, what can I do, she had a good life.

But best believe, if I get the drop on one of them, ain't gonna be no phone calls or ransoms or none of that. If I'm beefing with you, then I'm beefing with everyone and everything you love. I'm going to murder your wife, your girl, your mom, your newborn baby, whoever. If you fuck with me, anyone I see you with is going to die with you. That's my word!

I know it sounds ugly, Pops, but I'm getting older. Not old like you, you're a got-damn dinosaur in here, but I'm getting to a stage in my life where I just want to be comfortable. You know what I mean? And speaking of comfortable, I need that bottom bunk, Pops. My shoulder hurts and I ain't with all that climbing, so you're gonna have to move up to the top. I ain't playing! Get your shit and move!

MALIK

I'm 58 years old and I've spent over two-thirds of my life in prison. After serving eight of my twenty years in Stateville I was released and free for the first time since I was 14. I had become a man behind bars, but even better, I had become a Black Gangster, and I went home to an official Syndicate gangster party.

It was 1974. I still had close to 50-thousand dollars of my cut from the truck robbery. I was styling and profiling until I fell in love with that cocaine and the prestige of being a black gangster. I still felt I had something to prove and after a late night shoot-out with the Stones I got pulled over with my gat on me; still smoking. I was arrested after being free for only eleven months and sent back to Stateville for 10 more years.

I was 31 when I came home the second time. I had earned my stripes and moved up in the ranks of the Syndicate. I was elevated to a governor's position and placed in charge of the entire Southside. I ran a small empire that controlled the gambling and drug trade in the largest part of the city.

I had new Cadillacs, silk suits, and sexy women. I had respect and love and the Black Gangster Syndicate was a million-dollars-a-month-business, driven by fear and sustained by loyalty.

Then the Feds came. Indictments included wives and mothers and plea offers started out at 20 years. The fear had changed sides and loyalty was lost, as 'looking out for self' became the catch phrase of the year.

My prior arrest record and my position in the upper tier of the Syndicate made me a big fish. I was given a leadership role in a corrupt organization and charged with racketeering, drug trafficking, and conspiracy to murder. After a short trial, I was found guilty and sentenced to life in prison.

Like most people, I considered life in prison to be worse than death. I wanted to die. At least I thought I did and I began chasing death unconsciously, yet devoutly.

Back then prison was dangerous. It still is, but not like before when what you said could literally get you killed. I was a high-ranking Black Gangster and I had built most of my reputation inside the wall. I had done a lot of dirt and I had to defend myself often.

I've been shot at with zip guns, stabbed twice, and sliced with a razor six different times. I've been in four major riots where the State Police or National Guard had to be called in. I've witnessed convicts and guards die in some gruesome ways: hung from ceiling pipes, strangled with bags over their faces, and stabbed so many times their insides spilled out when the bodies were moved.

I've been put in 'holes' where you were not given a release date. You slept on the floor and the bathroom was a hole in the ground. I've been in 'holes' where you were fed bread and water twice-a-day and given a piece of meat every third day.

In the federal system, I spent my first 10 years in an ADX 'Super-Max,' which provides the highest security lock-down in the country. I was locked in my cell for 23 hours-a-day, copies of my mail were shown on a screen, showers were every three days, and my one hour of recreation was spent alone in a cement courtyard only slightly bigger than my cell. I actually went six years straight without any physical contact with another human being, not even a brushing of hands as the guards put my cuffs on.

I have scars over 70 percent of my body: Four on my face, which make me look older than what I am. I broke my hip in a fight when I was pushed down two flights of metal stairs so I walk slower than I should. I remain in good shape and even though I can still throw a crisp jab, my fighting days are long behind me.

I want to go home. I've been denied parole nine times, but I'm confident that my next hearing will be the one where they realize I'm no longer a threat to society—that I now have the potential and the willingness to contribute to society in a positive way.

I'm going into my 15th year without any misconducts. I've earned my masters degree in education and I'm a certified paralegal. I teach G.E.D. classes and I've initiated mentoring programs for the young guys just coming in. I've assisted many men in their legal struggles and I'm responsible for the overturned convictions of seven men who were doing life sentences like myself. The B.G.S. tattoo on my chest now stands for— Building, Growth and Success.

Some would say that my rehabilitation is due solely to my age. They say I've calmed down simply because I'm too old to still be a menace. Others believe that my becoming a Muslim and embracing the peaceful life of Al Islam was the beginning of my reformation. And those closest to me would swear I became a new man when I found love with a woman who I had fathered a child with while I was free, and who I had no idea was so beautiful until she returned to me with complete devotion and a plea for marriage even though my reunion with her physically may never happen.

In truth, all of these blessings contributed to my conversion. I became older and wiser. I submitted my life to the will of Allah. I found my soul mate and despite being behind bars, built a beautiful bond with her and my son. However, the real reason I retired my gangster stems from an unexpected encounter with a forgotten enemy and a sharpened lawn mower blade held against my jugular vein.

CARLOS

I got a little family out there, too. Well, I got my son and his mom. She alright I guess. She's better than most bitches out there. She got a good job and shit. And she takes good care of Lil' Los, but she also knows I'd kill her if she didn't.

I met her at a club and that was a fluke 'cause I don't even go to the club to meet bitches. Those days is over. Me and my niggas go to the club to start shit. I throw on some jeans, a tee-shirt and my Air Force Ones. Fuck all that dressing up shit; I wear whatever matches my pistol. Me and my mob be up in there just drinking, smoking weed and poppin', Ecstasy pills. We might grab a bitch's ass, but we ain't asking for their numbers and shit like that.

We were in there with the mad face on, hoping a nigga would say something wrong so we could shoot the whole club up. Ooh, I got this

Desert Eagle .45, Pops. It is so sweet and it will blow a nigga's chest through his back.

Anyway, my baby's mom was in the club about to fight some other bitch. She was wildin' out and I like that shit. Plus, she's a bad bitch, she looks good. Not that I fuck with ugly bitches, well, sometimes, if it's late and I'm on that horny-wet, I might run up in a baby-barracuda, but not raw-dog; not without a condom. Oh, hell no! I can't imagine having a baby to an ugly-ass broad.

I mean what kind of life are you giving your child. My son, Lil' Carlos is cute as hell, but if his mom was ugly, ah man, my son would grow up and want to kill me.

I could see him now, 13 or 14 years old, coming up to me like "Dad can we talk for a minute? Damn, Dad, look at Mom. She is a got-damn animal. What the fuck was you thinking about? And now I'm all fucked up, ugly as all outdoors, because your drunk ass had sex with a monster. Look what you've done to me!"

I couldn't live with myself if I did that to my little soldier. My little nigga is gonna be fly just like me. Yo, Pops, my son is only four and he already knows how to cuss like a mothafucka. I be telling him to call his mom a bitch and he do it. That shit be funny as hell. She'll pop his mouth and he'll say it again. She'll hit him harder and he'll start crying and still say it. I be on my back buggin' for real.

Me and my baby's mom ain't together, but she still does her job. She knows I don't play and I will whup her ass if she doesn't play her position. Every once in a while she'll get sensitive on me and write me a long letter asking me to change my ways. I don't even answer that shit. I'll write back one sentence—*Where the fuck is the money I asked for?* That's it. She knows better than that, sending me a long-ass letter. I can't eat no letter. Send that money!

That's what kills me about these fake thugs in here. They suppose to be gangstas and they sittin' around writing 20-page letters to their girls. They writing novels to these hoes like it's a bunch of shit to talk about. You're in jail, nigga. The same shit happens everyday. I hope their girls leave them and fuck their best friends.

Then, when they don't have a girl anymore, they wanna take a bunch of pictures and send them to 'Pen Pals for Prisoners' or some other shit on the internet.

Why they do that, Pops? If you can't get love from a whore you already know, how you gonna get it from a stranger? The only people that write back is fat bitches, church bitches, *fat–church* bitches, or gay men.

And I know for a fact these niggas be writing back to the faggots. You can tell. Just look at these friendly-ass niggas in here, always asking; 'how you doin?' and 'is you alright?'

No, I ain't alright. We in jail! Why the fuck is you so happy? Why are you always smiling? Is you a faggot or something? I tell them to get from around me quick. All the time smiling like some got-damn gumps.

I'm glad you told me you got a wife and shit, 'cause you be smiling sometimes too, and ain't nothing worse than an old faggot.

MALIK

When a man is raised in a jungle he feels as if he has no choice but to become an animal. He believes his survival depends on it. And if something never brings a man joy, he will never truly value it, even if that something is life itself. I was an animal. I was a beast with a hardened heart and no respect for life. But with experience comes knowledge and with knowledge came understanding. If a man can live long enough he will eventually experience, know, and understand that he wasn't created to be an animal, even when raised in a jungle.

There are many reasons offered to explain the tragic condition of black men in America. Some are genuine and justified. Some are just poor excuses. I believe the root of our problem is we forgot our role as men. We forgot how to be fathers and husbands, role models and leaders. And being that we forgot these things, the generation that followed never learned. I look at Carlos and I blame myself. I see my failure as a man to set a righteous example because I know Carlos looked up to someone who was just like me or maybe someone worse.

It is only by Allah's mercy that my son is not the same way. He was definitely on that path. As I was gaining knowledge of self and discovering the benevolence of God, my son was chasing after the reputation I left on the streets. He was trying his best to be like me, because it is a son's nature to idolize his father, good or bad. Imagine if more of us were good.

My wife recognized my son's longing to be a part of me and she tracked me down for that reason alone. The love came soon after; when she saw I was no longer a boy pretending to be a gangster because I didn't know how to be a man.

I was still learning, but I was also able to start teaching. With my son it was difficult at first. There was bitterness and disappointment on both ends. But I refused to give up or let go even though at times I felt like I was trying to hug my son with my handcuffs on and he wouldn't respond because the embrace wasn't as tight as he needed.

Eventually, he realized his hands were free and that he didn't have to pull away; that he had the power to make the hug tighter. That's what he did and for that I say, Allahu Akbar! God is great!

One of the five pillars of my faith is Zakat, which means charity. Most people think of charity as giving money to a needy cause, but charity is that and so much more. Charity is love for ones fellow human beings, it is kindness, tolerance, compassion, and it is the giving of one's self to someone in need.

That is what I have learned and what I intend to do for the remainder of my years, whether it be from behind these walls or on the streets. Allah knows best!

God willing, Carlos here will one day realize his brothers aren't niggas and his sisters aren't bitches and he is not an animal. He is a man with a purpose in life. I only pray his lesson comes at a lesser price than my own. Speaking of prayer it is time for my Salaat.

CARLOS

Damn, Pops! I ain't trying to hear all that Dr. King-Malcolm X-shit. I call niggas niggas because they're niggas and bitches is bitches, plain and simple. I'm a nigga, my baby's mom is a bitch. Shit, my mom is a bitch. I love her, but she's a bitch too. The only knowledge a nigga needs is to know he ain't shit. I ain't shit. You definitely ain't shit. My son, your son, they ain't shit either.

You talk about dads being there like that means something. Well, it doesn't. Dads ain't shit either and having one around just makes a nigga soft. We in the projects on super-struggle-status, and we see a lil' nigga playing catch with his dad. That shit is weak and when we see him by himself we're gonna beat his ass for having something we don't.

I ain't never had nothing, so I don't care about nothing. Life is one day, Pops. That's it. You could die any day so why not live like you want to and do whatever it takes so the next man dies right now and you get to see another day. You saw that guard come by to tell me Mr. Dave is gonna pull through, like I should be happy I'm not gonna get a murder charge. I wish he would of died. Now he's another nigga I have to watch my back with. I knew I should've sliced all the way across his throat. Damn!

It ain't nothing. Just another reason for me to stay on point. See, that's the difference between real niggas and fake niggas. I'm a real mothafucka so I do real things. And I stay real with myself. I know I've done some foul shit. I've done some dirty, ignorant shit almost every day of my life, even to my homies. My own niggas done seen me wild out on them.

We might rob someone together and I'll turn around and take everything. I won't give them nothing and my attitude is whatever. If they don't like it, so what. However they want to do it, let's rock. I will lay them down in a heartbeat and shoot holes in their casket at the funeral. That's how I do and they all know it.

They usually laugh it off, but I know they hurtin' inside and they'd shoot me in my back if I turn around long enough. So I watch them every time they come around me 'cause I know they're waiting for me to slip, but I don't give a fuck.

You hear me, Pops!? Damn, old niggas is disrespectful. I'm trying to talk to you and you ain't even listening. How long you going to pray? You've been on your knees for like five minutes. I ain't trying to hear all that chanting and shit. Get up and talk to me. Damn, nigga, you ignoring me? Get up! I said, umph! Get up!

Ah, I didn't even kick you that hard. I just tapped you, Pops. You only fell over 'cause you was off balance. Come on, get up. Yes, you are finished! That '*Rockman-Shayton*' shit is giving me a headache and you keep talkin' about Allah and Muhammed. Man, fuck them niggas too!

You heard me. Fuck Allah, God, Jesus, whoever! Fuck all of them! I'm God in here! What? You raising up like you don't like what I said, like you want to do something. What, nigga? Say something, anything. I will beat your old ass in here. What? Oh, I didn't think so. Get your ass broke up in here fuckin' with me. Matter of fact, I should smack the shit out of you for even raising up to me. Uhmm!

MALIK

I can't believe this boy hit me in my face. But the metal taste of blood in my mouth and my split lip proves that he did. He slapped me like I was a female, unworthy or too delicate for an actual punch. Worse than that, he interrupted my prayer, kicked me in my ribs while I was prostrating to Allah, and threw my prayer rug under the toilet. His disrespect reminds me some lessons can only be learned the hard way and I fear that before the night is over one of us will die.

CARLOS

That nigga Pops is funny. I give him a little love tap and now he wants to curl up in his bunk and not even speak to me. He's an old, soft-ass nigga. Come to find out he ain't even suppose to be in the 'hole.' He's in here as a holdover while being transferred to another institution. Probably one with a lesser security. I bet he's probably in here for tax evasion or something soft like that.

I keep laughing 'cause he looked like he was 'bout to cry after I smacked him. I would of choked him out if he'd started crying, but he just turned away and spit a little blood in the toilet. I tried to hand him his rug, but he just climbed on his bunk and turned towards the wall.

Oh well, fuck him! He don't have to say nothin' to me. I ain't trying to listen to all that positive bullshit about not calling my brothers niggas and how his son is in college and how we should give of ourselves. Shiitt, ain't no one gave me a got-damn thing and the only thing I'm giving out is grief.

So, if he's mad or hurt, so what. I don't give a damn. Let him be mad at his Allah or the guards, 'cause they the ones who put him in the cell with a killa.

MALIK

I was still in Stateville waiting for the feds to transfer me. The movie theater was packed like a slave ship and when me and my folks got up to leave we noticed about a dozen convicts who didn't stir when the lights came up. They sat motionless, some with their heads hung forward kissing their own chests and others slumped over sideways, blood trickling to the floor. They were bad gamblers who owed debts and good fighters who owed rematches, or just victims of a predatory environment, either way, they were all dead. Movie theatre murders were routine. There was even a sign on the door that said, 'ENTER AT YOUR OWN RISK,' but 12 dead in one night was a bit extreme, so I left two of my lieutenants there to investigate and make sure the Syndicate was safe.

I walked back to my cell alone and got ready to take a shower. I started undressing which meant taking out the two blades I carried, one of them a foot-long, machine shop-sharpened, double-edged lawn mower blade I kept tucked in my waist down the side of my thigh. I began to peel away the 15 one-inch thick National Geographic magazines taped around my chest and back, as armor against would be assassins.

I wrapped a towel around my waist, stepped into my boots and reached under my mattress for the small shank I always took to the shower with me. It wasn't where I usually kept it and as I stretched my hand further I heard someone behind me. Before I could turn around he rushed me against the bed so that I was sprawled on my stomach with my face in the pillow and my arms pinned beneath me.

I had never been raped, but I'd seen it happen a few times and this was how it usually started. I was tensing myself getting ready to buck backwards with all my strength when the unmistakable feel of cold steel pressed against my throat. All of my strength faded.

CARLOS

It's almost three in the morning. The guards just walked by and counted. I'm laying on my left side facing the door 'cause my shoulder is killin' me. Those bullshit Motrins ain't helping with the pain and I couldn't sleep for nothing. Every time I close my eyes I see the muscle nigga that bit me. I wanted to kill that nigga and it was burning me up that I didn't. Shit, I hit Mr. Dave twice and he didn't die. I felt like a sucka for real.

I heard Pops moving around above me and when I looked up, half of his body was leaning over the edge of the bunk. I figured he had to use the bathroom, but the way he was trying to get down was crazy. I smiled and started thinking how funny it would be if he fell and busted his old ass.

But he didn't fall. Somehow he managed to grip his bed and swing his legs so that when he let go he landed on top of me, trapping my body in between his legs and diggin' his hand into the stitches in my shoulder. When I tried to look up at him I caught a glimpse of the two razors he held against my neck. He must've broke them out of the razors they gave us to shave with, but I wasn't thinking about that. All I could think about was how this old fucker jumped down here like he was 13 years old.

MALIK

All I could think about was how this cat got into my cell and got the jump on me with my own knife. He bent down and whispered in my ear, telling me to be quiet. I didn't recognize his voice so I asked him who he was. I felt the sharp blade cut into my flesh and a teardrop of blood slid down my neck.

He told me to shut up and listen. He said years ago I tried to kill his cousin; that I stabbed his cousin over three dollars and for that alone I deserve to die. He told me that when he tried to stop me from taking an innocent man's life, a good man's life, that I had cut him too. And for that I deserve to die.

I had done so much I still didn't know or remember what he was talking about. That is until he reminded me of how I had stomped him and spit in his face, and according to him, for that too, I deserve to die.

CARLOS

This old nigga is crazy! He's on top of me whispering about debts being paid and revenge and how some nigga named Fat Cat owed three dollars. What the fuck!? I'm feeling his hot breath on my cheek and he got the razors right at my vein and I want to slam his old ass on the floor, but his legs are strong as hell and I can't move. Plus, the way he keeps saying, 'for that you deserve to die,' lets me know this nigga really wants to kill me.

MALIK

He told me he wasn't going to kill me. He said it sadly like he regretted the words even before they left his mouth. He said that for 10 years he dreamt of killing me and had planned all kinds of ways to do it, but Fat Cat—who had went home and become a good, steady, 9-to-5 working man and family man—made him promise not to kill me, even if the opportunity presented itself. Now he was having trouble with that promise and he had to keep taking deep breaths as he said over and over again, 'I promised Fat Cat.'

CARLOS

Pops was crying as he talked in my ear, whispering, 'I promised Fat Cat.' Then he started saying some type of speech that sounded like he made up just for me.

He said he could see I didn't love or respect life, but he wouldn't be responsible for ending mine while I was so ignorant ...

MALIK

With the blade still at my throat, he told me I better realize at this very moment he was saving my life; that although I deserve to die he was giving me a chance to deserve to live ...

CARLOS

Pops said that one day I will meet someone who also deserves to die, who is a walking disease amongst men, and I, too, must abandon my first instinct to kill this brother and instead save his life so that he too, may one day realize the power of living ...

MALIK

He then took the knife and cut a two-inch gash in my cheek and said, 'this is for the spit in my face ...'

CARLOS

Pops took one of the razors and cut into my cheek and said, 'this is for slapping my face ...'

MALIK

He grabbed my arm in a ferocious grip and said, 'Live by the sword, die by the sword,' as he sliced across the back of my forearm in the same spot I had cut him many years before ...

CARLOS

Pops sliced the razor across my arm and said, 'this is to remind you that you've blocked the sword that you were meant to die by ...'

MALIK

And whenever you look at it you better remember you are still alive so you can one day save a life ...

CARLOS

Pops bent my chin back and I could feel the bloody razor biting against my neck. He looked into my eyes and I could tell that everything he'd said was rehearsed from some other time and only now did he see me and in his eyes was pure hate. He swallowed and licked his cracked lips and whispered real, real low, 'make the promise or choose death.'

I'm Carlos Briggs! I'm a got-damn gangsta, a soldier ... you all know how I rock. Death before dishonor is the code, right? I wanted to say fuck you, old nigga, but for the first time in my life I was scared, and I can admit I wasn't ready to die. I saw flashes of my son and it made me weak.

Pops was biting his lip, and he was sweating hard even though the cell was cool. He was ready and that scared me even more. Scared me so much that I couldn't find my voice. I couldn't say nothing. Even as pops screamed in my face, 'Make the promise!' I stayed silent, while death sat over me, ready to claim another nigga. Damn!!

(FIVE YEARS LATER)

Shooting Suspect Arrested at
Area Hospital

In a bizarre end to a three-day, citywide manhunt, a 15-year-old, Southside boy was arrested without incident in the emergency room of City General Hospital. The juvenile, whose name is being withheld due to his age, was charged with three counts of attempted homicide after allegedly shooting into a crowd of spectators at a high school football game this past Saturday, three people were wounded.

According to sources, the shooting may have been a rite of gang initiation. Two of the victims were treated for minor injuries and released immediately. The third victim, nine-year-old Carlos Demond

Briggs Jr. was shot in his face and remains hospitalized at the Mercy Medical Center in serious but stable condition. Dr. Frank Clark stated that the bullet went through the boy's cheek and lodged under his tongue. The bullet has been removed and Carlos Jr. is expected to make a full recovery.

The police report states the shooting suspect walked into City

General's emergency room around 3 a.m. yesterday. He had a deep gash on the left side of his face and was bleeding profusely from his right arm.

The staff at City General was unaware the victim was wanted.

Authorities were called as standard procedure requires police notification when there is evidence of possible foul play. "It was obvious the young man was attacked and cut deep with something extremely sharp," a nurse said under condition of anonymity.

It remains unknown as to how the suspect procured his injuries, which required 22 stitches for his face and 130 stitches for his arm. "The suspect was dazed and barely coherent at the time of his arrest," Police stated.

"We asked him what happened and he whispered something about 'deserving to die' and 'blocking a sword.' As we cuffed him, he chanted the words, 'I promise' over and over. The suspect was taken to the Youth Detention Center pending his arraignment, where he will most likely be charged as an adult.

Ex-Gang Leader Paroled After 30 Years

Malik Abdul Ibn Johnson formerly known as John Johnson was released from Federal Prison yesterday after serving more than 30 years of a life sentence.

Johnson, 63, a one-time lieutenant in the notorious Black Gangster Syndicate, was sentenced to life in prison after being found guilty of racketeering and conspiracy to commit murder. Until yesterday, he had been denied parole 14 times.

While incarcerated, Mr. Johnson earned a master's degree in education and numerous certificates and citations. He is credited with starting a non-profit organization promoting peace, education, and rehabilitation for inner-city youth. "Malik Johnson has changed his life during his lengthy incarceration" stated Shawn Jordan, head of the new Federal Parole Commission. "We could no longer in good conscience ignore the fact that Malik Johnson is now able, and most of all, willing to be a benefit to society. He has earned a second chance," Mr. Jordan concluded.

Johnson, along with his wife and son walked out of the prison arm in arm.

When asked what he would do now that he was free, Mr. Johnson smiled and said, "I'm going to love my family and do my part to help change the world. I want to teach our children how to live in peace ... and how to build growth and success."

The Hand I Was Dealt

You see, I'm only playing the hand I was dealt.
I've been rolling set dice my whole life, chasing my point like that elusive first high.
My soul is on the line and I'm flipping a two-headed coin and calling tails every time.
I'm just playing the hand I was dealt.
I left my bible in my backpack, but I got my gun tucked in my belt.
I'm a 3-time offender, a career criminal.
My record is slow-song long, my jacket is thick like a Triple-Fat Goose.
I'm a faithful fugitive with no future and I keep a few felonies folded up in my front pocket right next to a picture of my girl and a quarter-ounce of 'that boy.'
Yeah, you heard me, I'm still riding dirty.
The streets root for me like I'm Rocky Balboa running full speed, crowds of caught-up kids right behind me, waiting for me to run out of breath, callously claiming that they got next, but I ain't done yet.
I'm still playing this hand I was dealt
Snake Eyes!
That 3-bang knock, teams of cops with red beams on their glocks screaming … STOP!
But. I Can't. Go. Back.
Back to chow lines and count times, hard looks and smut books, random urine tests and 8-foot slums, hidden razors cutting my gums.
I'm playing this hand out!
I'm asking for a hit with 17 showing.
I'm drawing too late into an inside straight.
I'm flipping that same coin and I swear on everything I love, it better come up tails this time.
I'm not folding!
I'm taking the safety off my gun and looking into the wide eyes of a nervous cop.
His trigger-finger itching, almost like he's wishing that I'll place my bet, that he can play Russian when I spin the roulette.
He wants me out of the game, laid to rest.

He wants me in a dark suit, my hands folded on my chest, my face caked up with make-up.
My girl at my viewing screaming,
BABY, WAKE UP!
Her hot tears falling on my cold cheeks like summer storm raindrops landing on glass.
But, I'm playing this hand out.
I can't fold now!
I'm picking 12 jurors that silently sit in the cold casing of a .40 caliber clip.
I got a 50/50 chance and guess what?
I'm taking it!
I love the odds, so I defy the Gods and bet all that I have on me being fast enough
To pull my ----
BOOM!
Damn! Heads again!
Well, at least the whole world will know how I felt
'cause my tombstone will read:
HE PLAYED THE HAND HE WAS DEALT!!!!

More Everyday

Yesterday, I lost my Daddy. It was Christmas Eve and I was sitting on the kitchen floor eating a cookie shaped like a candy cane. It was soft. My Nana just made them in the oven so it was warm, and good, too.

My Daddy came in and put snow down Mommy's shirt. Now that was funny. Him and Mommy were laughing, but Nana was looking at Daddy real mean. She had that look like when I'm being bad at church, but Daddy doesn't go to church with us so it couldn't be that.

"I hear you're selling that poison," Nana said.

"What?" Mommy yelled. Her voice was like a bee when it gets stuck between the window and the screen. "I know you're not selling again, Dee?"

My Daddy's name is Daryl Ray, but every one calls him Dee or D.R.

"Calm down," Daddy said. "I was just making some quick money so I could give my Lil' Man a good Christmas."

He was talking about me. I'm his little man.

"You can't give him anything if you're gone for 10 or 20 years!" Mommy screamed.

Ooh, and she said a bad word; but Nana didn't say anything; she was so busy fussing at Daddy, too.

I was getting mad. Daddy was just sitting there and Nana and Mommy were both over top of him pointing and yelling. I was about to go in there and tell them to leave him alone, but Daddy had that look I get when I accidentally wet myself.

Maybe that's what happened. I should go in there and tease Daddy like he does to me; *Ah, did Daddy pee-pee in his panties?* No, Nana would get me if I did that.

Nana had her faded, old Bible in her hand, holding it tight and sayin' something about serving two masters. When she wasn't snapping at my Daddy, her mouth was squeezed tight like she was eating lots of sour candies.

Mommy just kept shaking her head saying, "I can't believe this, Dee. You promised." She looked real sad.

I couldn't understand why they were so angry. They said Daddy might go to jail if he didn't stop selling, but we could just go with him. I thought I would just ease in there and tell them that, so they would stop yelling, but when Mommy saw me, she started crying and that made me cry too.

"Look at him," she pleaded. "Look at your son. Did he ask for a pair of Air Jordans or a leather coat that costs hundreds of dollars and won't even fit him next year?"

"Come here, Man," she dropped to one knee and pulled me into her arms. "Do you want a big electric car and a gold chain with your name on it?" she asked me through her tears.

I thought about the car, but she cried and shook her head, so I cried and shook mine, too. I don't want anything that hurts my Mommy.

"See?" Mommy said as if I had solved the whole thing. Nana stood there nodding her head in agreement.

See, Daddy? I asked quietly as I walked over to him. He was sitting on the edge of the couch, with his elbows on his knees, holding his head in his hands. Maybe he had a headache. I squeezed in between his arms and gave him a hug. He hugged me to him and I kissed his cheek. I tasted the salt from a tear and was surprised. I never knew that daddies cried.

"All he wants is for his father to be around; to be there for him as he grows up," Nana said.

"How do I do that?" Daddy snapped. I think he forgot I was in his arms. He sat me down beside him and stood up.

"Huh?" he continued. "Tell me how can I be a father if I can't provide for my son? How can I even be a man when my family still lives with you?"

My Daddy had his fists balled up, he was so mad.

"I have a high school diploma and I can't find a job anywhere. And notice I didn't say a decent job, because right now I'd take anything, but there's nothing out there!

"Then there's these kids," Daddy shook his head and took a deep breath. "Fourteen and fifteen-year-old kids driving 'BMW's' and Lincoln Navigators. They're out there making thousands of dollars a night, and I'm sick to my stomach, because if the Temp Agency doesn't find me some work this week, I have to borrow money from my mother-in-law, just so I can buy a Happy Meal for my son and pretend like I'm putting food on the table."

"Are you that foolish?" Nana asked him. "Half those kids will be in jail or dead by next year. Do you want that?"

Mommy walked up to Daddy and held his face in her hands. She was talking softly and looking at him the way she looks at me when I'm struggling to tie my shoe or trying to reach the cereal box on the kitchen table.

"Baby, this is just temporary," she insisted in a sweet tone. "We knew it would be hard when Lil' Man was born, and with us getting married right after we graduated, but our blessings are coming, we have to trust God."

Then she smiled and kissed Daddy on the lips. My Mommy is the prettiest, smartest woman in the whole wide world.

"You're going to block those blessings if you're out there selling drugs," Nana was still fussing. "I'm sure if you spent some of that extra time you've been spending on the streets, looking a little harder for a job, you'd find one, because they are out there."

Ooh, now Daddy said a bad word. He was leaving and he was going away for 10 or 20 years. I ran to get my coat. I was going with him.

"You're son is behind you!" Mommy shouted.

"I'm only going to the store," Daddy threw back without stopping.

"He wants to go with you, Dee!"

Daddy turned around ready to scream some more, but I was on his heels and when he looked down at me, I held out my coat and gave him my *pretty please Daddy* look. I have one for Mommy and Nana, too; theirs doesn't always work, but I get Daddy every time.

"You want to go with me, Lil' Man?" he asked while bending down. I nodded my head while still holding on to the 'look.' He didn't smile as he pulled my hat and gloves from the sleeve of my coat. He looked real serious as he zippered me up.

Are we going to sell the drugs, Daddy? I was curious so I asked. It looked like Daddy might really cry then. He looked sad, even sadder than me when I don't want to take a nap. I felt bad and was about to cry too. But I felt Daddy's big hand holding up my chin so I could look into his eyes.

"No, Lil' Man," Daddy said, still serious. "That's a no-no. Daddy won't be doing that anymore, okay?"

He looked hard at me to make sure I understood. I wanted to show him that I did, but I didn't. He smiled at me and said, "What did I tell you about keeping your head up?"

Daddy always tells me to keep my head up. So I looked all the way up at him, smiling, hoping my tears would fall back in and they did.

"How old is my Lil' Man?" Daddy asked.

Three, I said real quick and held up three fingers, trying hard to keep my littlest finger down.

"You love me?" he asked.

More everyday, I answered. *You love me?* I asked back.

"More everyday," he said.

That was our special little thing; we said it all the time. Daddy was smiling at me while putting on his hat. My neck was starting to hurt from looking up at him. I started lowering my head, and Daddy scooped me into his arms.

"Didn't I tell you to keep your head up?" he said while tickling me through my coat. I squealed with delight as he carried me out the door.

I had to squint my eyes when we stepped outside. The snow made everything look real bright. It wasn't dark yet, but the sun was going down and the sky was that pretty crayon-blue color. Some of the houses had their Christmas lights on and they were beautiful.

Daddy put me down so I could walk. I stomped the ground, loving how the snow felt crushing under my boots.

Daddy was laughing at me when Keon from across the street, he's 11 years old and bad, threw a snowball that went right over my Daddy's shoulder. I thought Daddy would be angry, but he laughed and said, "Oh yeah? Hey, Keon, you just started a war." He turned to me and said, "Lil' Man, get down by that car and make me some snowballs."

I ran and got down beside the car door. I was mad at Mommy for getting me gloves with no fingers. It's hard making snowballs with mittens, but I was trying.

Daddy was leaning over the car, making snowballs from the snow on the roof. He would throw them as soon as he made them.

"Come on, Lil' Man, I need some ammunition," he chuckled.

I jumped up and handed him my three pathetic snowballs, each the size and shape of a plum.

Daddy smashed all three into one and as I watched, he threw it and hit Keon on the back of his leg.

"Yeah boy!" Daddy shouted as he held out his hands.

Yeah boy! I repeated while hitting his hands with my own.

"Uh oh!" Daddy said. He snatched me up and started running, carrying me like a football.

Keon was joined by four of the other neighborhood kids. All of them are bad too. They started chasing us, but my Daddy is the fastest man in the world. Once we turned the corner they were no longer behind us. Daddy was still laughing when he put me down.

The store was right across the street. We were almost there. I was hoping Daddy would buy me a lollipop. Ooh, maybe one with gum in the middle. I'm not supposed to have gum, but Daddy will get me that kind as long as I promise not to take it out of my mouth in front of Mommy or Nana.

"Come on, Dee?" a weird looking man was talking to my Daddy. He was real skinny and his hands hung down to his knees, right in front of me. His big hands were dirty and shaky. He had to be cold, 'cause he didn't have a coat on; just two shirts and a scarf.

I looked up and saw that his lips were white—whiter than the snow—and he was dark-skinned. He had tears stuck in the corner of his eyes. The tears had dried up and looked rotten or spoiled.

Daddy said, "No!" over and over. Finally the man staggered across the street to a skinny lady with a big stomach. Ooh, she had a baby in her belly, I could tell. The man told her no and she got upset and walked away. She wasn't wearing a coat either.

"Yo, Dee! My man, D.R.!" This other guy was calling my Daddy. He looked nicer though, he had on a bigger coat like mine and a big, shiny, gold cross was hanging around his neck.

"Are you sure?" he was saying and he sounded disappointed. "If you're money ain't right, I can front you what you need and you can pay me later."

"Nah, that's okay," Daddy said, sounding disappointed also. "I'm going to chill, see how this job thing turns out, but I'll call you if I change my mind."

Come on Daddy, I was thinking as I tugged at his hand. I wanted my lollipop and the store was still across the street.

Daddy wasn't listening to me. When I looked up at him to see what was wrong, everything went in slow motion. The wind blew some snow off of a tree and I watched it sprinkle slowly like those glass balls you shake up. I saw an empty potato chips bag half buried in the snow; the half sticking up danced with the breeze. Everything was quiet. Daddy was staring at a big, long car, driving so slow it was walking.

Someone yelled from the car, "I told you 'bout working my corner!" The words did somersaults in my ears. Then ...

Boom! Boom! Boom! I was scared because it was so loud. I tried to see where the loud booms came from, but my Daddy was falling and pulling me with him.

It sounded like thunder, but closer. I was lying there, it was cold and I was still scared. I wanted to get up, but my Daddy's arm was holding me down.

Daddy's eyes were wide and not blinking. He tried to scream, but couldn't. He was crying, saying, "I love you, Lil' Man, I love you!" I kept answering, *More Everyday*, but he couldn't hear me.

Then I saw the blood. It was all over everything. I touched it and it felt hot and sticky. I was really, really scared then. I wanted to hug my Daddy, but somebody picked me up and carried me away.

I wasn't scared anymore, I wasn't cold, I wasn't even crying. I could still hear my Daddy screaming that he loves me, so I kept answering, *More Everyday*, while looking at the sky and its pretty, crayon-blue color.

Yesterday, I lost my Daddy, but I still see him all the time. God lets me watch over him. I send him things every now and then—a good memory, a butterfly, a nice dream. Today, I'm going to send him a real big rainbow, just for him.

My Daddy's a little older now; yesterday lasted a bit longer for him than it did for me. He used to cry a lot, but he's doing better now. At first he was sad because he thought our time together was too short. Isn't that silly? God said that I had to come home first so Daddy would take the right path and make it home, too.

Look! That's him right there. He's going into that Boys Club to speak with the kids about saying no to drugs and gangs, and staying in school ... you know positive things.

He's a ... a ... Hey, Uncle Gabriel what is my Daddy called again? Oh yeah, he's a guidance counselor for at-risk teens. He also helps guys who used to sell drugs find jobs when they get out of prison so they won't sell again. Yep, that's my Daddy! I'm so proud of him.

I'm going to check on my Mommy, too. There she is, still pretty as ever. She's taking my brother and sister to visit Nana. Wow, they look great. My brother and sister never met me, but Daddy told them all about me and they will see me soon.

See, my family will be here tomorrow and I'm so excited. But tomorrow is far away for them, so if you happen to see my Daddy before then, tell him to keep his head up ... I don't want him to miss his rainbow.

The Good Brother

His handcuffs were painfully tight. The shackles on his feet bit into his ankles without mercy. The bus ride had lasted more than 12 hours. Ricky Osborn was cold, tired and hungry. He was fed only once: Four slices of bread, two slices of cheese, a bag of potato chips and an apple. Paper cups and a water cooler sat in the back of the bus next to the bathroom, but his ankles were cut so raw he made the trip only once.

Throughout the day, they'd made several stops to load and unload prisoners at different institutions. Ricky felt a wave of relief wash over him when he saw his designated prison finally come into view. It stood atop of some Indian-named mountain, surrounded by a thick layer of fog, huge and intimidating like a fortified castle.

The over-crowded bus climbed the steep and winding road then stopped at the receiving gate. The engine cut off and sputtered like an old man's cough.

A burly, full-bearded guard wobbled up the steps with a clipboard in hand and started calling names through the wad of tobacco he had stuffed in his mouth.

"Osborn, Richard!" he yelled when he reached Ricky's name.

Ricky grimaced as he stood up. He recited his ID number and began a slow, painful shuffle to the front of the bus.

"I see dey gat the bear-traps on ya pritty tight, eh?" the guard spoke with a backwoods drawl.

Ricky nodded without looking at the officer's face. He didn't want to see the twisted smile or the dirty-brown drip of tobacco juice dribbling down the guard's chin. Ricky had done time before and even though his first bid was only two years, it was long enough for him to learn that most C.O.s got a perverse joy from seeing prisoners in pain. He considered them to be racist and mean and pictured them burning bugs with a magnifying glass even as grown men.

"Officer Swain," the big guard called over to the gate. "Come loosen up this man's leg irons. Some prick tried to cut his ankles off." That rare display of sympathy surprised Ricky, but he hid his shock behind a blank face. He stole a quick glance at the C.O.'s nametag, which read Sgt. Warren. He mumbled his thanks and turned around so that C.O. Swain would have better access to the lock on his ankles.

"Price, Bryan!" Sgt. Warren continued his roll-call.

A rail-thin, light complexioned man, whose baby face was splashed with freckles, stood up and clutched his over-sized pants against his stomach to keep them from falling down.

"2-1-2, 2-5-3, 4-1-7-4," he stated as he bopped down the aisle.

"And what number is dat, Mr. Price?" Sgt. Warren asked patiently.

"That's my phone number in New York, Son. Why, you need the math for my cell phone too?" There was some nervous laughter from the few inmates still on the bus.

"I reckon this is your firs' time in, Mr. Price?"

"Oh, no, no, no, Son. I just did six weeks in Rikers. True story, B. It is mad serious on the Island."

"I'm sure it iz, Mr. Price," Sgt. Warren agreed sarcastically. "But I guarantee ya; it's also very serious in here. First of all, I'm Sergeant William Warren. You'll 'dress me as Sergeant or Sir. I'm not your home-boy, your brother, your cuzin, your fam'ly, and definitely not your *son*. We clear?"

"Yes, Sir."

"Now, when I call your name, you give me your pris'ner identification number.

Alright?"

"Yes, Sir."

"Price, Bryan!"

The young New Yorker frowned in deep thought. He looked down as if the numbers he needed could be found on the dirty floor of the bus. "Son, I mean Sir, is that like my social security number? Because I don't know it by heart, but it starts with a one, right?"

"Come here young man," Sgt. Warren shook his head and took out his ink pen. "This here is your ID number," he said while writing the eight numbers on the palm of Price's hand. "While you're here, it's more 'portant than your name, so mem-o-rize it."

Price stepped off the bus and got in line behind Ricky. "What's the deal, Son? My name is BK. You know, for Brooklyn. That's where I'm from; Brooklyn, New York, so everyone calls me BK."

"I'm Ricky," he answered although he wasn't in the mood for chit-chat. It was the middle of January and it was freezing. They were dressed in tee shirts, thin khaki pants, and Bruce Lee slip on shoes. The mountain air had a stinging chill and Ricky wanted only to get inside.

"Yo, it's b ... biting out here, Son." BK shivered behind him. Ricky nodded his agreement. He looked back and watched as the last inmate got off the bus. Sgt. Warren gave the word for them to be taken inside.

They were herded into a spacious bull-pen with a cement floor, three metal benches and a metal toilet that wouldn't flush. They spent the next four hours being photographed, fingerprinted, and interviewed.

Ricky sat in the cramped office of some psychologist whose name he couldn't pronounce. The doctor had a doughy face and his skin was the color of paper. His eyes were bloodshot and he looked almost as tired as Ricky felt.

"Are you having any thoughts of suicide, Mr. Osborn?" the doctor asked while eyeing Ricky's intake form, his pen poised to check the yes or no box.

"No Sir," Ricky answered. He wasn't thinking of killing himself, but he did feel the need for some type of physical pain: A vice grip screwed in at his temples; the figure four leg-lock; Chinese water torture; anything to distract him from the emotional agony sitting in the middle of his chest like a hot piece of sharp metal.

Ricky had good reason to be disappointed with himself. He had been released from his first prison term over three years ago and he was doing well. He was working full-time at Wal-Mart, living with his fiancée, Tangela, and helping to raise their three children. He was paying bills and living in the routine world of washing dishes, reading bedtime stories, and chaperoning field trips. He was a square and he knew it, but he wasn't looking over his shoulder anymore, so he was content. At least he thought so until Tone came through the checkout line with a thousand dollars worth of X-Box games and a book-sized billfold to pay for them.

Ricky and Tone had gone to school together until Tone dropped out and became a successful drug dealer. Tone was wearing a velour tracksuit underneath a three-quarter length Sean John leather coat. He had diamonds in his ears, around his neck, and on his wrists. His girlfriend wore a full-length, snow-white mink and was prettier than most movie stars. Even his son, who was no older than eleven, was wearing a platinum chain and ID bracelet that probably cost more than Ricky would make in a year.

Tone paid for the games without even speaking to his old classmate. He then breezed through the automatic doors, his perfect family in tow, without waiting for his change. Ricky stared at the 32 dollars and ten cents that Tone had left as a piteous tip and he hated him. Hated him for having the life he so desperately wanted.

That night while driving home in his 94 Cavalier, Ricky came up with his great idea— a one time only, stick and move, drug run. He called it his 'holiday hustle.' He didn't want to compete with Tone; he simply needed some quick money. A little something extra to give the kids a wonderful Christmas. He could buy Tangela one of those Chinchilla coats and maybe trade up on the Cavalier, get a Blazer or something. That's all. He didn't think he was asking for much. He'd do his thing for a month and then get out. In Ricky's mind, the plan was fool-proof.

Ricky cashed his next check, bought two ounces of crack, and hit the block like a ten-year-old on the first day of school. It was a Friday night, the first week of November and the block was a bee hive of drug-fiends spending their first-of-the-month checks in careless intervals that had no chance of making it to Saturday morning.

Ricky doubled his paycheck in less than three hours. A little after 11 p.m., he called it a night and drove home with heavy pockets and an ambitious smile on his face. His 'run' had started out perfectly.

Unfortunately, it also ended quickly. Two weeks—and two quarter ounce sales to an undercover cop—later, Ricky was arrested at home during an early morning drug sweep. His house was clean; no drugs or guns, but the two seven-gram sales and his prior conviction had him facing up to ten years in prison. His public defender managed to get him a five-year plea-bargain offer and Ricky accepted it with a mixed sense of resentment and relief.

"Is there any reason why you can't be placed in population?" the pale psychologist interrupted Ricky's self-lament.

"Uh, no Sir."

"Okay, good luck. Please send the next man in."

Ricky was escorted back to the crowded bullpen. The smell of musky men and stale urine made his empty stomach queasy. He leaned against the gray-green wall and watched as BK stood atop of the clogged toilet and entertained the other convicts with witty one-liners, and hilarious stories.

BK was one of those guys you couldn't help but like. He was a natural comedian who loved to make people laugh. Everything he did was animated and most of what he said was exaggerated. His Brooklyn accent was obvious, and he spoke 100 percent New York City slang. He addressed people as Son or B, Shorty or Ma and swore everything he said was a 'true story.'

"Yo, Ricky! What Psych did you have, Son?" BK asked when he noticed Ricky was back in the cell.

"I had the white dude."

"Ah, snap, you mean the kid that look like a ghost," he shook his head disappointed. "You should of seen the lady, Son. Yo, B, true story, shorty is thick like a baby pony." A few of the other convicts nodded their agreement and BK continued. "I was peepin' Ma's style while she was doing my interview. All of a sudden she stopped writing and said, 'Why you keep looking in my eyes like that?'"

BK paused and scanned the room to make sure he had everyone's attention. The corners of his mouth turned up slyly. "When Brooklyn's in the house, oh my God!" he sang out. "Son, you know I'm trying to crush something. I said, listen Ma, I was taught to always look a woman in her eyes, that way you can get a glimpse of what her soul might taste like. Yo, she liked that. I licked my lips real slow, Son, like I'm L.L. Cool J. And that's my word; she reached over and put her hand on my thigh."

"Yeah right!" someone shouted and it was followed by other murmurings of disbelief.

"True story," BK continued unfazed by the crowd's doubt. "Shorty was looking into my eyes like she in love and she was rubbing on my thigh real slow, working her way up my leg. She was talking all soft like she wanted me, B, and she leaned close to me. I'm telling you, Son, she wanted me to kiss her."

A few of the inmates laughed out loud while the rest looked on anxiously. "Did you kiss her?" a bald headed guy in the back asked for everyone.

BK jumped down from the toilet and looked at him like he was crazy. He then surveyed the room as if making sure there weren't any listening devices. After walking around the crowded cell with wide suspicious eyes, BK stood back up on his nasty throne satisfied that he could share his shadiest secrets with them.

"Yo, Son, true story, she was ready. She rolled her chair closer to me and closed her eyes as she leaned in towards me. I ... I ..." BK could see that they were hanging on every word and let them hang for a few seconds.

"What happened, BK?" a tall guy asked impatiently.

"I leaned in and our noses touched, but I couldn't do it."

"Ah, man!" There was a collective sigh of disapproval.

"Son, her breath smelled like pickled baby-poop and hot train smoke."

"So what!" The crowd said through their laughter.

"You wouldn't say that if it was your eyebrows she almost singed off. Yo, Son, her breath smelled like she had a butt-naked stripper dancing on her tongue." The men laughed harder. "True story, B. I could see a big nasty broad with a fat butt and hairy under arms dancing in her mouth. Son, she's sweating and she ain't showered in three days and she doing splits on shorty's tongue. Yo, B, she smell like barbeque chitterlings and a bag of feet."

Ricky felt his eyes water, he was laughing so hard. The other men were bent over howling as they stomped their feet and clapped each other on the back.

"True story, Son. I've seen strippers like that." BK said with a straight face. "And if you want to see one too, get that lady doctor to smile." Then he laughed a low, musical chuckle that invited all those within hearing range to laugh with him, which they did.

Ricky sat at the end of the bench, trying to get comfortable as he drifted in and out of an awkward slumber. It was after the 10 p.m. count when they were finally assigned to a unit. C.O. Swain called their names in alphabetical order, which led to Ricky and BK— Osborn and Price— being placed in the same unit.

They followed the C.O. up two flights of stairs and down a long, wide hallway that passed the Commissary, the Barber Shop and the Chow Hall. Ricky could tell BK was nervous. His eyes were darting everywhere as if he was trying to remember landmarks in case he got lost later on.

Ricky wanted to reassure him, let him know this wasn't Rikers Island, and as long as he played it cool he'd be alright. But Ricky was dealing with his own demons as they marched down the empty corridor.

He was hoping his money traveled with him and wondering how long it would be before he could go to the store. And he was anxious about a phone call. He hadn't spoken with Tangela since his sentencing and needed to hear her voice. He needed to tell her how much he loved her and that he was sorry. He wanted to talk to his sons and his baby girl and assure them he was fine.

"Ricky," BK whispered as C.O. Swain left them in front of the 12-man dorm that BK was assigned to. "This is me right here, Son." BK switched his bedroll to his other hand and hiked his pants back up at the same time. "I'll see you tomorrow, right?"

"Yeah, no doubt," Ricky gave him a pound. "Be easy." He held the door open and watched BK creep into the quiet dorm and set his things on the one empty bed. BK threw him a two-finger peace sign and started making his bed. Ricky let the door close softly. He adjusted his own bedroll and started down the hall to where his room should be.

He passed a dark TV room where a handful of inmates were watching the news. The TV light flickered against the convicts' faces making their features hard like Mardi Gras masks. Ricky followed the room numbers to the end of the hall until he reached 217. He checked the name tag he was told to place over the door — *Osborn, R. 217 Upper.* He slid the index card into its frame. He was about to open the door when he noticed a man on his knees, bent over his bunk in prayer.

Sharp, painful images flashed across Ricky's mind. Memories so old, the average 30-year-old-man would have forgotten them long ago. For Ricky, the memories were like permanent scars he could point to as proof of how rough his life had been. He closed his eyes as his father's voice exploded in his head like a migraine.

"'And the prayer of faith shall save the sick and the Lord shall raise him up.'" That's right, Richard, fold your hands just like that. 'And if he hath committed sins, they shall be forgiven him'. Close your eyes, Son and get your mind on God. No, not like that, Richard. Keep your hands together." His father's voice was stern and Ricky imagined God's voice sounded exactly the same.

"No, no, no Richard! Listen to your brother. David, start over again."

David, who was five years older than Ricky and in Ricky's eyes the greatest person ever, next to Spider-Man, pinched Ricky's arm while their father wasn't looking. "Just say it with me," David whispered with encouragement.

"Our Father which art in Heaven."

"Our Father wish are is Heaven."

"No, Richard!" their father shouted, "This is unacceptable, David.

I'm going downstairs and if your brother doesn't know this prayer by the time dinner is ready, then neither of you will eat. Am I understood?"

"Yes, Father," they answered together.

When their father left the room, David jumped up and did a fair impersonation of his father's bow–legged walk. "No, no, no, Richard, unacceptable!" he imitated his fathers scowl and made his voice as deep as it could go. "If you don't know the prayer then you don't eat." He then leaned closer to Ricky and whispered conspiratorially, "If he's cooking, we need to be praying that the food will taste good."

Ricky rolled onto his side and held his hands over his mouth to stifle his laughter. David tickled him until he dropped his hands and laughed out loud.

David and Ricky didn't eat until nine o'clock that evening. The pork chops were dry and the macaroni and cheese were cold and rubbery. But their father sat at the table with them; offering a rare smile. Ricky had learned the Lord's Prayer and recited it perfectly three times in a row. Ricky was two years old.

Five minutes passed while Ricky was lost in thought. He waited another five minutes and still the man did not move. Ricky wondered if the man had fallen asleep in that position. He started to tap on the door. An older black man with a long face stepped out from the room across the hall on his way to the bathroom. He eyed Ricky suspiciously at first and then relaxed when he noticed the bedroll and Ricky's fresh-off-the-bus attire. He greeted Ricky with a stiff nod and headed down the hall.

After a few steps, he turned back around and said, "You may as well go on in. If you're waiting for Brother James to finish praying you'll be out here all night."

That was all the motivation Ricky needed. He turned the doorknob and eased into the shadowy room. He laid his things on the end of the bed and seriously considered climbing up on the bunk, lying down on the bare mattress with his bedroll as a pillow and sleeping until someone forced him to wake up. He glanced at his cellmate still deep in prayer. As his eyes adjusted to the dim lighting, he noticed the rest of the room.

The cell was wider than most due to its corner location. There was a sink and mirror next to a door-less closet with spacious shelves set behind a clothing bar. A wooden desk sat beneath a window that looked out onto the wall of another unit it. The desk was submerged with big, thick books: Bibles, Concordances, dictionaries, and thesauruses. There were books by T.D. Jakes, Iyanla Vanzant, James Baldwin and Alice Walker.

Ricky zeroed in on the center of the cluttered desk. He noticed a five by seven picture frame with a professional photograph of a young woman and a small boy. The picture was an extreme close-up of their faces pressed together affectionately. It highlighted their butter-soft cinnamon complexions and spirited smiles. They were beautiful.

Ricky knew intuitively that the persons in that picture belonged to the man praying at the edge of the bed. He immediately thought about Tangela, Devante, Lamar and Nyisha. He shook his head with a tiny sigh, stepped onto the bed ladder and began to make up his bed.

Ricky was tying a knot in his sheet so it would fit the narrow mattress when his cellmate rose slowly to his feet. The man was about the same age as Ricky. He stood six feet even and had an athletic build. He was dark brown and clean-shaven with naturally curly hair cut low. He blinked his squinty eyes and offered Ricky a tired, but sincere smile.

"Peace, brother," his voice was falsetto soft. "My name is James Morris. Everyone calls me Brother James."

Ricky stepped off of the bed ladder and extended his hand. "My name's Ricky."

Brother James took Ricky's hand and pulled him into a tight hug. Good to meet you, Brother Ricky. God bless you."

"Yeah, good to meet you too," Ricky mumbled as he pulled out of the uncomfortable embrace.

Brother James began moving things in the closet to make room for Ricky. "It's so late. I didn't think they were going to take me up on my offer."

"What offer?" Ricky asked.

"It's nothing really. I've been in for quite some time now. After 10 years they gave me single-cell status. When I heard they were having problems finding beds for you all, I offered to take a cellie, temporarily."

Ricky nodded slowly, wondering how you say thanks for a bed in prison.

"When it's overcrowded like this I've seen them set beds in the gym, the TV rooms, and in the hallways. Imagine coming in and having to sleep in the hall?" Brother James slid some more books into the closet and then turned to Ricky with a bright smile. "At least this way you can start your time out a little more comfortable."

"I appreciate it and I'll make sure I stay out your way since you're used to being in here by yourself."

Brother James stood still and stared at Ricky seriously. He didn't say anything, he eyed Ricky as if he'd seen him before and was trying to remember where. The scrutiny made Ricky even more uneasy. He rolled his eyes from left to right and then looked behind him to see what Brother James had locked in on.

"Have you ever read a book that made you cry?" Brother James asked.

Ricky shook his head, barely able to hide his annoyance.

"God is a wonderful God indeed," Brother James gazed dreamily at the Bible lying on his bed. "Of course, there are stories in the Bible that bring tears. Some sad tears and oh, so many joyful tears.

"I just finished reading Maya Angelou's *I Know Why the Caged Bird Sings,* and Wow! I must have cried ten times while reading it. My wife sent it for Christmas and I can tell by the author's picture she is a woman inspired by God. Have you ever read any of her books?"

"Can't say that I have," Ricky answered through a yawn. He was valiantly fighting the urge to laugh, scream, or do both.

"Well, you're welcome to it. Any of these books," he pointed to the desk and the closet. "You have to find ways to make the most of your time here. You have to open up so God can cleanse—"

"I know how to do time," Ricky cut him off.

"Okay, brother. Well, if you need anything, please don't hesitate to ask."

"I'm fine. All I need is a pillow and a good night's sleep."

"You don't have a pillow? That's right. They took it out of here because no one was using the bed," Brother James said sadly. His face clouded over as if they were talking about a missing child and not just a pillow. "I think there's one in the supply closet. I'll go get it for you."

"No, that's alright," Ricky protested. "I can wait until tomorrow."

"It's nothing. Besides, I have to put some mail in the box," he grabbed two letters from off the desk, gave Ricky a quick smile and slid out the door.

Ricky cursed his luck. It was bad enough to be locked up two hours away from home, but to be put in a cell with a man who hugs and talks about crying over books was cruel and unusual punishment.

He walked over to the sink to wash up. He'd taken a shower during his processing where they made everyone use a lice-killing shampoo, but his face felt dry and ashy. He let the steaming, hot water run over his washcloth and after wringing it out held the scalding cloth against his

99

face and felt his pores open instantly. He drug the rag across his face and blinked wearily at his reflection.

His dark brown eyes were heavy and ringed with shadows. His lips were dry and cracking. His hair was an inch too thick for his waves to be seen. Even his skin color, which was usually a rich shade of pure honey, had taken on a grayish pallor. Worst of all, he had lost weight, and at 6'1", 175 pounds, he was already on the left side of skinny.

Ricky was stressing. He missed his family and just thinking about his five year sentence, sent his appetite AWOL. If he could just talk to Tangela and make sure she understood what he had been trying to do. If he could be sure she will forgive him, well, then he could focus on the little things like eating.

Ricky stepped away from the sink. The door busted open and banged against the wall loudly. A short, barrel-chested man with thick tattooed arms stood in the doorway.

"Hey, slim, where you from?" His voice was deep and scratchy, as if he'd been smoking cigarettes since he was a baby.

Ricky felt a ball of fear rise from his stomach. He swallowed it back down. He returned the stranger's hostile gaze, knowing from experience that any sign of weakness would be exploited. "Yo, where *you* from?" he countered forcefully. "And why you busting in people's rooms like that?"

The short muscle-man narrowed his eyes at Ricky and gritted on him hard. Ricky held his breath along with a defiant grit of his own. Seconds crawled by while they sized each other up. The stranger took a step into the room and Ricky turned to face him.

"There was a young New York kid in the dorm who said he came in with someone from the Burg." The aggression in his voice was still evident. "And since you have enough heart to stand there looking at me like you want drama, it must be you."

Ricky licked his dry lips and blinked once. "Yeah, I'm from the Burg," he jutted his chin out as if to say, *So What!*

To his surprise, the stocky inmate with the words *DEATH BEFORE DISHONOR* tattooed on his forearm looked at Ricky and smiled.

"Do you know how long it's been since I had a homie locked up with me?

I'm from the Burg, too. I'm from the Third Ward."

Ricky remained skeptical, but he could sense his anxiety evaporating as he noted the friendly tone in the raspy voice of his 'homie.' "I'm from the Fifth Ward, by the park."

"Yo, slim, that's right around the way. What's your name?"

"Ricky Osborn."

"Osborn, Osborn? I don't remember any Osborns. But you know who I am, right?"

Ricky looked him up and down. He took in the box-braids mashed flat against his round head, the wide nose, the beady eyes, the fishy lips traced with a thin goatee, and the cement blocks that formed his upper body resting on legs the size of number two pencils. Ricky almost laughed out loud when he realized his new homie had the official California Body—all chest and arms with no legs.

"You do look familiar," Ricky lied.

"Yo, it's Frizz! You know, Bernard Franklin. Frizz!"

"Franklin? I know that name, but I can't re—"

"I been down for a while so you probably don't remember me. Plus, I'm a few years older than you."

"I turned 30 a few months ago," Ricky answered absent-mindedly while trying to place the name Franklin. There was something at the tip of his sub-conscious like words to an old song, but he couldn't grab it.

"Yeah, and see, I'm almost 37. You were only 20 when I fell. Finally, I got someone from the home team with me. I know you got pictures of them freaky girls out there," Frizz's voice was dripping with anticipation.

"Not yet, but I can have my cousin send some in."

"That's money. Yo, in the morning I'm going to lace you with everything you need until you get to the store."

Ricky wasn't sure he wanted to be indebted to Frizz. He didn't like owing people period, and the name Franklin was giving him vibes that suggested it would be best to keep Frizz at a safe distance. "I'm good, man. I appreciate the offer, but I don't need anything."

"Stop playing, Ricky. You can't go to the store until next week, and I ain't gonna let you take something from someone else when you got a homie right here in the unit with you. I got you, so don't worry about nothing. We family. We all we got. Remember that."

Ricky threw on a plastic smile as he tried to figure out why everything Frizz said sounded like a threat. Maybe it was his voice, how he talked, or how he looked. Ricky noticed that Frizz had his hand extended for a pound. He blinked away his trepidation and tapped Frizz's fist with his own.

Frizz glanced at his own reflection in the mirror. He made his chest muscles jump, smiled, and then turned his attention back to Ricky. "It's kind of late and I have to be in the kitchen at four a.m.. But yo, we gonna get together tomorrow, right?"

"No doubt! I'll get with you tomorrow."

As Frizz was turning to leave, Brother James stepped into the doorway with a worn pillow under his arm. Frizz saw Brother James standing there, turned back to Ricky and in a stage whisper loud enough for the men in the TV room to hear, said, "Damn, they put you in the cell with the good brother?"

Ricky kept his face blank while Frizz stood there blocking the doorway. "Excuse me, Brother Franklin."

Frizz rolled his eyes and wheeled around to face Brother James. "Frizz! My name is Frizz! You know like F-R-izz!"

"Pardon me, Brother ... Frizz. I'm trying to get into my room."

Frizz turned back towards Ricky, "Alright homie," he said homie with the pride of a father saying son or maybe a son saying Dad. "I'll see you tomorrow." He hit his fist against his chest and turned sideways to step past Brother James. "That's my peoples in there, Preacher Man. Don't start nothing won't be nothing!"

Frizz strolled off with his arms out in front of him like he was carrying an imaginary treasure chest. He bounced from side to side, shifting his weight from one leg to the other. Ricky watched him go, expecting his knees to buckle at any minute.

"You have to excuse my friend," Ricky muttered as he thanked Brother James for the pillow. "He's a little burnt out, but he seems like good people."

Brother James studied Ricky with that same intense gaze. Ricky felt as if his soul could be seen from the outside. "There was a time when I first got saved, that I didn't want anyone to touch me," Brother James spoke slow and soft. Ricky had to lean in closer to catch every word. "I didn't want them to make me dirty, and I really believed they could steal my joy. I was calling myself saved, but I was still lost. God is love!" His voice skipped an octave and his eyes lit up. "Once you realize and understand that, Wow! All you want to do is love. And the word says, 'Love is patient, love is kind, it keeps no record of wrongs.' Love is God, and God is eternal, so when you love like God loves, well then, everyone is good people."

Brother James sat down at the desk and began writing. He didn't expect a response, which was fine by Ricky since he didn't know what to say. He climbed into his bunk bone-tired but couldn't sleep. The butterflies in his stomach whispered 'what ifs' as he stared at the ceiling. His guilt clung to him like the finger print ink and conjured up heartsick images of Tangela and his kids that bought tears to his eyes.

He glanced over at Brother James, who was huddled at the desk writing intently. He felt a mixture of envy and pity. In his eyes, Brother James was still lost; especially if he really believed God is love. Ricky knew first hand that God's love was fleeting at best. He had his brother David as proof.

***

Ricky soon remembered prison life has a distinct rhythm. It is usually a monotonous drone, but it can speed up like a racing pulse and pause dramatically when the beat is interrupted by clashing cymbals. Ricky regained his groove and after a few weeks, was two-stepping with the best of them.

He went to the store and stacked his locker with a three month supply of food and cosmetics: He was hired as a compound orderly— an easy job detail that consisted of sweeping cigarette butts for an hour every day— and best of all; he'd gotten a chance to speak to Tangela and the kids.

The prison phone system was set up for collect calls only. Ricky's home phone had a long distance-block on it due to the twice-a-week calls he'd made during his first sentence. He harassed his counselor for a week and was granted an emergency call.

Ricky laughed loudly when his oldest son, Devante, answered the phone and said, "Speak!" which was Ricky's customary greeting. He pictured his 10-year-old son playing 'man of the house.' He spoke with Devante and his seven-year-old son Lamar. His baby girl, Sierra, got on the phone and sang a song by some group called the Cheeta Girls. When she finished singing, she passed the phone to her mother and Ricky heard her tiny voice say, "Don't cry, Mommy. Daddy's on the phone."

Ricky felt his breath catch as soon as she said hello. Her voice was like the whispering of a seashell. Ricky closed his eyes and tried to savor every word.

She assured him the kids were fine and that she wasn't mad at him anymore, just disappointed. She sounded distant and Ricky knew she wasn't telling him everything. She promised to come see him in two weeks and he would have to wait until then to assess her emotional state and try to make things right between them.

"You know I love you, Tee?" he asked with a strained voice. There was a few seconds of crushing silence.

"I know. I love you, too." Tangela's voice rang hollow. Ricky forced a phony smile as he hung up and handed the phone back to his counselor. He walked out of the office dizzy with despair and went looking for Frizz and BK to distract him from his depression.

The three of them formed an unexpected fraternity even though Frizz did not like guys from New York. When Ricky asked why, he shrugged his huge shoulders and in his sandpaper voice said, "They think they better than everyone."

BK on the other hand took to Frizz right away. He considered Frizz the most comical thug he'd ever met, but admired him openly. BK worked the same kitchen shift as Frizz and spent early morning hours beguiling him with made-up stories about handguns that shot 200 rounds in six seconds and pop stars who stalked him at night clubs.

Frizz tolerated BK because he was young and funny and because he clung to Ricky like a pesky little brother. However he rarely passed up an opportunity to taunt BK about his "shady and crooked" birthplace and remind him he was only welcomed into the circle because he was Ricky's boy.

BK endured Frizz's disdain with the disregard of a superstar being heckled by a bum. He knew deep down Frizz liked him. Everyone liked BK. He was a thorough young kid who knew how to have fun. Of course, there were times when BK returned Frizz's teasing with his own. And since he was much wittier than Frizz, Ricky usually had to intervene before Frizz made good on his threat to "choke the little nigga out." Ricky genuinely cared for BK, but he also kept him around as a balance to the negative and stormy vibes that emanated from Frizz like a bad odor.

Frizz was burnt out. He was 5'6" and had an aggressive Napoleon complex. He challenged people to fight at least three times a day. He was insecure and wanted people to like him, but he talked to everyone with a nasty disrespect. He cut lines, took food out of peoples hands, and turned the TV without any consideration for those who were watching it first.

Ricky tried to focus on his positive traits. Frizz was generous to a fault. He would come into the TV room during football games and pass out candy bars to everyone in there or open five or six bags of chips for the room to share. He also encouraged everyone in the weight room to push harder, and spotted anyone who wanted to lift more than their usual.

He was overprotective of Ricky and stayed on a mission to impress him. He treated Ricky like a big brother and a little brother at the same time. He got jealous if Ricky paid too much attention to someone else. He also deferred to Ricky about the smallest decisions: "Homie, you want to walk the track or watch videos?" Whatever Ricky said, became law enforced by Frizz.

Ricky became more acquainted with the other prisoners and learned that Frizz hadn't been as aggressive or boisterous prior to Ricky coming there. They playfully blamed him for Frizz's evolution from a baby beast to a full-grown monster. Ricky knew they were telling the truth, he just couldn't figure out how he could have that type of influence on a man 6 years older and 50 pounds heavier than him.

On the opposite end of Ricky's jail house spectrum was the good Brother James. Ricky would leave Frizz and BK at the poker table or in the TV room and come back to his cell where Brother James would be holding Bible Study in the hallway outside their door. Ricky would hold in his sigh and navigate through the circle of men, saying 'excuse me' ten or more times until finally reaching the door.

Initially, Ricky believed Brother James was crazy. Not your typical, lost-in-the-head-madness, but that tiny flame-about-to-burn-out-crazy. The 'crazy' that comes from traumatic experiences or from being incarcerated too long. After a few weeks of casual conversations that always began with "Praise God" and ended with "Let brotherly love continue." Ricky decided that not only was Brother James crazy, he was one of those over-zealous fanatics who used religion the same way addicts used drugs. He pictured Brother James walking out of jail and into the first strip-bar he sees, hell-bent on wiping away 15 years of hymns and scriptures with sweaty, smoky, alcohol-induced fornication.

Ricky watched him with a discerning eye, waiting to see the hypocrisy, the contradictions. They never came, and eventually Ricky had to accept his first impressions were wrong and that Brother James was exactly what he claimed and portrayed to be every hour of the day— a man who loves God.

Brother James worked as a clerk in the Chapel. He was Chaplain Parker's right hand and he did everything from formatting the church programs to setting up the chairs for each religious service. He was also the choir director. His voice was said to be so powerful and amazingly pure that any mention of him singing a solo would bring the atheists and agnostics to Sunday morning service.

Outside of church, Brother James taught a manhood mentoring class geared to new inmates who were still mad at the world. He ran a heart-healthy exercise class for overweight prisoners and tutored GED students one-on-one at night. He was also responsible for an annual Run-a-thon that raised money for cancer.

Brother James was 33 years old and had spent the last 12 of those years locked up. Yet, he carried himself as if life was wonderful and every day a blessing indeed. He smiled all the time and never cursed. He called everyone brother or sister and was always polite. He was respected by all inmates and by most of the prison staff. He projected a worldly wisdom and quoted scripture without sounding preachy. He gave sound advice on anything he could and if he didn't have an answer he was honest enough to say so.

He didn't watch much TV. The exceptions were BET Gospel, an occasional football game— he was a die-hard Cowboys fan— and the World News.

It was in the TV room that Ricky first noticed how much respect and admiration the other inmates had for Brother James. Rap videos were on BET. Ricky sat in the back of the room with his headphones blasting. The throbbing baselines and gritty lyrics were like a mind-numbing narcotic helping him to forget he was once again confined behind barbed-wire fences with angry men who sharpen toothbrushes for battle and no longer remember how it feels to cry.

Brother James eased into the TV room. A heavy-set Spanish guy immediately stood up and turned the channel to the ABC News. Ricky sprung to his feet prepared to protest. Brother James placed a light, restraining hand on his shoulder. "Thank you, Brother Rodriguez," he said with a bright smile. "But I can't stay, so you all enjoy your music." He turned towards Ricky and kneeled down as Ricky slumped back in his seat.

"Brother Ricky, you received some mail. I set it on your bed under your pillow."

"Thank you," Ricky muttered as he eyed the back of Rodriguez's head, willing him to turn it back to BET before he missed the new Jay-Z video.

"I have some turkey and cheese wraps that Brother Mike made for me. He gave me six of them and I can only eat three. Well, I could probably eat more than three, but I have a six-pack in the temple."

Ricky looked at him with a shocked expression and Brother James laughed like a little boy. "No, no, Brother Ricky. The good brother isn't drinking alcohol. I'm talking about my body; that's the temple. And this here," he grinned while rubbing his stomach, "is the six-pack."

Ricky laughed with Brother James. "Just put the ones you can't eat in my bowl. My six-pack can afford it."

"Oh, you call that a six-pack?" Brother James winced comically. "I thought it was a swimming pool for your ribs."

They cracked up and Ricky was surprised at the diversity and depth of Brother James' personality. Ricky watched him exit, saying "God bless you" to everyone he passed.

It wasn't until Brother James left the room, that a slim, dark-skinned man with a Virginia accent turned the TV back to Rap City. A Lil Jon video with a crunk baseline was in the middle of an exotic display of half-naked women all built like triple-scooped ice cream cones.

"It might jus' be me," the Southern brother spoke up. "But don't Brother James make you feel guilty when he's around? You don't wanna cuss, you try not to think evil thoughts, and you damn sure can't enjoy these thick-ass girl's right therrre!" He pointed to the TV and the entire room laughed with him, except Ricky's laugh was filled with pride and admiration. He knew his cellie was held in high regards.

Ricky lay in bed at night, watching a real-life rendition of the Godfather movie with a Christian twist. Grown men came to their room and spoke to Brother James in hushed tones. They asked for anything; a stamp, a can of tuna, advice about a rebellious child.

Brother James quoted from the book of Hebrews and told his friends to let brotherly love continue, while Ricky chased sleep relentlessly. He missed his family. Ricky hadn't seen Tangela and the kids in six weeks. The phone was still blocked and the letters he received were distant, cool, and brief. The last one was a one paragraph memo that said something had come up and she would try to come see him in two weeks.

Ricky was miserable. He wrote three and four page letters declaring his love for her and the children and made poetic promises to marry her as soon as he could.

Her letters were short progress reports on the kids. She didn't say if she was mad at him or if she missed him or anything. The, *Love Tee* at the end of each note was like urine in the swimming pool he wanted to drown himself in—it added insult to injury.

Ricky was fed up. If that's how she wanted to do it, fine by him. He'd lick his wounds, pop his collar and do his time by himself, solo like a prisoner of war. And if that didn't work, well, he had Frizz and BK.

The three of them sat in Ricky's room with two pencil-thick joints of hydro-ponic marijuana. It was raining outside and the dorm that Frizz and BK slept in was crowded with inmates getting off work. Ricky didn't want to smoke weed in Brother James' room, but he really wanted to smoke, he needed to smoke, and like Frizz said, it was his room, too.

"Yo, Son, word to my motha. You think you stressin', imagine how I feel." BK was leaning against the desk holding one a joint between his thumb and forefinger. "Last year around this time I was at the Source Awards."

Frizz coughed out a laugh, "Homie, why this little fool always lying?"

"Frizz. B, this is real talk. Hear me out." BK passed the joint to Ricky who was giggling at how BK had called Frizz, a frisbee. The hydro had him feeling good. The sweet poignant scent refused to leave through the open window and intensified his high.

"True story, Son," BK continued. "I was at the Source Awards dipped. I had that Armani on, cleaner than the Board of Health. I had the 32-inch platinum chain, with the Roli bezeled out, B. I was a walking light show; diamond ice cubes in my ears, Son. I had—"

"Diamonds?!" You … you ain't even got no commissary," Frizz cut him off.

"You see what I mean, Son. I can't even talk without Frizz-B sayin' something. With his strong-face self."

Ricky looked over at Frizz and noticed that his face did look strong. He fell out in a fit of laughter as Frizz and BK traded insults like professional comedians. Ricky lost all control when BK stood up and impersonated Frizz's walk.

"Frizz, you're like the real life Shrek, Son. You all brolic, but you ain't got no legs. You must have a strong butt to hold up all that weight."

Frizz stopped laughing and bent his eyes at BK. "Hold up! What you doin' looking at my butt?" His tone was menacing.

BK poked his lips out with disgust and disbelief. "Stop playing, Son. Ain't no one looking at your butt."

Frizz eyed him down then turned to Ricky for corroboration. Ricky shook his head to assure Frizz no one's been looking at him like that. Ricky took a long pull of the joint before they could blow his buzz. He fought the urge to laugh as he visualized Frizz talking like Shrek.

Frizz accepted the joint from Ricky. His eyes glazed over as he inhaled deep. "Funny freckled-face nigga," he blew out a breath of smoke that billowed toward the ceiling and took the tension with it. "What else happened at the Source Awards?"

A relieved BK picked up right on cue. "It was bananas, Son. True story. I get inside and there's a famous shorty sittin' in my seat. You won't believe who was in my seat."

Ricky had a silly grin on his face as he waited for BK to say Beyonce, Ashanti or Jennifer Lopez.

"Who?" Frizz asked with zero patience.

"Nah, Son. It's too crazy. Word to motha, it's a true story, but you won't believe me."

"Just tell us who, BK." Ricky was getting frustrated as well.

When BK finally answered them, Ricky and Frizz fell out in a fit of raucous laughter.

"What?" BK looked perplexed. "Son, that's my word. Oprah Winfrey was sitting in my seat."

"At the Source Awards?"

"Yeah, at the Source Awards, B. And she had on a sexy dress with the high slit up the side."

"And what you do?" They asked as tears sprang from their eyes.

"What you mean? I asked her to move."

They laughed even harder.

"Son, she started beefin' with me. Oprah told me to bounce. She said I was blocking her view of 50 cent—"

"Stop! Please stop him Frizz." Ricky was on his knees.

"It's not funny, B. Ma caused a scene." BK had the nerve to look hurt. "She said she could buy me and then give me away to charity."

Frizz started coughing up what sounded like a lung. "Then...what happened?" He managed to get out.

"Word to motha I was in my feelings, B. I was 'bout to put hands on Oprah, but the dude Chuck D from Public Enemy was sittin' in front of us and he was like, "chill out, kid." Then he offered her a seat beside him. His man? Yo Son, his man with the clock, Flava Flav. He started buggin'; he said he was going to get in my business after the show."

Ricky and Frizz had to hold each other up; their stomachs had balled up from laughing so hard. "Then what?" Ricky urged him to continue.

"Nothing, B. I broke out of there a little early. Not that I was scared, Son, but I was on parole and ... well yo, Flav is bigger than he seems on TV."

They laughed so long they had to relight the second joint. Frizz held it up to his eyes and studied the burning tip. He was entranced by the tiny orange glow. Ricky and BK noticed him at the same time. Before they could tease him about it, the sound of the doorknob turning caught their attention. A brittle silence fell and nobody moved as Brother James walked in the room.

"Man!" Frizz let out a breath of relief. "I thought it was a C.O., but no, it's only Bishop T.D. James."

BK chuckled while Ricky stared at Brother James with a defiant smirk.

Brother James scanned the room. His face wrinkled in disgust as he smelled the marijuana that lingered heavy in the air like a whore's perfume. "I would like for you to take your reefer and leave." He fought to keep his voice steady.

"Don't even trip, Preacher Man," Frizz said smugly. "This ain't just your room. It's my homie's room too, and we're only trying to bless the cell. You know all about blessings, right?" Frizz took another drag of the almost gone doobie. "Well, this here is the cess that Buddah blessed."

Brother James ignored him and kept his attention on Ricky. "I can't believe you could be this disrespectful."

"How is it disrespectful?" Ricky sounded offended. "This is my room, too. Just 'cause I'm not into the things you in to doesn't mean there's not things I wanna do." Ricky sounded high even to his own ears. He looked at BK who gave a half shrug and said, "Word, Son."

"What you want to do jeopardizes my freedom," Brother James spoke patiently, but his mouth was set tight. "You're doing something that could effect when I go home to my wife and son. If the officers come in here, they're not going to ask whose weed it is. I'm going down with you, because of what *you* wanna do. Is that how you—"

"We ain't with all that soft shit," Frizz cut him off. "Take it how you want. We doing us!"

Brother James kept his eyes on Ricky whose nonchalant expression made it clear he agreed with Frizz. Brother James closed his eyes, said a quick prayer, and then shut the door behind him.

"That's word life, Son," BK smiled as Brother James sat on his bed and took off his sneakers. "That's what you do, just hit some of this hydro and fall back."

Ricky and Frizz traded confused looks as Brother James put on his boots and talked to himself in a pensive voice.

"The root of the righteous shall not be moved." Brother James laced his boots as tight as they would go. "Deliver me from the workers of wickedness. O God, defend me from those who rise against me." He stood up and grabbed his gloves from his coat pocket. "The righteous cry and the Lord heareth, and delivereth them out of all their troubles." He slid on his gloves and faced Frizz, Ricky and BK. Their cotton dry mouths formed small O's of surprise.

"I think he wants to fight something, Son."

"That's exactly what I want to do," Brother James said evenly. "Since you don't want to leave, we're going to settle this the old-fashioned way."

Frizz and BK busted out laughing.

"Oh yeah," Frizz slurred as he struggled to his feet. His legs felt rubbery from being high and sitting down for the last two hours, but he was always ready for a fight. "I ain't whooped a choir boy in years. Let's do it."

Frizz pushed the chair against the desk. BK slid towards the window to give them room. Brother James kept his back to the door, put his left foot in front of his right pivot and threw up his hands.

"Hold on Frizz," Ricky spoke through his haze. There was something familiar about Brother James' stance. His jaw was clenched and the whites of his eyes flicked with determination. He held his left hand high, so he could jab and turn his elbow for defense. His right hand was tucked close to his chin in perfect position to throw a six-inch hook once he got inside. His shoulders, although square, were at an angle—that hard to see which hand is coming— angle. Ricky saw it right away; the good brother knew how to fight.

"Let it go, homie." Ricky stepped in between them. "We 'spose to go get something to munch on anyway." Frizz didn't protest when Ricky gently pushed him back and Ricky wondered if Frizz had noticed the same thing he had.

"It's your lucky day, Preacher Man!" Frizz mumbled as he snatched his hat from off the desk.

Brother James dropped his guards and stood beside the door as Frizz and BK stalked out of the room. Ricky reached over Brother James' shoulder to grab his coat. Their faces were only inches apart. Brother James could smell the marijuana, sticky and stale on Ricky's breath. When their eyes met, Brother James smiled and said, "The weed isn't going to help you remove the bitterness from your heart. For the joy you seek, brother, is already inside of you."

Ricky shook his head, twisted his mouth into an amused smile, and walked out into the hallway where Frizz and BK were waiting.

That night Ricky climbed into bed after the count. The window was still open and the smell of disinfectant was strong in the room. He knew Brother James had missed choir practice to clean out the cell.

Ricky's high had washed away without warning, leaving in its place a pool of guilt. He cleared his throat twice in an attempt to apologize to Brother James, who sat at the desk reading his Bible. He couldn't find the words or the heart to say them. Instead, he rolled over and stared at the back of his eyelids until finally falling into a fitful sleep.

He woke up the next morning with a sewer in his mouth and a subway running through his head. He spent a half hour on the toilet and ended up being 20 minutes late for work. His boss, Seargent McClain, jumped all over him right away, berating him like a disobedient child and refusing to accept any excuses. When he brought up how sweet the compound orderlies had it— to only work for one hour and get paid for a full day— Ricky couldn't hold his tongue any longer.

"Wow, a whole 12 cents an hour, 84 cents a day," Ricky scoffed. "I'd give you 84 cents a day if I didn't have to come here for an hour."

"Oh, you want to be a wise ass?" Sgt. McClain flushed red with anger. "Go to the Lieutenants' office for the works."

Ricky sauntered off gratefully until he remembered that the 'works' meant being strip-searched for contraband, breathalyzed for alcohol, and worst of all, he'd have to give a urine sample to be tested for drugs.

Ricky sat in the Lieutenants' office in a clammy, cold sweat. He ran through his mind the many sanctions a dirty urine would earn him: Loss of good days, loss of visiting privileges, 30 days locked up in the SHU (Segregated Housing Unit), and a random urine test twice a week for the rest of his sentence. "Damn!" he thought.

Lt. Stevenson, a tall, sober man with a military bearing and the only black Lieutenant on the compound, looked up as if he'd just remembered Ricky was still there. "Can you go yet, Osborn?"

"Uh, not yet, Sir. Let me drink some more water." Ricky walked to the water fountain. He was stalling. He'd been in the Lieutenants' office for over an hour. He'd been stripped and breathalyzed, but he was trying to delay the urine test, futilely hoping that if he waited long enough, the hydro-marijuana would miraculously disappear from his system. He took only a small sip of water. He had drunk so much in the last hour; his bladder was kissing his lungs.

He sat down and fought to keep his legs still. He felt like he might go on himself any minute. Lt. Stevenson glanced at him then returned to his paperwork. Ricky practiced in his mind how he would explain to

Tangela why he couldn't have any visits. He closed his eyes for a second and when he opened them he saw Brother James peering through the glass door. Their eyes met momentarily. Brother James shook his head slowly and walked away.

"At least he'll have his cell back to himself," Ricky mumbled under his breath. He suppressed a bitter smile as he pictured Brother James celebrating by throwing Ricky's things out into the hallway and inventing his own scriptures; "Thou shall not smoke the unholy trees in room 217."

Ricky heard the door open and was surprised to see Brother James had returned.

"Praise God!" Brother James stepped into the office, his radiant smile lighting up the room. "How are you, Brother Stevenson?"

"I'm blessed, Brother James. How are you?"

"The grace of God is sufficient for me."

They exchanged pleasantries about their families. Ricky listened to their conversation, once again awed by Brother James' ability to evoke the same respect from a Lieutenant that he received from his Bible study faithfuls.

"I wanted to remind you Brother that the church's anniversary service will be held in the evening this year."

Lt. Stevenson bent closer to Brother James and lowered his voice, "I've already been approved for overtime on that day. I wouldn't miss it for the world."

"And you know Chaplain Parker would be at your door if you did," Brother James warned and they both laughed.

"I'm sure you and that amazing choir have something special planned."

"God willing, it's going to be beautiful. Speaking of choirs, I need to get to rehearsal right now." Brother James glanced over at Ricky, who had his eyes glued to the floor. "Brother Stevenson, I notice you have my cellmate in here. Surely he's not in any trouble is he?"

"No, not really. McClain sent him through the works for being late this morning. I'm just waiting for him to pee in a cup."

Brother James breathed a sharp sigh as he realized the seriousness of Ricky's situation. Ricky met his gaze with a defeated frown on his face.

"I sure could use him at rehearsal, Brother Stevenson."

"Sure. Osborn can you go now?" Lt. Stevenson asked.

"No, Sir," Ricky answered a little too quickly. "See, I had just went before I came to work. Actually that's why I was late."

"Can you vouch for him, Brother James?"

Brother James kept his eyes trained on Ricky and answered without hesitation, "Yes, I can vouch for him."

"Alright, Osborn. But don't tell McClain you didn't give a urine. And don't be late for work anymore."

"Yes, Sir!" Ricky stood up and held the door open for Brother James.

"Thank you, Brother Stevenson, and God bless." Brother James tightened his scarf and stepped outside with Ricky.

"Man, you're like the Governor in here," Ricky said as he blew into his hands to keep them warm.

"You should have your gloves on, Brother Ricky, especially when you work outside."

"I know. I was rushing this morning and forgot them."

Brother James reached inside his coat pocket and pulled out Ricky's gloves. "I saw them in your chair and thought you might need them."

Ricky slipped on the gloves and took a deep breath of cold air. A shiver ran through him, more from the shame he felt than the 20 degree weather. Yesterday, he acted like a nut-case and treated this man with complete disdain. Today, that same man came out in the cold to bring him his gloves and ended up rescuing him from a serious situation that would have had some ugly consequences. Ricky felt like a jerk.

"I really appreciate what you did back there. And about yesterday, well, that 'dro had me buggin'. I know we shouldn't have been smoking in the room. I was wrong for—"

"I must also apologize for my behavior yesterday. It was completely out of my character to want to resort to violence."

"No, no," Ricky insisted. "We were in the wrong and you were right to wanna get your hands dirty."

"That's not my way, Brother. There was a time when I tried to solve all my problems with violence, but God has shown me a better way and I have to trust His way no matter what the circumstances."

Ricky looked up at a bright sun that offered no warmth. He was sorry about his actions, but didn't want to hear about God's way. He reached for the door that led to their unit. "I have to go. Thanks again for getting me out of that jam."

"Brother Ricky, please do not make me a liar. I told Brother Stevenson that I need your help and I do."

"For what? The choir? Are you serious?" He looked at Brother James like he was crazy. "I can't sing."

"Yes, you can sing," Brother James smiled knowingly. "You may not like to sing, or want to sing, but I have heard you with your headphones on going note for note with Gerald Levert, Usher, and R. Kelly. Oh, and you must really like that 'House is not a Home' piece, because when that song came on I thought Luther Vandross was in the cell with me."

"You need to stop playing," Ricky smiled at the compliment. He had no idea that Brother James was hip to any other types of music besides Gospel.

"I do not play when it comes to music."

"But I have to use the bathroom real bad."

"I'm sure you do," Brother James winked. "There's a bathroom in the Chapel and it's a lot closer than the one in the unit."

Ricky hunched his shoulders against the wind, a reluctant smile tugged at the corner of his mouth. "I'll go, but I ain't singing, especially in no choir."

"That's perfectly alright, just be my ears and help me find the weak spots."

"What makes you think I can do that?" Ricky asked as they reached the chapel door.

"Because you have to be able to hear notes in order to sing them. Besides," he added as he opened the door and pointed Ricky to the bathroom. "God told me."

"Whatever," Ricky muttered as he turned into the bathroom.

The chapel was actually a long, wide, well-lit rectangular room that could be divided into four separate sections. It bore little resemblance to a real church, which was intentional since all practicing religions shared the space.

Ricky stood in the doorway watching the 20 or so inmates milling about. A few of them stood at the piano trying to match their voices with the keys. Others bent over long, black cords, connecting electric and bass guitars to amplifiers and mixing boards. Drums were being set up and mics were being tested, but as soon as Brother James entered the room, all activities ceased.

The brothers stood up and greeted him as if he'd just returned from an arduous voyage at sea. He flashed his signature smile, embraced a select few, inquired about sick family members and encouraged all to let 'brotherly love continue.' When everyone was standing, he motioned to the center of the room and said, "Let's pray!"

Ricky stood out of respect, but kept his head up and his eyes open. He watched the men with a tiny pinch of jealousy as they held hands and punctuated Brother James' prayer with "Amens" and "Yes, Lords." The prayer was short and to the point. Brother James asked God to forgive their sins, cleanse their hearts, and accept their praise as they glorify His precious, holy name.

After they said Amen, Brother James became very serious. Ricky sat down in a far off corner of the room and watched as the choir formed a two-tiered line in front of Brother James. He looked each of them in their eyes and then stared past them at the rubber plant that stood near the window. When he was satisfied they were ready, he lifted one hand in the air and said, "Order My Steps, on three."

The drummer tapped his sticks three times to count them in. They sang! In perfect harmony. Ricky was taken aback. Electric currents shot through him and made the fine hairs on his arms stand straight. He hadn't heard singing that dynamic in a long time. His soul felt light and free as he listened with voracious ears.

He watched Brother James make circles with his hands and hold them to his eyes like binoculars to tell the choir to keep their eyes on him. He waved a hand to the band and stopped the music, then pointed to the different sections for an a capella harmony that shifted from baritone to alto. He brought the music back in, one instrument at a time, building a captivating crescendo that flowed fluidly; a wave roaring unhindered as it crashes ashore.

Ricky closed his eyes, and like a child who knows there's a springy mattress behind him, fell comfortably into his past.

"You have to sing the solo, Richard," his Mother said in a voice sweeter than wind chimes.

"But, this is David's song, Mom. David has the solos." Ricky was ten years old. He'd been singing in the choir since he was four, but had never sung a solo. He didn't feel he was ready to go at it alone. Not in front of so many people.

"It's your time now, Richard." She bent down and straightened his tie. "God has blessed you with a beautiful voice and it's time for you to share that gift. Are you ready to use your gift for God, Richard?"

"Yes, Mother," Ricky swallowed in effort to loosen his tie.

"Still no word?" His Father walked in mopping his brow with a handkerchief.

"He said he's not coming dear," his Mother answered. "You gave him the choice and he chose not to come. He's not... coming!" She brushed away a stubborn tear with a gloved hand.

"Lord have mercy! I try and do all that I—"

"David's not coming?" Ricky interrupted his father.

"No, son, he's not coming. Your brother is listening to the voices of false teachers and has gone astray. We will pray for his return, but we must continue to serve God."

Ricky was more than confused. David was all he had, his only link to the real world. Their father saying he had gone astray was like saying David had jumped off the edge of the earth. It just wasn't possible.

"Richard!" His father's voice was thick with emotion. "You must stand steadfast. There is nothing to cry about. You wipe your eyes and go on out there and glorify God. You magnify our Lord and Savior. Can you ... can you do that for me?

"Yes, Father," Ricky answered in a trembling voice. He wandered to the front of the stage and missed his cue to start singing. The pianist had to start over twice before he finally opened his mouth and gave voice to the song; 'That Old rugged Cross.'

He cried the whole way through. Big, rain drop tears that coerced the congregation to cry with him. Even as they marveled at the little boy with the deep soulful voice. They said he sounded as if the finger of God was on him, but Ricky didn't feel God. He was thinking of his older brother and wishing he was there to hear him, too.

"Could you hear him, Brother Ricky? Could you hear him from over there?"

Ricky hadn't heard anything. He looked at Brother James with a disoriented and inquiring gaze.

"Was Brother Timothy loud enough?" Brother James asked as he stood next to a diminutive brother with a face like a hawk.

"No, I couldn't hear him." Ricky answered.

"You see, brother? You have to sing from your soul, with passion and love. Every song, every note. Your voice is needed for the body to be complete." Brother James started towards Ricky with Brother Timothy on his heels.

"Brother James," Timothy's voice was high and nasal. "You think I could maybe do a solo this week?"

Brother James stopped cold and the look on his face was undiluted disappointment. He turned around and faced Brother Timothy. "Maybe next week," he said simply and watched Brother Timothy sulk back to the group.

"He has such a wonderful voice, but he's still singing for man's applause instead of for God." Brother James shook his head and sighed. "As soon as he can go one week without asking for a solo, he'll get one. I thought he was going to make it this week."

"You all sound real good," Ricky stated.

"All glory to God, brother. This next song is the one I need you to pay close attention to. It's new to us and we've been having problems with the timing and the harmony. Can you help us out?"

"I don't know what I can do to help, but sure, I'll listen."

"That's great," Brother James smiled and then strode back to the choir. "Okay Brothers. 'Sing' on three!"

The choir took their places with drug-feet and hung-heads. It was obvious they weren't very excited about the song. After the first five stops and restarts, Ricky understood why. The song was complicated. The verses had a lot of words and needed to be sung with a sharp choppiness. The bridge was smooth and brilliantly composed, but didn't match the tempo. And the climax of the song involved the whole choir harmonizing the 'si' of sing back and forth, so fast that when done right it would sound like an infinite tide of melody that covered the musical scale.

Instead it sounded like a group of stuttering children.

"Brothers, brothers, please just listen," Brother James implored. "It's on the down-beat, like this, si, si- si, si- si, si- si, sing, siiinngg!" Brother James executed every note crystal clear and it came out perfectly. "Okay? Now, let's try it again."

Ricky tucked his chin in his chest and tried his best to keep his laughter in check. Now they sounded like a bunch of drunk Mexicans. Brother James held his hand up to stop them and then raked his fingers through his tight curls. He looked at Ricky with pleading eyes, shook his head and walked away.

"You alright?" Ricky met him at the window.

"The Word says, 'I will sing of all the excellent things the Lord has done.' That's what this song is about—singing," Brother James sighed. "I'm fine Brother. I just want them to get it."

"There are too many harmonies and it's throwing the timing off," Ricky said evenly. "Why not give them the same notes in different octaves and let them do the bridge in unison?"

"That would make it easier for them," Brother James contemplated. "It's worth a try."

Brother James went over the new parts with each group and even as they practiced they sounded better. Their attitudes improved as well. When Brother James said, "Sing, on three," confident faces beamed back at him. The drum sticks clicked thrice and sing they did; all the way to the end of the song.

No one said anything. They looked at Brother James expectantly. He stared at something over their heads, his expression uncertain. "One more time," he whispered.

They sounded even better the second time. Their voices were clipped and precise. On key and on time. Even the 'si- si, sing' became a backand-forth serve and volley that rose and fell with the intensity of a rhythmic roller-coaster. When they finished, Brother James laughed and clapped, and said, "Beautiful, Brothers! Praise God! Very, very beautiful!"

The choir basked in Brother James' approval. They hugged, clapped and congratulated each other on a job well done. Ricky smiled at their jubilation. He tried to remember the last time he was a part of something so special. Brother James caught his eye and mouthed the words 'Thank You.' Ricky waved him off to say it was nothing, but deep down he knew it was.

****

That weekend, Ricky was called for a visit. It took him less than 20 minutes to shower, dress, and walk to the visiting hall. After handing over his ID and being thoroughly pat-searched, he stepped into the visiting room, nervous and excited like a freshman at the senior prom.

It was only nine a.m. and the visiting room was already crowded. The smell of loud perfumes and microwaved popcorn filled the air. Ricky scanned the room for his family and almost broke into a run when he finally spotted them in the children's playroom. Tangela sat in a small plastic chair while Devante, Lamar, and Nyisha ran around the game-filled room with the other children.

Tangela wore an all black pant suit, cream-colored boots, and a matching belt. Her hair was braided with micro extensions and pulled back into a pony tail that revealed all the features of her pretty, round face. A light layer of lip gloss was her only make up.

She turned her head, caught him studying her and gave him a smile that took ten years off her age. She gathered the kids together and pointed at him through the glass. "Look, there's Daddy."

The children crashed through the door with Nyisha in the lead, screaming "Daddy!" Ricky dropped to one knee and held his arms open. His kids barreled into him and hugged him like he was home base in a game of tag. Ricky held them tight, loving their smell and the feel of their hair against his face. He didn't want to let go.

"I can't breeve, Daddy," Nyisha gasped into his neck and they all laughed as Ricky opened his arms to release them.

Tangela stood in front of him and Ricky fought the urge to hug her legs while on his knees. He stood up and saw the tears crawling down her face. Her mouth was a shiny pout and when he grabbed her hand, he felt her trembling.

"I am so, so sorry, Tee." Ricky looked into her eyes hoping she would see his sincerity.

Tangela sniffed and wiped her eyes with her left hand. Ricky felt a mix of guilt and hope when he noticed she was still wearing the 800 dollar engagement ring he had given her years ago. Her lips parted, but no words came out; only a peppermint scented sigh.

"Please Tee, please, don't leave me. Don't give up, baby. I will make this up to you, I promise. Just please don't leave me."

Tangela made a noise that could have been a cough or a laugh. She flung herself into his arms and hugged him tight around the neck. "Boy, I'm not going any where. But I am so pissed at you."

Ricky immersed himself in her embrace. He tried to get lost in her arms, her warmth, and her love. He felt one of the kids tugging on his pant legs and yelled out, "I can't breeve, Mommy!"

The kids laughed and tried to pull their mother away as Ricky held her even tighter.

In the playroom, Ricky talked wrestling with his boys and played a game of 'I Declare War' with his daughter where fives beat everything since that's how old she was. They ate little pizzas and Ricky fed Tangela his pepperonis. One of the other parents put the Lion King video on and the kids sat down Indian-style to watch the Disney classic.

"I'm sorry it took me so long to get up here," Tangela laid her head on his shoulder.

"I was sick," Ricky admitted. "I thought you didn't want to see me. I couldn't blame you either. I know I messed up, Tee." He felt her glance up but pressed on. "And if you can't do this ... I understand. But when I come home I'm beating up whoever you're with and taking you back." He was only half joking.

"Baby, I said I'm not going anywhere. I don't want to be with anyone else and you should know that by now. It's just things are real tight. I had to get new brakes for the car and I'm behind on most of the bills."

Ricky shook his head. This was the part he hated the most: His family struggling and him unable to do anything to help. "What are the bills looking like?"

Tangela lifted her head and took a deep breath. "The credit card is maxed. I have to give the telephone company another 200 dollars to get the long distance and collect back on. And I'm a month behind on Nyisha's school tuition. It was either that or the rent.

Ricky didn't know what to say. Tangela made decent money as a caregiver at the Edison Senior Center, but their lifestyle was dependent upon two incomes and his was now missing in action.

"I'm sorry, Tee. I wanted to get us a truck and get you one of those Chinchillas," he mumbled.

"Oh yeah? Well, I want to give you a *chin* check." She poked his head with her finger. "That was stupid, Ricky. Stupid! Did I ask you for a Chinchilla? You are not a drug dealer, Ricky. That's why you get caught whenever you try ... because you are so much more than that."

Ricky wiped away her tears and wrapped his arms around her. "I know baby. You're right and I swear to you I'm done. Never again." He hugged her as she tried to say something and her words got lost in his chest.

"What did you say?" He asked while brushing a kiss across her forehead.

"I said I might have to start dancing again."

Ricky winced and almost bit his tongue. Tangela danced topless while he was serving his first sentence and didn't tell him until after she'd been doing it for three months. It caused so much friction between them that Ricky threatened to have someone take the kids from her if she didn't quit. She responded by saying that was fine with her, because she could use the break. She quit only after Ricky wrote her a letter from the mindset of their one-year-old daughter expressing her desire to be just like Mommy.

"Hear me out Ricky," she felt him tense up and spoke softly while rubbing his hand. "It would only be three nights a week and I could make enough tips to catch everything up within two months. What do you think?"

Ricky tried to even out his breathing, but when he spoke, his words still fell like icicles. "Why are you even asking when you're going to do it no matter what I say?"

"That's not fair, Ricky. We were in a different place back then. You put hustling in front of everything. Selling was more important than me and the kids. Then you went to jail, so I really didn't care what you thought or said." Ricky tried to let go of her hand and she held it tighter. "But we're not those same two people. We've grown. And our love has grown. I know who you are and if you tell me not to do something, I won't do it."

"I don't want you stripping." Ricky pouted.

"Okay."

Ricky looked at her to make sure she was serious. Satisfied that she was, he hugged her and kissed her on the mouth. "That's right, you heard her correctly. Her man said no and she said okay." He gave her a macho grin. "Cause she knows what it is and what I say is law and if—"

"Ow!" Ricky rubbed the shoulder she punched. "I was just playing, Tee. Ooh, you hit hard." He smiled at her and hugged her again. "Don't worry, baby. I'll think of something."

"Well, I did get a call from your father," she confessed and waited for Ricky to respond. He stared ahead, his face was blank, but his nose flared. "He wants to see the kids and he offered to help out while you're away."

"No." Ricky spoke so low Tangela barely heard him.

"I know how you feel, but your father could make things a lot easier for us, and we could—"

"I said, No!"

"Why not, Ricky? It's been so long."

Before he could answer he noticed his sons tussling over a Lego car. Lamar won the tug of war and as he held the toy against his chest, Devante kicked him in his leg and shouted, "I wish I had a gun so I could shoot you in your face and you'll be dead!"

"Devante!" Tangela and Ricky both exclaimed.

The whole room heard him and it wasn't so much the words that shocked them, it was the venom in his voice as he said them. It sounded as if he meant every word.

"Come here, Devante!" Ricky demanded.

"No!" Devante screamed. "You're in jail, and you can't do nothing to me."

Ricky stood to his feet and Devante ran for the door. He swerved around his little sister and banged right into a well-dressed, brown-skinned boy who was a little taller than himself.

"Honor thy father and mother, that it may be well with thee," the boy quoted as he caught Devante from falling.

Ricky reached for his son who shrieked "No" and scurried into the boy's arms. Ricky let Tangela pull him back to his seat as they watched the young boy put his arm around Devante's shoulders and walk him to the rear of the room while talking into his ear.

"He's angry, Ricky." Tangela rubbed his back. "He misses you a lot and he's just lashing out."

Ricky didn't say anything. His emotions were roiling and he felt inadequate as a father. He didn't know what to do. He let Nyisha crawl onto his lap and held her as he watched Devante and Lamar huddle up with the Bible quoting pre-teen.

The three boys were locked in a deep discussion. Ricky and Tangela watched them with an amused embarrassment as the clean-cut little boy talked to their sons with expansive hand gestures and jerky head motions. Devante and Lamar listened with rapt attention. As Ricky was about to call them over, the three of them linked hands and approached him purposefully.

"My name is Jimmy," the youngen extended his hand to Ricky as he introduced himself.

Ricky shook his small hand and held in his laugh. "Ricky Osborn. Pleased to meet ya, Jimmy!" He used his best soap opera voice.

"Praise God, the pleasure is mine." Jimmy answered seriously. "Mr. and Mrs. Osborn, your sons have something they want to say. Go ahead, little brother," he nudged Devante.

Devante glanced at his parents and then found something very interesting about his sleeve. Jimmy looked to Lamar, who shrugged his little shoulders and started easing back to the Lion King.

Jimmy nodded his head as if he expected as much. "Your sons are upset with you Mr. Osborn," he said evenly. "Especially Devante. He says you were in jail before, and you promised never to leave them again. He believes he did something wrong and that's why you're here."

Ricky faced Devante, "Did you say all that, son?"

Devante stared at the floor and nodded slightly. "You did promise," he whispered.

Ricky felt his heart drop. This was his first born, his first understanding of life's purpose. He could recall every minute of the eight hour labor and delivery that brought him into this world. He couldn't take it if Devante was ashamed of him.

"I'm sorry I didn't keep my promise, D., but it's not your fault. Daddy did something stupid. I broke the law and I have to pay the consequences. But you, Lamar, and Nyisha; you didn't do anything wrong. Don't ever think that—"

"God has a path for everyone," Jimmy chimed in. "This is your father's path. God's ways are not man's, but he will not give you more than you can handle. You will not suffer burdens—"

"Okay little homie," Ricky stated a bit harshly. "We appreciate your help but we can handle it from here."

"Don't be rude Ricky!" Tangela scolded him and smiled at Jimmy.

"How old are you young man?"

"I'm 12 years old, ma'am. I'll be 13 this summer."

"You are very intelligent for your age. Very mature."

"It's only through the grace of God, Mrs. Osborn."

Ricky slid Nyisha onto Tangela's lap. Something about Jimmy's last statement sent a chill down his back. He hugged Devante and assured him that everything would be alright. He looked up and asked Jimmy what his last name was.

Before Jimmy could answer, Ricky's suspicion proved true. Brother James opened the door to the playroom and the intelligent, mature Jimmy yelled out, "Daddy!" like any other 12-year-old son.

Ricky watched them embrace and couldn't believe he hadn't seen the resemblance right away. Not only did Jimmy have his father's complexion, eyes and good grade of hair, but he spoke with the exact same cadence. They also shared that bright smile that said, 'Everything is going to be alright.'

"You must be Sister Tangela." Brother James shook her hand. "I hope you know that the love this man has for you is obvious every time he says your name."

Tangela giggled and snuggled closer to Ricky.

"Tee, this is my roommate, Brother James."

"Nice to meet you Brother James. Your son is a darling."

Jimmy turned shy in his father's presence. "I was just ministering to their sons a little bit."

"That's excellent, son, for the Bible says: "Preach the word; be prepared in season and out of season; correct, rebuke and encourage—"

"With great patience and careful instruction," Jimmy finished the verse and then noticed his mother outside the playroom looking for him and his father. "We're in here, Mom!" he called while holding the door open for her.

An unmistakable hush fell over the playroom; even the children stopped what they were doing and gaped at the radiant woman walking in.

"Mommy, is that Princess Jasmine?" A little girl's voice punctured the silence.

Brother James introduced his wife as Sister Karen Morris. She flashed even white teeth as she said, Hello. She was tall and graceful with Asian eyes and toffee-colored skin. She wore a conservative skirt suit that was meant to convey professional career woman, but on her statuesque frame still came off as sexy.

"I've heard so much about you Brother Ricky," her southern accent was sweet. "You have such a beautiful family."

"Thank you," Ricky glanced at Brother James.

Brother James had his eyes on Jimmy who was building Legos with Devante and Lamar. Karen noticed it too and explained to Ricky and Tangela how rare it was for Jimmy to sit down and play like a normal little boy. "He's always so serious," she sighed.

"I wonder where he gets that from?" Ricky emphasized as him and Karen looked at Brother James accusingly.

Brother James looked up, unfazed and innocent, "Isn't there a rap song that says, 'he get it from his Momma?"

Karen pinched him and they all laughed.

"Well, if you need our two boys to help bring the kid out of him, you're welcome to take them." Ricky grinned.

"Anytime!" Tangela added with a laugh.

"Your boys are little angels," Karen replied. "I'd love to take them home with me along with that sweet baby girl on your lap."

"Be careful," Ricky looked at Brother James. "Tangela used to keep bags packed in the trunk of the car for people who said that."

"Let's stay in here, honey. Let Jimmy play for a while. Is that alright?"

"Sure." Brother James grabbed two of the little chairs so he and his wife could sit down. Karen and Tangela talked 'Girl Talk' until Ricky and Brother James started complaining about the lack of attention.

Nyisha woke up and asked Ricky to tell her a story, then called her brothers and Jimmy over so they could hear, too. The boys sat in a half circle at Ricky's feet listening with wide eyes and adding sound effects when asked. Nyisha cried twice during the story and kept interrupting to ask if the baby- brother bunny rabbit was gonna be alright.

When Ricky finished the story they all clapped. Jimmy raced to his parents. "Dad, Mom! It was an excellent story. It had rabbits, but it was really about brothers and sisters and how they should always love and protect each other no matter what. Man, I can't wait 'til y'all give me a brother or sister."

"Jimmy!" Karen exclaimed.

"I feel you on that one, Son."

"James!"

"What? I do look forward to expanding our family. I want at least two more boys and four girls. Seven total. That's not bad."

"Not bad? If you want six more children, they better all come at the same time."

Brother James smiled boyishly. "Karen, honey, the Word says 'Wives submit to your Husbands.'"

"And I do that naturally, honey. But the command that comes with that is for husbands to love your wives like your own body. So, we can have as many children as you want as long as you find a way for your body to carry them."

"Ooh, she got you with that one, Dad!"

"You're supposed to be on my side." Brother James pulled Jimmy into a head lock and tussled his little curls playfully.

Visitation was about to end. Tangela held on to Ricky's arm while the kids cleaned up their toys. "What about your Dad?" she asked.

"He can see the kids, but we don't need anything from him."

"Guess I better pullout my cow-girl outfit," she laughed but Ricky didn't crack a smile. "I'm joking, Ricky. I'm not going to go against what you said. If Daddy Rabbit is focused, Mommy Bunny will always follow his lead." She kissed him softly.

"I love you so much, Tee. Please, just trust me. I'll think of something."

She nodded her head and looked up at him with a loving gaze that melted him. He kissed her long and hard until their breathing became short and Nyisha tugged on their pant legs.

Ricky helped the boys put on their coats. He hugged and kissed them goodbye, urging them to behave for their mother. Over their heads he watched as Brother James held Jimmy by the shoulders and spoke to him earnestly like a coach to a quarterback. They hugged tight and when they let go, they simultaneously wiped their wet eyes.

Ricky and Brother James stood in line together waving goodbye and blowing kisses to their loved ones as they waited for their ID's. Jimmy stood in the doorway and looked back at his father. He pointed to the sky and closed his eyes, then took that same hand and placed it over his heart. He opened his eyes and smiled triumphantly at his father then ran to catch up with his mother.

"That's his way of saying God is love. He made it up himself," Brother James said proudly.

They walked back to their room in silence; sweet and sad thoughts settling on their consciences like morning dew.

Count had cleared and dinner announced, yet Ricky and Brother James hadn't moved from their beds. "I don't think I've ever seen you sit still for so long," Ricky said.

"Visits always drain me, brother. It's like you put all of your energy out in the open and when they leave they take some of you with them."

"I know what you mean."

"You have a beautiful family, Brother Ricky."

"Thanks. So do you. Your son is a chip off the old block."

"That he is," Brother James agreed.

"Kids grow up so fast these days, I had a talk with my oldest today, and it felt like I was talking to a grown man. He's only 10!"

"I think I have one of those same talks with Jimmy every visit."

"Yeah, but you've probably always been a good father and you know just what to say. I realize I haven't been the best dad."

"Brother Ricky, you are still being molded by God's great hands, and it is evident you're a good father. Your sons look up to you and your daughter adores you. You even had my Jimmy remembering he's still a kid. That's not an easy task."

"I'm not a good father, Brother James. Trust me."

"Do you love your kids?"

"Yes, of course, but—"

"Would you do everything in your power to keep them from being hurt?"

"Yeah, man!"

"Well, then you're a good father."

Ricky let out a frustrated sigh. "You don't understand. I sold drugs. I set a bad example, Brother James. I used to pick up my sons from school right after I picked up a package. I met customers in the park while I was playing with my kids. I helped them with their homework then used the same calculator to tally up my hustling figures.

"I've exposed my boys to some ugly situations. One time, I took them to the movies to see 'Finding Nemo' and I snuck two bottles of beer in the theatre with me." Ricky heard Brother James gasp. "That's not even the worst of it. I poured the beer into an empty soda cup and sat it on the floor.

"Devante and Lamar drank from my cup for the first half of the movie. They were only six and four. They kept asking me to take them to the bathroom, back and forth at least four times and I still didn't realize they were getting drunk.

"When I took them to the bathroom for the fifth time, they refused to wash their hands. They locked themselves in a stall and took off all their clothes. They said they were hot. When they finally opened the door, they dashed into the lobby butt-naked. They were yelling and screaming that they were Indians and tackled the metal poles that hold the velvet ropes. Now, what kind of father lets his babies get drunk?"

Brother James didn't answer and Ricky pictured him shaking his head in disgust. He felt the bed move and heard what sounded like a low moan. He leaned over his bunk and peered down at Brother James who was holding a pillow to his face and reeling with laughter.

"Ah, no! I don't believe this," Ricky stated with mock indignation. "Not the good brother. Unh, unh! Laughing at another man's pain and sorrow."

"It ... it probably wasn't funny then. But ...when you were telling me what happened ... I got a visual of your boys, running ... and ... yelling ... What did they drink, some ... some Colt 45?"

"No!" Ricky tried to sound hurt, but began laughing himself. "It was Heineken."

"Oh, oh, the good stuff," Brother James remarked and they both laughed even harder.

"Seriously," Brother James stated when they had finally calmed down. "Don't you realize how lucky you are? You've been blessed to be able to do such important things with your children. Even in your negative lifestyle you were still playing with them, helping with homework, taking them to parks and," he cleared his throat "to the movies. You were living foul and making bad choices, but you were still being a father. A good father."

Brother James stared off out the blurry window. "I've been in jail all of my son's life and every experience we've shared has been in visiting rooms.

"Jimmy had his first recital when he was seven years old. He wanted me to be there so bad he prayed for God to let me out even if only for two hours. It was the biggest revival of the year. He soloed 'Amazing Grace' with a symphony behind him and brought the house down.

"The next day, Karen brought him to visit me. He wore his little tuxedo from the night before and went around the visiting room passing out hand made tickets to a free concert recital. The other visitors became his audience. He stood in front of the vending machines and sung his little heart out.

"I cried when he finished and he thought I didn't like it. He cried too and said he sounded better with the music. I hugged him tight and told him how beautiful he sang; and that I cried because I was happy." Brother James let a tear slip as the memories played out in his mind like a silent film. Ricky felt his own eyes get misty as he imagined the joy and pain of Brother James' life.

"You've been in jail a long time," Ricky said. "I don't want to get all in your business, but it seems like you and your wife have a beautiful, strong marriage. Has she been with you for your whole bid?"

"Yes, she has, Brother Ricky. Praise God. He blessed me with my soul mate and we have never doubted that. Of course, we had our little rough patches and there were times when I encouraged her to maybe find a friend, but she is a Godly woman who respects the vows she made. Even though she would have been perfectly justified if she walked away when I came to jail."

"What do you mean?" Ricky was confused.

"I met Karen while I was on the run in Atlanta. I had shot a man over a dice game. A dice game!" Brother James closed his eyes and looked up. "Praise God who forgives all things. Hallelujah! Praise God! That man survived, but at the time I was wanted for attempted murder."

"Karen was a senior at Clark University. She was so different from the girls I was used to." His whole face lit up as he thought back. "She was gorgeous, yet humble. She was smart and independent. I was 19 years old and accustomed to getting what I wanted. She became a challenge to me and since I was the thug she had been warned about, I was a challenge to her as well.

"Neither of us realized we were falling in love until she became pregnant and I proposed to her on the spot. Not out of obligation, but out of selfishly wanting to be with her for the rest of my life. We got married and lived happily for seven months."

"You never told her you were wanted?"

"I never told her."

"How'd you get caught?"

Brother James sighed and yielded a closed mouth smile. "God's grace and my mother." Brother James stood up and began to pace. "I never knew my father, and my grand parents died before I was born. It was just me and my mom. She's only 16 years older than me, so we were very close. My mom was also very focused. She used the insurance money from my grandparents to buy a house for us and then worked two, sometimes three jobs to make sure we lived comfortably.

"I remember riding the bus with her; me on my way to school, her on her way to work. On the way home, she helped me with my homework, then we stopped at a store to buy things for dinner. We cooked together and took turns doing the dishes. She read to me at night or sometimes if she was too tired, I read to her.

"As I got older I spent a lot of time at home by myself. My mom worked a graveyard shift and I stayed out as long as I wanted. I got hooked on the rush of being in the streets and eventually they became my home.

"My mother has always been a Christian. As she got older her faith matured. She stopped smoking and drinking, she didn't curse and ultimately didn't put up with a son who chased after worldly things. We fought. I left. For a while we only spoke on holidays and that usually ended up badly.

I received a call from my mother after being gone for 18 months. She told me she had breast cancer. She had to have a mastectomy and wanted me there with her in case things didn't go well."

Brother James sat back down on his bunk. He was quiet for so long, Ricky wondered if he would continue.

"I was so ignorant and selfish," his voice quivered. "I actually hesitated to go be with my mother in her most difficult time. This woman, this beautiful woman who worked 12-hour shifts and still spent quality time with me when she was dead-tired. This woman, who loved me unconditionally; who screamed at me that the streets couldn't have me without a fight. And I ... I didn't go right away. Lord have mercy, I didn't rush to be with her.

"When I got there, they had already removed both breasts. I straggled in; she smiled and said, "I knew you would come." She pointed to her Bible and told me it was my turn to read to her. For three days, that's what I did. Whatever scripture she asked for, whatever Psalm she requested, I read it and although I couldn't see it at the time, she was ministering to me and guiding me into God's arms. I was reading to her, but the seeds were being planted in me.

"Word got out I was in town and the police came to the hospital to arrest me. My mother," Brother James nodded slowly. "My mother was still so beautiful. The chemo had taken 40 pounds and all of her hair. She was weak and sick, but she stood there, in between the cops and me. With tears streaming down her face she yelled at me that the wages of sin is death, but the gift of God is eternal. In a dry voice she ordered me to repent with Godly sorrow and accept Jesus Christ as my Lord and Savior. She refused to move until I agreed.

"I felt a peace so clear, so unmistakably good that I said yes without even thinking about it. My mother hugged me so tight it took two police officers to separate us.

"Ricky, I've had that peace ever since. It is a peace that assures me God is love. My mother's cancer went into a full remission. She's now a missionary of God's Church, teaching the Gospel in Africa. God is love. I have a wife who has stuck by me even though I lied to her, who has grown closer to God as I grew closer to Him, because God is love. And I have a son, who has only known me in visiting rooms and he is everything I could ever pray for a son to be. I tell you, God is love!" Brother James laid back on his pillow, his words hung in the air like a cool mist.

Ricky sat up, his emotions pulsing between peace and regret. "I've been with Tangela since Junior High School. Now and then we'd break up for a week or two, but we always made up. Somehow we knew we belonged together. Devante was born nine months after we graduated and I proposed to her right there in the hospital. Even without a ring she was the happiest woman alive, but I didn't follow through.

"I wanted a big wedding and we needed to save money. That was my first excuse, then Lamar was born and that set us back. I started selling and convinced myself I was doing the right thing. I was trying to get money for us to get married and buy a house.

"Tangela was patient for awhile, but eventually she got fed up. She threw me out of our apartment, so I finally bought her a ring to get back in. A year later, she was ready to give up again, but she got pregnant with Nyisha. Then, I went to jail and told her to move on; that I was nothing and didn't deserve her. But she chose to ride it out with me. Like always, she had my back."

"A love like that is rare, Brother Ricky. It is a blessing indeed."

"Yes, I know," Ricky admitted.

"If you don't mind me asking, why have you not married this wonderful woman who has loved you for over half of your life?"

Ricky bit back his first reply, which was to say he did mind him asking. He contemplated lying, but opted instead for the truth, which even to his ears sounded like a lame excuse.

"When I was locked up the first time, she ... she started stripping. I think she might have cheated on me."

Brother James stood up and stared at Ricky. He had his head tilted as if he expected to hear more. "Is that it?"

"I was only doing two years," Ricky said defensively.

"Brother Ricky, even if she did cheat, if you chose to forgive her, then the slate has to be wiped clean."

"I tried, but sometimes I picture her with another nig-. Another man. I just can't ... I get sick."

"As much as I hate to do it, let me play devil's advocate for a minute."

"Devil's what?"

"Just listen, brother. Do you know for sure she cheated on you?" Brother James asked and Ricky shook his head reluctantly. "Did you ever cheat on her?"

Ricky looked away and Brother James took that as a yes.

"If the shoe was on the other foot would you have remained faithful to her while she served only two years?"

"Yeah," Ricky blurted out. "I would've held her down." Brother James looked at him with raised eyebrows. "What? I would've sent her money and took the kids to see her and not ... cheat on her." Brother James eyed him skeptically, the corners of his mouth turned up slightly. "Okay! I might have dipped here and there, but she wouldn't have known about it. And besides, it's different for men."

Brother James shook his head. His smile faded. "Whatever you put into something is what you get back. When we did whatever wrong that put us in here, we didn't have some invisible contract that said our wives, girlfriends, family or whoever has to do this time with us."

"Hold up, if she's your wife, she has to honor her vows and keep—"

"No, she doesn't and in most states she can request an automatic divorce when the husband has committed a felony. So, for any woman to take on the vast responsibility of loving a man in jail, she should be placed in a category with angels.

"Think about everything they go through: The lonely nights when they'd settle for a simple phone call. Sometimes that call doesn't come until the next day when they're all cried out. Think about the financial struggles, the days when the children are too much; and watching their friends go on dates when all they have to look forward to is a letter, maybe.

"Think of all the things they sacrifice while waiting for us. Not only making love, but morning kisses, foot rubs, massages, or just being able to talk to their soul mate after a bad day at work."

Ricky was astounded. He thought of the many times he had called only to find Tangela crying. When he asked her what was wrong, she always said nothing. In his ignorance, he believed her.

"We had a beautiful visit today," Brother James continued. "Of course, it helped remind our angels that their labor and love is not in vain. But think, Brother Ricky, about what they have to go through to come see us: Finding something acceptable to wear, getting the children ready, the drive, the search to get in, the ignorant guards—God forgive them—who treat them like they are criminals too.

"And still they force beautiful smiles so we won't worry. How often do we say thank you? Not often enough. We're too busy thinking they owe us something because of all the money we spent on them. They don't owe us anything!

"This prison life is horrible and for anyone to share your pain while you do time is worth more money than we could ever spend. And do you know why they do it?" Ricky shook his head.

"They do it because they see something ... *someone* inside of us that we don't even realize is there. You referred to Tangela as a true rider because she's willing to do anything for you, but imagine if you were guiding her to do the right things, the things that are beautiful in the sight of God. Imagine if you taught her how to follow your example and to love you the way she witnesses you loving God. That is how families overcome any and all obstacles ... That is what God intended for families to ..."

Ricky heard the words God and family and he immediately tuned out what Brother James was saying. He felt a harsh winter wind and smelled his mother's perfume stinging his nostrils. Brother James was still speaking, but Ricky was listening to the voices from his past.

"He is no longer a part of this family!" his father's voice was resolute.

"Your brother has chosen to take sides with the enemy," his mother added, although she sounded unconvinced.

"Mother, Father, he's sick. He needs—"

"He needs to bend before the throne of God and beg for forgiveness. And until he does, he's an outcast and is unwelcome in our home."

Ricky looked at his father with suspicious eyes; trying not to see a hypocrite. His mother grabbed his hand and her fingers felt cold and sharp like talons.

"We know what you've been doing, Richard," she grimaced against the wind, and to Ricky, her lipstick made her mouth look nasty like the smile of a witch. "It's okay, we understand and we forgive you."

"But it stops now," his father cut in. "You will not let your brother into our home. Not to change clothes, eat, or anything. You will not give him money, and you—"

"David needs our help!" Ricky shouted at his parents for the first time in his 14 years of existence. It felt good.

"And you will not say his name in my presence," his father said crisply and then turned on his heels to go.

Ricky's mother stood eye to eye with him and spoke as she pulled out her handkerchief and made a show of wiping wind-tears from Ricky's eyes. "We still love your brother, but we've placed him in God's hands. We have to trust God, Richard. Please obey your father or … you will be choosing sides with the enemy as well.

She walked away and Ricky watched her slip her claw inside his father's arm as they stood side by side glaring at him with an air of impatience.

Ricky stared at the ground; hurt and confused. He didn't want to disobey his parents nor be a traitor to his brother. He wrapped his scarf tightly around his neck wishing it was a noose. With slow steps he caught up with his parents.

"… about your parents much, Brother Ricky?"

"What?" Ricky turned his attention back to Brother James. I didn't hear you."

"I asked if your parents are still alive, because you don't talk about them much."

Ricky climbed down from his bunk and slid on his shower shoes. He opened the door to go use the bathroom. He gave Brother James a stony look. "Yes, my parents are still alive. No, I don't talk about them." The door closed behind him with a hush.

Ricky heard BK's loud and excited voice as he was walking back from the bathroom. He stepped into the dayroom and saw about 15 inmates standing around Frizz's poker game. Ricky shouldered his way through the crowd to see what the excitement was about.

When he reached the table, he saw that Frizz and BK were locked in a hand of straight seven. With five cards dealt, Frizz had an ace and a pair of sixes showing, BK had a jack and two deuces. When BK saw Ricky behind him he lifted the corners of his two hole cards and revealed two more deuces. Four of a kind—very hard to beat.

"Son, I own a helicopter. True story! I got a six seater heli with the Louis Vuitton interior." BK kept a straight face as the spectators laughed. "My money long like a slow song, Frizz. Whatever you bet, I'm gonna call, Son."

Frizz checked his hole cards again and then looked at BK with contempt. "Let's bet street money then," his gruff voice was serious. "Let's see how deep your pockets are for real. There's 80 dollars worth of stamps in the pot, I bet 50 dollars cash money."

Ricky caught the quick flash of disbelief in BK's eyes, but BK played it off right away. "Son, I'm still spending money from 1980 and that's mad crazy, B, since I wasn't born until 1981. I call 50 pesos, a half a football field, whatever B, I got that!"

Ricky shook his head and felt a premonition of things about to get worse. Frizz turned out the sixth card, a nine for BK and another ace for himself. He sneered at BK and said, "the two pairs bet 100 dollars."

It was obvious to everyone watching that Frizz had a full-house and he was assuming BK had three of a kind or a smaller full-house. BK laughed and pointed at Frizz's cards. "Ah, isn't that so cute." The crowd chuckled at his boldness. "Frizz, Son, trust me, two pairs ain't enough, make it light on yourself."

"The bet is one hundred dollars, call or fold," Frizz said icily.

"That's how you wanna do it, Son? Word life? I call the Benjamin and raise you…"

The inmates reacted raucously when they heard BK say raise. They started whispering amongst themselves what they thought BK had in the hole. Ricky watched with the dread of witnessing a car accident.

"You raise me what?" Frizz barked.

"I raise you … ten stamps," BK laughed hard as he threw a half-a-book of stamps into the pot. "Yo, Son, I had you. Ricky, did you see his face? He thought I was gonna bet my Death Row pendant. What? True story, Son. I was on the 'The Row' for six months. Me and Suge fell out over me rocking a New York Giants jersey. Son, I was just reppin' the home team, Big Blue. I didn't know it was that serious. He told me to bounce, but he let me keep my pendant."

"Stupid, lyin'-ass, New York-nigga," Frizz mumbled as he ripped off ten stamps. "You want to raise me? I call your 10 punk-ass stamps and I raise you 100 dollars."

"Yeah, Son? I call your hunned and raise you a hunned more."

"I call that hundred and raise you a hundred."

They went back and forth until the pot was at 2500 dollars. Ricky hit the table and urged them to get it over with.

Frizz dealt the final card down low. Ricky couldn't see what Frizz got, but BK was handed a six of hearts. Count time was in ten minutes so they reluctantly agreed to check the final bet and turn out their cards.

"Yo, Son, I love you like a play cousin, so I'll take an IOU for the quarter stack. As the late, great Biggie Smalls once said, 'sure do, two twenty-twos in my shoes!'" Bk turned out his four deuces, stood up and slapped hands with the crowd.

Frizz looked at the four of a kind unfazed. He grinned at BK and turned over his three hole cards— a king and two sixes. "Twenty twos are such small guns and niggas that carry them usually get killed. Just like you. Get them four sixes off your ass!" He laughed like a comic book villain and slapped hands with the crowd himself.

BK looked around like a child lost in a cemetery. The convicts offered insincere condolences and headed back to their rooms for count.

"That's a real heart breaker, New York," Frizz stated as he scooped up his pot. "But I don't take IOU's, so when can you get that money to me?"

Ricky waited until everyone had left, then nudged BK. With his eyes he directed Bk's attention to the cards still on the table.

"I know, Ricky. Four deuces, I had to stay in. Son is just mad lucky."

"What were your hole cards, BK?" Ricky asked. Frizz cut his eyes at him, his expression was accusatory.

"My hole cards? I had the deuces ..." it dawned on him as Frizz gathered all the cards together. "And a six. Oh, snap, Son! This kid pulled the oochie-wallie on me. How he have four sixes, when I had one in the hole? Damn, Frizz, how could you cheat me?" His hurt was genuine.

"I didn't cheat you. I never saw a six in your hand. You owe me 2500 dollars and I want my money."

"I saw the six and you don't owe him nothing," Ricky challenged.

"Damn homie, you siding with this next nigga? What's up with you?"

"What's up with you? You know BK is my peoples. Cheating him is like cheating me." Ricky screwed his face up in disgust. "I'm starting to wonder about all the times I lost at this table."

Frizz swelled up and pointed at Ricky. "Are you saying I'd cheat my own homie? We from the same spot and you accusing me of cheating you? This New Yorker ain't shit to me, but you're like my brother."

That's when it clicked. Ricky had recognized the name Franklin, but it wasn't until Frizz said brother, that he remembered why it left such a bad taste in his mouth. "Us being from the same spot don't mean a thing, and I don't want to be like a brother to you, especially since I know you snitched on your own brother."

Frizz winced as if he'd been struck. He stood with his fists balled up. His eyes blazed furiously. "So, now I'm a snitch, huh? You're saying I'm hot? Well, if I am, that makes you a bitch for not checking me in from day one." Frizz got up in Ricky's face. "But no, you ate with me and smoked with me. So I can't be too hot unless you're hot too."

Ricky pushed Frizz out of his face. Frizz glared at him.

Ricky glared back poised for whatever. He felt none of the fear from the first time they had squared off. A few inmates came back to see what all the commotion was.

"Yo, Ricky, come on, Son. They called count and it ain't worth it," BK grabbed Ricky's arm. Ricky glowered at Frizz as he strolled out of the dayroom.

Ricky and BK were halfway down the hall. Frizz crept up behind them and swung a solid, right hay-maker that caught Ricky flush on his ear and jaw. Ricky instantly heard bells as he staggered against the wall.

"You gonna put your hands on me and walk away like you the man or something! You got me twisted, homie!"

"What is you doing, Son? How you gonna snuff Ricky from behind? That's real weak, Frizz." BK stood in between them. "That's bullshit, Son!"

"You're next, New York," Frizz pushed BK out of the way and threw up his hands. "Let's go, Ricky!"

Ricky shook off the stinging in his ear and looked at Frizz through watery eyes. He ignored BK and the inmates who seemed to come from out of the walls. He disregarded the fact he was wearing shower shoes and that it was count time. He stood in the boxer's stance that David had shown him when they boxed at the Boys Club and focused on Frizz.

Frizz held his hands low and wide. Ricky used his reach advantage and hit Frizz with three straight jabs. The blows didn't hurt Frizz, but they embarrassed and angered him. He responded with slow, wild hooks that hit nothing but air.

Ricky stepped inside and hit Frizz with an over-hand right, but he tripped over his shower shoe as he stepped back. Frizz grabbed him around the waist and rushed him against the wall. Ricky lost his wind from the impact. Frizz dropped low and tried to scoop Ricky off his feet so he could slam him to the floor.

Ricky stretched out across Frizz's back and tried to spread his legs out of Frizz's reach. He swung desperate, ineffective blows at Frizz's solid body. His feet slid on the floor and Frizz was finally able to grab one of Ricky's legs. He felt his balance giving away. He was going down and he knew he'd have no chance if Frizz got him on the ground.

Ricky swung a looping upper-cut that hit Frizz in the mouth and knocked out his front tooth. Frizz let go of Ricky's leg and held his hands to his bleeding mouth. Ricky's hand was cut across the knuckle and felt like he had touched a hot stove.

Someone yelled that the guards were coming, but Frizz wasn't trying to hear that. He spat out his tooth with a gob of blood and rushed at Ricky in a blind rage. Ricky side-stepped his attack and hammered him with a right-hook that floored him.

Brother James made it down the hall just as C.O.s Swain and Riley were putting the cuffs on Ricky and a half-dazed Frizz. "You alright?" he asked Ricky as C.O. Swain walked him down the hall.

Ricky glanced at him and nodded yes, but Brother James noticed his eyes had said no.

Ricky spent that first night in the SHU trying to decipher the messy graffiti that stained the walls of his cold cell. He laid on his bunk gently touching his face to check for swelling and stayed up half the night contemplating what he could have done differently. Eventually his exhaustion won out and he fell into a dreamless sleep.

He woke up the next morning with a stiff back and an angry red bruise on the curve of his jaw. He ate cold oatmeal and toast that was cooked on only one side. There were no windows and he had no idea what time it was. He found a two-year-old Ebony magazine and read it twice. Lunch was a thin slice of roast beef, watery mashed potatoes and dry peas. He ate it all.

He wore the standard thin orange jumpsuit and was cold. He stood up on the top bunk and stuffed magazine pages into the AC vent that blasted out ice-cold air. As he packed the vent he heard what sounded like hands clapping and organ music coming out of the air vent that sat directly above the AC.

He leaned his ear to the vent and sure enough, he heard music and then a voice. He slid the lever to open the blades of the vent and the voice came through loud and clear.

"... yet God, in his infinite mercy, rescued us and placed us back on the path of righteousness. Where we could become fathers and husbands instead of drug dealers and thieves, where we could become sons of the most high God." Ricky recognized the booming voice of Chaplain Parker and remembered that most of the SHU was right under the Chapel. "Brother James, please leads us in special music."

Ricky felt his breath catch. He stared at the vent as if he could see his cellmate's bright smile and waited for his voice to float out of the metal shaft. There was a round of applause and Ricky heard the mic being removed from its stand.

"Praise God!" Brother James commanded and the applause grew louder. "Hallelujah, praise God! You could have been dead, asleep in your bed, but God has blessed you to see another day." There were shouts of Amen and Hallelujah. "For this is the day that the Lord has made and I will rejoice and be glad in it." Praise shouts shot through the vent like a flock of birds. Ricky sat on the bunk, his back against the wall hugging his knees to his chest even though he no longer felt the cold.

"Brothers, I know I've said this before and I will say it again," Brother James spoke earnestly. "When you see us up here singing, it is not to entertain you. The choir and I are here to minister to you with song. The Word of God says make a joyful noise, and when we sing, it isn't for the applause, but for the glory of God. I pray that you hear us and feel the love we have for God; that you join in and help us to worship and praise our Lord and Savior Jesus Christ. Somebody out there feels like he is all alone, like no one feels his pain. Listen brother, and know that God is always with you."

Ricky waited for the music to start, but it didn't. There were ten seconds of complete silence. Ricky played with the vent lever to make sure it was still open. He heard the intake of a subtle breath and felt his spirit move as Brother James sang the first note.

"Whyyy ... should I feel discouraged? Why should the shaaa-dows come?" He was singing a capella and each word was a song by itself with a beginning, a climax, and an end. Ricky was amazed. He had heard Brother James sing light notes for the choir to follow, but he had no idea that his voice was so rich and commanding. *"When Jesus is my portion, my constant friend is he. His eye is on the sparrow and I know he watches me."*

It was David's favorite song. The first one he had learned and he could sing it effortlessly. Ricky closed his eyes and tried to keep the images at bay. When he opened his eyes he was 15 years old, on his back porch, staring at his drug-addicted brother, who was singing to him in a feverish search for sympathy.

"I sing, because...I'm happy. I sing because I'm free," David smiled at his younger brother as he cried out in a sweet melodic. "His eye is on the spar...row, and I know he watches me."

Ricky eyed his brother with love and pity, respect and disgust. David was still handsome, but he was smaller and frail. He wore the same clothes Ricky had given him a week ago and he smelled like spoiled vegetables.

"I can't let you in, David. I'm sorry, bro, but I can't do it."

"Please, Ricky!" David begged. Ricky wanted to hit him and shake him until he promised to be his big brother again. "I just need to rest for a few hours. And I need a shower, little brother. Come on, Ricky."

"I can't, I promised Mom and Dad."

"I don't have anywhere else to go."

"You took mom's bracelet, last time. You got me in trouble and, and you stole from our mother." David didn't deny it and that made Ricky angrier.

143

"Just go, David.   Get out of here!   Please, go get yourself together!"

David stared at his feet for a few seconds then looked up at his brother, who used to look up to him. "Okay, Ricky. I'm going to do that." He held his hands up to say goodbye and as he walked away, he started singing again, "I sing be...cause I'm happy, I sing because I'm free..."

"His eye is on the sparrow. And ... I ... know ..., I said, I know ... he watches ...me," Brother James held the last note long enough for the applause to rise, die down, and crescendo once more.

Ricky hugged himself and tried to shake off the eerie harmony of Brother James and his brother David. He turned away from the vent as hot tears overflowed his eyes. He cried hard. He cried until his throat ached and his eyes stung too much to cry anymore.

Ricky and Frizz were sanctioned to 15 days in the SHU and they had to spend the last three days of their sentence in a cell together to prove they could remain on the same compound without further incident.

After a few hours of tense, mono-syllabic conversation, Frizz broke the ice by showing Ricky his new tooth.

"They gave me a May Bach," he smiled as he compared his dental bridge to the most expensive Mercedes Benz. "The other one had a cavity and was loose, that's why it came out so easy. And you caught me with a good one."

Ricky cast him a jaded look and Frizz knew he was thinking of that first punch he'd thrown from behind. "My bad for stealing you. I know it was against the code and I deserved to get my ass kicked," he snorted. "I ain't lost too many fights, but I guess I can accept an 'L' if it comes from a homie. We are still homies, right?"

Ricky nodded his head slowly and gave Frizz a tight smile. "As long as BK's debt is squashed and you tell me how you got that extra six in there."

"Did you see his face?" Frizz bellowed. "Yo, his eyes and his freckles got bigger. If no one was around he would of cried."

Ricky laughed with him. Even though there was blood shed, their fight felt more like something brothers go through; where you have to make up sooner or later. They spent the three days playing chess and reminiscing about home.

"I didn't snitch on my brother," Frizz said out of the blue. It was their last night in the SHU and Frizz's voice was huskier than usual. "We got pulled over with 18 ounces of crack and they set our bail at five-hundred-thousand dollars apiece.

"Bobby came up with the idea. He's 4 years older than me and he was the boss. He told me to pretend like I was going to cooperate so I could get my bail reduced, get out and tie up some loose ends. We had money to collect; people to intimidate, you know, those were the things I was good at.

"I hired good lawyers and we went to trial. We lost and since I reneged on the deal, they gave me the max. You don't get 15 years if you tell, Ricky."

"I apologize. I didn't know. I just remember the newspaper saying, 'Brother against Brother.'"

"Yeah, they really blew it up in the press, but the streets knew the real deal. You were probably too young back then. It's alright." Frizz looked Ricky in the eye. "My brother only got eight years. He's been home almost three now, and I ain't got one letter or one dime from him. He knows I'm struggling and he don't do ... That's why I look at you like a brother, 'cause I don't have anyone else."

They were released the next day and they walked back to the unit together in good spirits, laughing as they tried to keep from falling on the ice that hid beneath a fresh layer of snow. Frizz went back to the dorm and within hours was back to his loud, boisterous self. Ricky walked into his room and Brother James stood up from the desk and pulled him into a powerful bear-hug. This time Ricky hugged back.

***

Over the next few weeks, Ricky adjusted to a new rhythm. The beat was slower, more serene. He could hear chords and strings and his stepping was a lot smoother now. BK moved to another unit and Ricky barely saw him, except in the kitchen. Frizz was running gambling tickets for basketball and Ricky wanted no part in that, so they'd eat together here and there, but usually Ricky could be found in his room reading or writing letters to Tangela and the kids.

He also spent a lot of time with Brother James. They played intense games of Scrabble, where Brother James would get righteously indignant about words from the Bible not being in the Scrabble dictionary. They had long, late-night conversations about family, fatherhood, life and love.

Ricky could barely feel the change in himself, but the growth in his relationship with Tangela was more than amazing and too remarkable to ignore. Tangela had managed to get the phone on and one night as they were about to hang up, she breathlessly whispered, "Ricky, I've fallen in love with you allover again." Ricky felt the same way.

The church's anniversary service was only a few days away and Brother James had their room looking like a campaign headquarters. Ricky laid on his bunk and watched with guilty pleasure as different sections of the choir came by every night to practice the difficult, new song Brother James had written for the special occasion.

Brother James had become anxious, demanding, and a bit insecure. The service was going to be held at night and all of the guest volunteers were invited. He wanted the service to be perfect. Every night that week, after the choir left, Brother James would second-guess the harmonies until Ricky would sing them with him to prove they fit. Then he'd sing the lead and ask Ricky's opinion on everything from the melody to the words.

The song was called 'I Will.' It was brilliant, beautiful, and profound. Brother James sung it with the passion of a preacher who knew if the words came out right, they could save somebody's life. The lyrics were inspiring and there was no doubt that Brother James had been filled with the spirit of God when he wrote them.

The song sunk into Ricky's sub-conscious and he found himself singing it all the time, adding his own little riffs here and there. Brother James heard him one night and begged Ricky to share the lead with him. Ricky declined adamantly. When Brother James pressed him about his reason for saying no, Ricky shrugged and simply said, "I don't do the church thing."

The 'church thing' was only part of Brother James' excitement. His 33rd birthday also fell on that weekend and he was looking forward to seeing Karen and Jimmy. He called his wife Thursday evening so they could pray and break their weekly fast. After teasing him about his old age approaching, Karen said she had a surprise for him and told him to hold on for a second.

"Happy Birthday, Jaymo!" His mother shouted into the phone.

"Mommy!" Brother James screamed with pure joy. Hearing his mother's voice and his childhood nickname was like a warm blanket around his soul.

"What's this foolishness I hear that I can't bring you any food? Who says I can't feed my Baby?"

Brother James laughed as he pictured his mom moving her neck like some young girl as she spoke. As a sanctified woman of God and after five years in Africa, Darlene Morris still had that outspoken, no-nonsense attitude that had earned her love and respect in the inner-city streets as well as the church.

"It's not that type of prison, Mom. They sell food here."

"Well, I don't eat wings from a machine," she pouted. "But as long as I get to see my Jaymo, I'll be alright."

"I can't believe that you're here. I've missed you so much."

"I know, I know. I missed you, too. There's this young Sudanese boy who looks just like you did at his age, and he clings to me so much. I know it was God's way of reminding me you're in good hands. That you are in God's hands ... I just can't wait to see you."

Brother James' voice was thick with emotion, "Yeah, Mom, me too."

"I've spent the last few days with my beautiful daughter-in-law. You are so blessed. If I would have known you were with her, I would have told you to stay on the lam."

"Mom!"

"I'm just kidding. God has had his way with you and look at you now! Oh, and my precious grand baby. He is so special. Why didn't you act like him when you were young? I wouldn't have any gray hair if you were that well-behaved."

"I was good, Mom!"

"Yeah, Right! Jaymo, did you know that your son has half the Psalms memorized? Ooh! And he has your voice, too. He sings like an Angel!"

"I know Mom. All glory to God."

"Amen!"

147

"Listen, my time is almost up—"

"Yes, Lord. Praise God. I know you are going to come home and be a beacon of light for these lost souls out here. God has plans for you and—"

"You're right, Mom. But I meant the phone is about to cut off."

"Oh, okay. Well, I love you and I'll see you tomorrow. God bless you and keep you. Here's Karen."

"I told you she'd be here," Karen said when she got the phone back.

"You sent her a ticket, didn't you?" Brother James asked knowingly.

"I had a little something left over from my Christmas bonus. It was nothing."

"I love you, Karen. You are truly my gift from God."

"Well, God created me from your rib. It is only natural that I stay at your side."

"Protecting my heart."

"As you protect mine."

Brother James smiled, "I love you, baby. I'll see you tomorrow."

"Wait, your son wants to—"

"Dad!" Jimmy grabbed the phone, out of breath. "I was outside. What you doing?"

"Nothing, son. But the phone is about to hang up. I miss you."

"I miss you, too. Hey Dad ... God is love!"

"Yes, He is. And I love you."

"I know. I love you, too—" the phone cut off.

Brother James woke up extra early the next morning. He needed to finish the programs for Sunday's service. There were two birthday cards on the floor in front of the door. He picked them up and read them on his way to the chapel. The first one was from the church. The front cover had an elderly music conductor instructing a group of musicians to blowout the many candles on his cake. The inside was signed by Chaplain Parker, the choir, and most of the congregation. It was completely covered with names, some overlapping each other and Brother James laughed as he read some of the tiny messages from his brothers.

The second card was from Ricky. Brother James pulled it out of the unsealed envelope and stopped walking as he read it. The cover was purple and gold and in a fancy cursive scrawl read, "For a Special

Friend on His Birthday." Inside, was a short poem, a few Hallmark words about friendship-and a handwritten, *'Happy B-Day Bro. James! Peace, Ricky."*

There was also a wallet sized photo inside. As Brother James held it up he felt a warm repose rush over him. The picture was one of those department store family portraits. Ricky and Tangela were seated; smiling with love in their eyes. Nyisha sat on her father's lap and held her mother's hand. Devante and Lamar stood at their sides wearing dress shirts and ties and flashing handsome smiles.

On the back of the picture Ricky had written: *To Bro. James, Thank you for helping me keep this together. One love, Ricky Osborn. PS. Remember, you can borrow the little ones whenever you want.* It was followed by a happy face.

Brother James put the cards in his folder and stepped outside to what he knew would be a beautiful day.

After lunch, Ricky stood at the side door of the kitchen talking to BK while waiting for Frizz.

"Son, I'm serious. Frizz put mad work in. Ole' funny-style nigga was mixin' eggs and milk and flour like he Martha Stewart, B. I tasted it and true story it taste like love, Son." BK smacked his lips. "He made a cake from scratch, B. Thugs don't do that. I'm telling you Ricky, ever since you put hands on him, he's soft now."

"Tell him that," Ricky said.

"No, Sir! And here he comes so don't say nothin', Ricky. I was just buggin'."

Frizz wobbled from the bakery with his apron stretched tight across his chest. He ducked down with the cake tucked by his waist like he was boot-legging a football. He handed the cake to Ricky and said, "I don't be baking for no good brothers, but since he's your roomie I made an exception. You got the banana banger with two layers of strawberry icing."

"And it's official, Son!" BK threw in.

"Good looking, Frizz." Ricky peeked around the corner, to make sure the coast was clear. "I have to go, but believe me, I really appreciate this."

"Ain't nothin', homie. We'll see you later."

"Son, on my birthday, I want a German-chocolate cake as tall as me. And I want a stripper to jump out the middle of my joint. Frizz, you can make that happen, B? You know about them strippers, Son. You keep one in your mouth. Let me borrow her, Frizz. Just for one day, Son. Cough her up. Ouch! Stop playin', Son."

Ricky quick-stepped down the hall, still laughing as he turned the corner where Brother Tim and two choir members were waiting for him.

"I told you he'd get it," Brother Tim exclaimed. "Look, brothers a real cake."

"Praise God," one of the brothers added as Ricky gave the cake to Brother Tim.

"Aren't you coming, Brother Ricky?"

"No, I have to stay in the unit during work hours, but you go ahead and enjoy. Knowing Brother James, he's only going to let you eat for ten minutes then it's back to rehearsing." Ricky softened his voice and smiled as he spoke, "Okay, brothers, 'Name Above all Names' on three!" he imitated Brother James perfectly and the choir brothers laughed as they started off for the chapel.

"God bless you, Brother Ricky," they chorused as they stepped outside.

Ricky was just waking up from a nap when Brother James rushed into the room and started getting ready for his visit. It was five minutes after four and visiting hours started right after the 4:30 count was cleared. Brother James grabbed his robe and raced back out for a quick shower. He returned in less than ten minutes and while getting ready, he tipped his chair over, dropped his deodorant twice and stubbed his toe on the locker.

"Where is your patience today, Brother James?" Ricky smiled as he sat up in his bunk.

"I am running so late," he said, flustered. "Did I wake you, brother?"

"No, I was up," Ricky climbed down the bunk ladder.

Brother James pulled his clothes from the closet and spoke with his back turned to Ricky. "That cake was delicious. I had no idea Brother Franklin could throw down like that."

"I'm glad you liked it."

"And thank you for the card and the beautiful picture of your family," Brother James smiled at Ricky. "You have truly helped make this one of the best birthdays I've ever had."

Ricky shook his head through a long yawn. "You do so much for everyone else; I just figured it would be nice for people to do for you, for one day at least."

Brother James looked at him seriously. "Thank you, Brother." Ricky shrugged and slid out of the room so Brother James could get dressed.

When the count was cleared, Ricky went to dinner. He left Brother James sitting on his bunk singing 'O Happy Day'; waiting for his name to be called. After dinner, Ricky met up with BK at the gym and watched an A-league basketball game that went into overtime.

After the game, he walked BK to his unit just so he could hear about the time BK got stuck up in Crown Heights by two teenage girls and their little brother. When he got back to the unit, he stopped at the phone and called Tangela.

It was 7:30 when he finally made it back to the cell. Brother James was still there. He was sitting on his bed with his Bible opened on his lap. As Ricky stepped inside the room, Brother James looked at him with a worried and wounded expression.

"What happened?" Ricky asked.

"I don't know, but something's wrong. I can feel it." His voice was calm, but there was no peace in his tone. He looked up and closed his eyes for a few seconds. "I can't get an answer at the house or on Karen's cell phone. They should have been here," he whispered.

"Maybe they're stuck in traffic," Ricky suggested.

Brother James nodded slowly as if he was willing to consider the possibility, then looked up and closed his eyes again. "Something is wrong, Brother Ricky."

"When was the last time you tried to call?"

Brother James looked at him strangely, trying to remember how long ago it was. "I don't know, maybe 20 minutes."

"You have to try again, right now!" Ricky felt a panic creeping into his own voice.

Brother James stood up quickly. "You're right. I'll be back." He came back in two minutes. "Still nothing," he brushed by Ricky and got on his knees to pray. Ricky stepped out the room to give him some privacy. He walked purposely to the officer's station to see if they had called for Brother James and he somehow didn't hear them.

As Ricky approached the officer's desk, C.O. Swain lifted the intercom microphone to his mouth. "Morris! Inmate James Morris! Please report to the—" he stopped when he noticed Ricky at the desk. "Osborn, is your cellie in the unit?"

Ricky nodded yes. "Is that his visit?"

"No, it's his job. They need him over at the Chaplain's office."

"For what?" Ricky shouted. "Did they say for what?" He forced himself to calm down.

"No, but it probably has something to do with that church festival thing they're doing this weekend." C.O. Swain reached for the mic again. I don't know, they just asked me to send him over."

"Alright, but don't call him again. I'll tell him myself." Ricky took heavy strides down the hall. He turned the corner and saw Brother James racing towards him while tucking in his shirt.

"They called me, Brother Ricky," he said with a relieved smile. "You were right. They were probably stuck in traffic."

Ricky put his hands on Brother James' shoulders. "It wasn't for the visit. They want you to go to the Chaplain's office."

Brother James shook his head and his smile faded like a sunset. "Did ... did they say why?"

"No."

"Will you come with me?"

"Of course."

"I don't know why I'm afraid. It may not be bad news," Brother James spoke to himself as they started towards the door. "God said he didn't give us the spirit of fear, but of power, and of love, and of a sound mind."

They walked into the chapel and Ricky could tell right away the news was bad. There were at least seven people loitering around the Chaplain's office. Lt. Stevenson was there, sipping coffee with two officers. The pale psychiatrist was there in a rumpled suit and accompanied by two nurses. Chaplain Parker stood in the doorway beside Sister Teresa, who was dressed in her full habit.

Brother James kept his eyes straight ahead and missed the sympathetic gazes from the red-rimmed eyes of the bystanders. Lt. Stevenson pulled Ricky aside as Chaplain Parker wrapped his arm around Brother James, guided him into the office and closed the door behind them.

"What happened?" Brother James ignored the chair that Chaplain Parker was pointing to.

"Please, sit down, Brother James."

"Sir, I don't want to sit down. Please, tell me what's wrong."

Chaplain Parker leaned his weight against his desk and stood in front of Brother James. He peered into the eyes of the young man he had grown to love like a son and a single tear escaped down his lined face.

"What happened?!" Brother James screamed as he felt his eyes welling up as well.

Chaplain Parker blew out a deep sigh. "There was an accident, son. The roads had ice patches and a deer jumped into the lane. Your wife swerved around ..."

Brother James felt his knees buckle. He was vaguely aware of Chaplain Parker hugging him to hold him up. He was on the edge of a cliff staring out at a stark, bare, endless abyss. "How bad?" He didn't know if he'd asked out loud or not, but Chaplain Parker's voice came to him like someone talking from behind a wall.

"They were coming up the steep side of the mountain, and when ... when they hit the ice, Lord have mercy. The car went over the guard rail and—"

Brother James pushed himself away from the chaplain. "No!" His tears fell unhindered. "Don't say it! Don't you dare say it! Don't Chaplain, please," his voice broke. Where's my mother? Where are my wife and my son? Where are they?! Please, Sir, please, tell me they're okay. Tell ... tell me they're going to be okay." Chaplain Parker reached for him, but Brother James stepped back and crossed his arms. "Tell me where my family is at," he quivered.

Chaplain Parker's heart dropped into his stomach. He stepped closer to Brother James. "They're gone, son. I'm so sorry, but they've gone home to glory."

The scream was heart-wrenching, like the strangled wail of a wild animal. Ricky started towards the door, but the C.O.s grabbed him. Lt. Stevenson and the Psych slid into the office. For the brief second the door was open, Ricky saw Brother James on his hands and knees crying so hard that his whole body convulsed. Chaplain Parker sat on his haunches, crying and cradling Brother James in his arms.

The nurses and Sister Teresa hugged each other and wept loudly. Ricky knew without asking; only death could cause such grief. He caught snippets from the tearful utterings of those waiting with him: A fifty-foot drop, all three killed instantly, a half burned monogrammed Bible that was supposed to be Brother James' birthday gift.

Ricky felt sick. After a few minutes, the office door opened back up. Chaplain Parker and Lt. Stevenson stumbled through the door holding Brother James up. His head hung down and he sobbed heavily.

"Brother James," Ricky took a step towards him and lifted his chin to look in his face. Brother James kept his head up, but looked past Ricky and stared at the pieces of his past shimmering like mirages in that deserted abyss. "I'm sorry, Brother James."

His eyes followed the voice. Brother James slowly focused in on Ricky's eyes. He blinked once, twice. His face broke like thick glass. "Oh God, they're dead. They're gone," his voice was like the crackling of a dying fire. "No, no, no," he chanted as the C.O.s carried him to the SHU.

"He doesn't want to be around anyone," Chaplain Parker explained. "We'll keep him in Administrative Detention for the night and I'll check on him in the morning."

Ricky couldn't think straight. He needed some air. He strode by unnoticed; stealing bits and pieces of their self-comforting condolences as he headed outside: "He giveth and taketh ...," "Such a tragedy ..." "So unfair ..." "...mysterious ways."

The words hit him in his back like sharp stones. He stepped outside and took his time walking back to the unit. He sloshed through the wet snow as the wind whipped at him. The agony he had witnessed chilled him to the bone and left him colder than the night air. He went to his room, turned off the light, laid on his back and stared at the darkness until his eyes stopped leaking and refused to stay open.

The next day came like a still-born baby delivered in a dark room. Sad. Depressive. Everyone crying except the baby itself. All morning, inmates came to the cell with long, tear-stained faces. They begged to know what happened to Brother James. Some of the church brothers stayed with Ricky to help explain the situation to Brother James' many friends.

By three o'clock, Ricky was drained. Most of the choir was gathered in his room trying to decide what to do about the anniversary service.

They went back and forth about whether or not the show should go on and who would sing what. They finally agreed that Brother James would've encouraged them to press on and that they would dedicate his song to the memory of the Morris family. Ricky almost clapped his hands when count time was announced and they all rushed out to their rooms.

When the count was clear, C.O. Swain stopped by to tell Ricky he was wanted at the Lieutenant's Office. C.O. Swain surveyed the cell with sad eyes and left without saying anything further.

Chaplain Parker was waiting for Ricky at the Lieutenants' Office. He was wearing his clothes from yesterday and it was evident he hadn't slept. He gave Ricky a limp hand-shake and looked at him through tired eyes. "I saw you last night, but I don't believe we've met."

"No, Sir, we haven't."

"And you're not a member of the church?"

Ricky eyed him with a hint of impatience since it was obvious the Chaplain already knew the answer.

"Okay, then," Chaplain Parker sighed after completing his half-hearted interrogation. "Brother James has asked to see you, and only you. I've arranged for you to be escorted to the SHU, where you can talk to him, maybe encourage him a bit," he frowned at Ricky, but was too tired for it to come off as intimidating. "You do know how to encourage, don't you?"

"I can try," Ricky muttered.

"Good man!" Chaplain Parker handed him a Bible and Ricky was surprised it didn't have its usual foreboding feel.

They walked to the SHU in silence. Chaplain Parker turned Ricky over to the beefy Sgt. Warren, who was still armed with a clipboard and a mouthful of Skoal. "You have to come and get 'em in an hour, Rev'rend."

Chaplain Parker nodded as he turned into the chapel.

Ricky followed Sgt. Warren down the steps into the processing room. He was patted down thoroughly and led to the last cell on the floor. After trying three wrong keys, Sgt. Warren opened the door and waved for Ricky to step inside. "You got 50 minutes. Hit the button if you need me before that." He locked the door and wobbled off.

Brother James sat on the bed with a ratty wool blanket draped over his shoulders. His eyes were puffy and he looked straight ahead; the thousand yard stare of a prisoner of war. His face had a sickly-green tint and he looked smaller, diminished.

"I never knew it was so cold down here," Brother James spoke in a hoarse, raspy whisper, his voice lost from crying all night.

"Yeah, they keep the AC pumping down here," Ricky spoke softly as he handed him the Bible.

Brother James sat the Bible down beside him without giving it a glance. "A few years ago, I had the flu," he let his gaze slide to the floor as he spoke. "Karen didn't like how I sounded when we talked on the phone. She made that three-hour drive just to come take care of me. She smuggled herbal tea and Thera-Flu into the visiting room and for three days nursed me back to health. When I called a few days later, she was sick. She had my flu. That's love, Ricky."

"Yes, it is," Ricky agreed as he sat down on the bunk with him. Brother James turned towards Ricky and looked through him as he spoke. "It's my fault. They were coming to visit me, they were ... Now, I've lost ..." he bit into his fist and started weeping. "I've lost them. The... the three people who I love more than my own life are gone. And it's my fault."

"No, Brother James, you can't blame yourself. You—"

"They were coming to see me!" He shouted and spittle gathered at the corners of his mouth. "They were coming to see me and now they're ... dead." Brother James stood up and paced. He clutched the folds of the blanket against his chest. "It's my fault. I must have done something wrong. I've been found lacking and God has taken everything from me. Everything I cherished, every ... everything I loved."

He looked up and let out a moan that sent chills through Ricky's whole body. "Why!?" he screamed at the ceiling. He looked at Ricky with an expression so confused, so filled with agony, that Ricky was forced to look away before getting lost in the misery that consumed his friend.

Brother James leaned against the wall, new tears falling slow. "Why?" he cried. "Please, Ricky, tell me why?"

"I don't know," Ricky shook his head, frustrated. He wanted to help, but didn't know what to say. "I'm sorry, I don't know."

"But you do." Brother James wiped away his tears and slid back onto the bed. He looked at Ricky with wide eyes glazed over with hurt and madness. "That's why I asked for you. Because you already know the secret."

"What secret?"

"You know," Brother James nudged him and grinned maliciously. "You already know that there really isn't a God."

Ricky closed his eyes and sighed deep. This was the last thing he expected. "You're hurting right now and—"

"No. You can tell me, Ricky. I'm ready to hear it. That's why you don't do the church thing isn't it? Because you already know there is no God." Brother James nodded as if he'd just solved the mystery of the Sphinx.

"I know you feel empty; like all hope is gone, but don't do this, Brother James. Now is the time for you to lean on God. More than—"

"What God!? What God, Ricky? You don't believe in God."

There was a thin silence as Ricky felt his past creep into the cell with them. He looked up in an effort to hold in his tears, then turned to Brother James and let them fall. "I do believe in God. I am the son of a Preacher. I've believed in God my whole life."

Brother James screwed up his face; about to say something, but Ricky rushed on. "I stopped loving God. I stopped believing in His love a long time ago. I know about some of what you're going through. It's not the same, but I know how it feels to lose someone close to you. I know how it feels to blame yourself.

"My brother David," Ricky's eyes sparkled as he said the name and his tears fell faster. "David was my older brother and he was my whole world. My parents were strict, real strict, but somehow David made ways for us to have fun and be happy. He had a free spirit and he did what he felt."

Ricky's lip trembled. It happened a long time ago, but the pain was still raw. "David started using drugs. He had an addictive personality and he went from weed to heroin within months. It got real bad. He was out of control. My parents kicked him out of the house and I was forbidden to help him in any way. They said he was no longer their son ... But he was still my brother. I couldn't just cut him off. I still needed him.

"I was my parents' last hope and they pressured me to be twice as good, twice as successful. I was expected to make up for David's failure.

I was ordered to be the good brother." Ricky shook his head violently, "But I still helped David. I loved him too much not to, even though I knew I was helping him to harm himself.

"One day, I held my ground about letting him in the house. He started walking away singing and I called him back. I gave him some money to get a cheap motel room and a change of clothes. I knew it was a risk giving him money. But I wanted ... I believed he would do the right ..." Ricky swallowed the lump in his throat and looked at Brother James through teary eyes.

"He used the money to buy dope. It was a bad batch and he ... he died. I blamed myself. I blamed my Mom and Dad. Mostly, I blamed God."

Brother James nodded his agreement. "You hear that, God?! We blame you!"

"I haven't spoken to my parents since David's funeral. It was like they represented some evil God who took my brother away. I left home, I left the church, and I lived life by my own rules. I stopped loving God and I didn't care if He loved me.

"But I missed Him. I remembered how wonderful it felt to have the peace of knowing Jesus and being saved. But I didn't want it anymore. I didn't believe I deserved it. I thought I could hurt God by withholding my love from Him. I thought I was justified, I thought I was right, but I was wrong."

Brother James squeezed his eyes tight and looked at Ricky as if he was a traitor. "You weren't wrong, Ricky. You were right. If there is a God up there, He is evil."

"God is not a God to tempt or do evil."

Brother James snorted, "Listen to you, quoting scriptures and all. You ..." he fell into a fit of hysterical laughter. "You ... you're the good brother now. No, no, no ... you were always the good brother ... you just didn't know it. Well, you-can-have-it!" His laughter faded into sobbing.

"It is because of you, Brother James that I want to be a good brother. God has used you to show me; remind me what brotherly love is, you have reminded me God is still alive, still—"

"Who cares if He's alive? My Mother is dead! My Wife and my ... my son are dead!" Brother James sank to the floor and the blanket puddled at his feet. "He's alive and they're dead."

Ricky kneeled down, wrapped the blanket around Brother James' shoulders, and thought about his father. He witnessed his father many times, ministering to people who had lost loved ones, people whose marriages had failed, whose children were sick. He saw his father take money from his own pockets to help pay doctor bills and funeral costs. He remembered how passionate his father preached and prayed and how his mother cried for every lost child as if they were from her very own womb. His parents were stern and God-fearing, but they were also very loving. Ricky felt a surge of adrenaline as revelation washed over him like baptismal water.

"Blessed are the mourners for they shall be comforted," he quoted to Brother James as he recalled the last conversation he had with his father at David's funeral. "My father did the eulogy and the burial ceremony. He did everything like it was just any other funeral. When it was over, I asked him why he wasn't crying and if he had ever loved David at all. My father's eyes sparked for a second and then he shook it off. He looked me in the eye and said he loved David the way God loved him. He said David and I were blessings from God. And like Abraham with Isaac, he had to be willing to give any and every blessing or gift from God, back to God. He had to trust God to provide, whether it be the restoration of a burned church on earth or the reunion with a son in heaven.

"My faith was never strong enough to accept that. It was easy for me to walk away from my parents and God. But you, Brother James, you're different." Brother James shook his head hard to deny it. "Yes, you are! Your faith is stronger than that grain of mustard seed. Your faith has already moved mountains, you are—"

"No! You're wrong!" he shouted and pushed Ricky away from him. "I can't wait for heaven! I can't accept that. I'm ..." he broke down. "I'm done! I'm done with God." He stood up and waved his clenched fists. "I'm done with you, God! I'm done with you! I'm ... I'm done." He fell against the wall exhausted, his whole being drained.

Ricky eyed him with sympathy and anguish. He wanted to do something, anything, but he had run out of words as well as time.

Sgt. Warren tapped on the door with his key. Brother James stood up slowly and shuffled back to the bed. His eyes resumed that far away look and though he had stopped crying, they were still watery, promising to flow forever if need be.

Sgt. Warren opened the door, his eyes sorrowful enough to fit right in. "I'm sorry Mr. Morris, but Mr. Osborn has to go now."

Brother James gave an imperceptible nod. As Ricky took a step to leave, Brother James grabbed him by his wrist with a trembling hand. "Tell me, good brother, what changed your mind? How can you forgive him now?"

"I heard a song," Ricky offered a small but genuine smile. "My brother's favorite song and he sung it to me through you, with the same passion and the same love for the same God."

Brother James looked at him skeptically and let go of his hand. He picked up the Bible and passed it to Ricky. "I won't be needing that. Maybe, I need a song, too."

"You just need some time to rest," Ricky said as Sgt. Warren ushered him out of the cell and locked the door. "If there's anything I can do, anything you need please let me know."

Brother James sat there with a vacant look on his face. "You hear me?!" Ricky yelled at the small window. "Anything you need, you let me know!" Brother James stared at nothing.

"We have to go," Sgt. Warren pressed.

Ricky gazed through the glass, willing Brother James to make eye contact one more time. But he didn't. With a heavy heart, Ricky pulled away from the door and followed Sgt. Warren down the hall.

Chaplain Parker stood outside waiting for him. Snow flurries swirled above him and landed on his black trench coat like diamond chips. "How did it go?" he asked.

Ricky shrugged. "He's hurting and he needs some time."

The chaplain nodded as if he expected as much. He looked up at the naked night sky and reminded Ricky of a little boy catching snow flakes on his face. They stood there in silence. Chaplain Parker noticed the Bible in Ricky's hand and could feel that Ricky had no intentions of giving it back.

"Will I see you in service tomorrow, Brother Osborn?"

"Yes, I'll be there."

"Well, praise God."

"Praise God," Ricky echoed as they shook hands and said farewell.

Ricky headed back to the unit with mixed emotions. He grieved for Brother James' loss and his heart was heavy, but his spirit felt light.

The wind pricked sharply, but the dampness of the snow felt refreshing against his skin. His pulse was strong and steady, the rhythm soothing and for some reason everything looked different to him. The world looked new.

When he got back to his room he sat down and opened a Bible for the first time in over 15 years. He read randomly and was surprised by how many scriptures he still remembered. He fell asleep with the Bible folded open on his chest, the words from Psalm 100 fresh in his mind.

While Ricky was reacquainting himself with the Word of God and then sleeping with the peace of a renewed salvation, Brother James paced a cold floor in his bare feet conversing with ghosts.

His mother laid on the bottom bunk with bloody bandages wrapped around her mutilated chest. She stared at Brother James with pleading eyes.

"I'm ... I'm sorry, Mom. I'm so sorry!" He kneeled down, reached for her hand and begged for forgiveness. To the third shift C.O. who checked on him every 15 minutes, it appeared as if he was praying.

Brother James knew what he was seeing couldn't be real, but he felt compelled to give in to them. The nightmarish images were better than reality. They distracted him from the cold, the nausea, and the pain in his chest that made him feel like his heart and lungs were ready to explode. Most of all, the illusions made him feel like he wasn't alone.

His wife stood at the door in her wedding gown. She looked elegant and sexy. The dress was form fitting and her shoulders were bare, her neck—long and slender—was graced with a string of pearls handed down for three generations. But her face was all wrong. Gone were the eyes that sparkled at the alter and the smile that made him say, "I DO!" before the preacher even began. Karen looked at him through flat brown stones that screamed, "Why!" Her mouth was set taut in an effort to keep from crying.

"I ... love you, Karen. You are my rib, my gift from God."

She turned her lifeless gaze towards the mirror and as Brother James followed her eyes he gasped and shot his hands to his mouth. The mirror held his son's reflection. Jimmy was wearing the tux from his recital, but he wasn't singing. He looked at Brother James from hooded eyes.

"Sing to me Jimmy. Let Daddy hear you sing. Sing for me, please!" Brother James screamed into the mirror. His mouth hung open as he watched his son shake his head no. Brother James spun around quickly, but Jimmy wasn't there, just the gray wall. He glanced to his bunk and his mother had faded away also. He turned around with his arms extended like a blind man, reaching out for Karen, but she, too, was gone. "NO!" he roared and banged on the cell door with both his fists.

"What's wrong?" The young C.O. asked after racing to the door.

"They're gone! They're gone! They're ... go—"

"I know," the officer said soothingly. "I'm sorry, Mr. Morris. Is there anything I can get you?"

"I ... I ... I want my picture," Brother James couldn't control his breathing. "Please ... get my picture. My ... my wife and ... my son. I want my picture! I want my picture! I want my pic—"

"Okay, okay, Mr. Morris. Please calm down. I can't leave right now, but as soon as my relief gets here I'll fetch your picture. Okay?"

Brother James nodded and leaned against the door. He watched the C.O. walk back to the front. He was afraid to turn around. Afraid his family would be in the cell with him, but even more afraid they wouldn't.

Ricky was already awake when the young C.O. came to his door and asked for the picture of Mr. Morris' wife and son. Ricky knew exactly what picture Brother James wanted. He grabbed the 5 by 7 frame from off the desk. "How's he doing?" Ricky inquired as he handed him the picture.

The C.O. shook his head and frowned. "The doc gave him a sedative last night and he still hasn't slept." He held the picture up. "Maybe this will help."

"Maybe," Ricky said to himself as the C.O. stepped off.

The anniversary service had originally been scheduled for that evening, but without Brother James in attendance, Chaplain Parker decided to go with the usual morning time and a more somber, reflective worship service. Ricky entered the crowded chapel at ten minutes before eight. Sister Tramayne was playing 'Center of my Joy' on the piano. Most of the congregation sat with their heads bowed in silent prayer. Ricky found an empty seat in the back and bowed his head as well.

***

Brother James stared at the picture of Karen and Jimmy. He clutched the frame with shaky hands; his tears splashing on the glass. He hugged the picture to his chest and let out a demented laugh as he talked to the beautiful faces that smiled at him. He slid the picture out of the frame, kissed it, and laid it gently on his pillow. "All together," he smiled with satisfaction as he studied the photograph. "All together." He turned his attention to the glass in the frame.

***

Chaplain Parker wasted no time. He unleashed a fiery sermon from the eleventh chapter of Hebrews. His voice was like an unexpected storm: Booming thunder, thick, heavy clouds rising and overflowing, his words were like rain falling— sometimes in torrents at other times just drizzling. He spoke of faith. How the prophets endured and survived by faith. Each verse, each prophet eulogized like close friends. As he got close to the end of the chapter, his voice became a whisper— the calm after the storm— as he spoke of those who had a good report through faith, yet didn't receive the promise. Those who were innocent and died faithful. "They will see paradise," Chaplain Parker exclaimed and most of the congregation wept, knowing he was also referring to the family that Brother James had lost.

***

Brother James was in a zone. The AC had been turned off and Chaplain Parker's voice blasted through the vent so clear Brother James felt like he was in the chapel with them. He sat on the bunk with a psychotic grin, hypnotized by the picture and by the glass in the frame. Chaplain Parker's voice was like the tinny sound of a slow song seeping out of someone else's headphones. It wasn't a distraction at all. "All together." He slid the glass from the wooden frame, stared at it for a few seconds and then broke it in half.

***

"God's way is the only way," Chaplain Parker continued. "He is the truth and the light. God says in Jeremiah that His thoughts for us are of peace and not evil and to give us a blessed end." Chaplain Parker looked out at the sad faces and sighed. "True faith demands that we praise God through all things, for God loves us and all things are through the Lord. We must not only possess faith, faith must possess us." He stepped away from the altar and sat down in the front row, there was no need for applause; the free-running tears were proof the message was received.

Brother Tim led the choir up front. They took their places and waited for him to lead them in *I Will*. Brother Tim grabbed the microphone from its stand and faced the crowd. He raised his right hand and then dropped it.

"Be-pleased-o-Lord, to-deliver-me: O-Lord-make-haste-to-help-me," the choir sang in perfect four-part harmony. Sister Tramayne brought the keys in right on cue. She played the soft melody for two bars and Ricky closed his eyes in anticipation of Brother Tim coming in with the lead. But he didn't come in. He stood there, frozen, holding the mic against his chest with tears gushing down his face. Sister Tramayne looked over the piano at the choir, who looked at Brother Tim, who looked at the floor. Before he knew what he was doing, Ricky was on his feet, heading down the center aisle.

***

Brother James held the longer piece of glass in his right hand. The broken end was jagged and sharp to the touch. He let his left arm lay across his knee exposing the thick radial artery in his wrist. This was the only way. He couldn't imagine living his life without Karen and Jimmy. The grief was choking him, crushing him. There was so much he wanted to do for his mother; so much he wanted to make up to her. He missed them all painfully.

He knew suicide was wrong. In his recent beliefs it was one of the worst sins. It was like spitting at God and saying I don't want this gift you gave me. Well, he didn't want it. Not anymore. Not without them. He glanced at the picture, "All together!" He took a deep breath and blinked away the tears. He pressed the glass to his wrist.

***

Ricky walked up to Brother Tim, "I got it," he whispered. Brother Tim gave him the mic and a thankful smile and stepped in with the choir. "Brother James loves to sing for the Lord." Ricky's voice was a light timbre through the microphone. "He wrote this next song, like all of his songs, as a tribute to God. He wanted to sing it to us. To inspire and encourage us." Ricky stared at the nodding heads and let them shout their Amens. "This morning, let us continue to praise God through song, but let us also sing to Brother James. Let us minister to him as he has done for us so many times. And the glory will be God's as always."

There was a collective sigh as the congregation sat up in their seats eager to hear one of Brother James' songs sung by a stranger to the church. Brother Tim raised his hand again, dropped it and added his own voice to that beautiful opening. Ricky let the piano play for a measure. He closed his eyes and opened his mouth in song.

"Who will-praise-you-Lord?" Ricky was back in his father's church, the preacher's youngest son with the soulful voice. *"I will, I said, I will,"* he sang each word, every note as if it was the last song he'd ever be allowed to sing. *"Everything we go through."*

"Go through," the choir echoed him.
"All that we have been through."
"Been through."
"Is for our good and the glory of God."

***

Brother James sprang to his feet and spun around looking for Ricky. The music pouring out of the vent could no longer be ignored and Ricky's voice rode a current of passion so pure and so clear, that Brother James would've sworn Ricky was in the cell with him. He spied the vent and squeezed his eyes shut in frustration. He gripped the glass so tight it cut into the palm of his hand. He fell to his knees and buried his head in between his arms. Ricky was singing to his soul, using his own song, his own words against him. "No, no, no!" Brother James stared at the vent and then at the glass and knew there was only one way to make the music stop.

***

"*Who-will-walk-with-you-Lord?*" Ricky held the last note the same way Brother James had shown him when they'd practiced together in the room.

"*I will,*" the choir sang softly.

"*I said who will worship you, Lord?*" Ricky took the note into the rafters and those who weren't standing already, jumped to their feet. "*Who will sing of the mercies of the Lord, Forever? For-ever-and-ever?*"

"*I will!*"

***

Brother James held the glass against his wrist, his hands shook and his body jerked with every sob. His knees ached on the cement floor. The pain in his head was unbearable. All he had to do was block out Ricky and the choir and drag the glass across his wrist with force. He was ready. He could do it. He just needed to look at the picture while committing himself into that forever sleep.

He knee-walked closer to the bed, ignoring the pain that shot into his legs. He vaguely heard Ricky coming to the end of the song, he was trilling the word earth and even as Brother James fought to block it out, it sent a ripple of chills through his body. He leaned on the bed, smiling at the picture. Then everything went quiet. Ricky, the choir, the music, it all stopped. The silence was louder and more disturbing than the song had been. Brother James peered at the vent, confused, wondering what happened to the end of the song.

***

Ricky waved his hands up and down, bringing the music choir to a halt. The crowd looked at him with hungry faces. Their spirits were high above them, dancing in a circle. The interruption was alarming and exciting.

Ricky turned to the choir and in a light voice sang, "*God-is-love. God-is-love.*"

The choir picked up the notes and joined him with a melodious chant. "*God-is-love, God is love.*"

Chaplain Parker added his deep baritone to the chorus and the congregation followed. "*GOD IS LOVE! ... GOD IS LOVE!*"

***

Brother James cried hard as the familiar voices swelled up and burst through the vent like flood waters through a breaking dam. *"God is Love!"* The voices filled the tiny cell and became the only air Brother James could breathe. *"God is Love!"* He looked at the picture and heard his wife's sultry tenor join in. *"God is Love!"* his mother's voice rang bittersweet. Like the rapid strumming of a harp added to a stirring symphony of soft strings, Jimmy's voice chimed in, *"God is Love!"*

Brother James stood up and turned to the mirror. Sure enough, Jimmy was there. Brother James watched— through blurry eyes and with a hopeless glee— as his son pointed to the sky and then touched his heart. He did it over and over, his voice matching his movements. *"God is Love! God is Love!"*

Brother James dropped the piece of glass. Jimmy smiled and faded away. *"God is Love!"* Brother James slammed his hands against his ears. *"God is Love! God is Love! God is Love!"* The vent was quiet, the symphony had ceased, but the voices reverberated inside of him. *"God is Love!"* His heartbeats were the words. *"God is Love!"* His rapid breaths were the words. *"God is Love!"* When he closed his eyes, he saw his son smiling, pointing to the sky and touching his chest. *"God is Love!"*

Brother James opened his eyes and saw the glass on the floor. It called him; begged for the warmth of his hand and the promise of fresh blood. "God is Love," he said, loud enough to know it was his voice. He kicked the piece of glass under the bed and heard it shatter against the wall. He backed away from the bed, from the picture, from the other half of the glass.

"God is Love!" he shook his head and laughed wildly until his laughter turned into sobbing. He slammed himself against the wall and slid down onto his side. He curled up in a fetal position and cried over and over in a hoarse voice, "God, help me!"

Ricky's voice trickled through the vent almost as if he had heard Brother James' cry. He was ending the song the way Brother James had intended. With no music, his voice strained and exhausted, he sang the bridge one last time, *"And God will be with you for-ever, unto the ends of the earth ..."*

A few days later, Chaplain Parker and Lieutenant Stevenson escorted Brother James to his wife and son's funeral. His mother's body was cremated and her ashes sent to Africa. He was then transferred to the State Mental Institution, where he could finish out his sentence while receiving the help he needed to cope with his loss.

Ricky sat at the desk. He remembered the hundreds of inmates and staff members who gathered at the dining hall windows and watched Brother James leave. They cheered and pounded on the windows, most of them screaming, "Let Brotherly love continue."

Ricky smiled at the memory and turned back to the blank piece of paper in front of him. He wanted to write about all the things he had learned from Brother James; like how being a good brother means bearing good fruit. He wanted to write about his love for God being restored. He wanted to write about singing again; about his friends, Frizz and BK and his mission to set a good example for them the way Brother James had done for him. He wanted to write about his desire to be a great father and a wonderful husband. Most of all, he wanted to apologize.

Ricky held the pen steady, took a deep breath and began writing ...

Dear Mom and Dad,

SHINE

I stand before you with a humble heart and an open mind, and with a spirit from God that commands me to shine.

I once was lost with no direction and blamed others for my imperfections,

Like skipping rocks in a shallow lake,

I was casting stones at my own reflection.

I rejected my protection and pursued a lifestyle that was wild and thought I found forgiveness in the smile of my first child.

I believed I could be baptized by the tears she cried and that her saying Da-Da automatically made me a man.

I thought I was shining.

Like many of you, I was raised by the cold streets that sold treats to lost souls who don't sleep.

I was reared where you find fiends and crime scenes,

Where love is handed out in small portions and orphans have abortions, where money is an idol-god and we trust in greed and lust and guns that bust.

We don't know what to believe in so like heathens we war for no reason.

I was caught up in the devil's way of thinking, and I've looked death in the eye many times without blinking,

Never realizing my life is a gift that I'm obligated to the Lord to do something with

I am supposed to shine.

So, now, I surround myself with apostles and disciples

Who strap-up with Bibles and shoot scriptures from gospels and epistles like they used to shoot pistols.

I'm talking about official saints who know it doesn't matter if our reverend or pastor is man or woman, black or white, Baptist or Methodist as long as their method is filled with messages from God and for God.

The only God!

The God of second chances, who we praise no matter what our circumstances.

The God who saved me, who removed my bitterness and hate.
The God who told me to wait.
The God who told me to shine.
The God who loves me so much,
He sent His only begotten son to die
And my God is not a man that He should lie,
And if you still don't know why just listen here while I paint the
picture clear …

An 8-year old boy, the oldest of four.
They all sleep on one mattress that lies on the floor.
He awakes Sunday morning; the smell of urine has him coughing,
a spaghetti-pot on the stove, he heats water to wash up in.
He puts on high-water pants and the only dress shirt to his name,
and a clip on tie that he hopes will hide the stains.
His sock has a hole that his big toe pokes through.
Breakfast is a slice of bread with syrup soaked through.
He tip-toes into his mother's bedroom, feeling guilty as he goes,
knowing her room is her only sanctuary from a life filled with woes.
He taps her shoulder and she opens pretty eyes filled with glaze,
the ugly mix of an alcohol and drug-induced haze.
In his child like innocence he smiles at her proudly,
barely noticing the stranger who sleeps beside her snoring loudly.
A van pulls up out front; Mr. Fox blows the horn.
His best friend Avery leans out the window and yells for him to come on.
He needs money for the offering; he gives his mother a poke,
she turns away from him annoyed and tells him she's broke.
Him and his brothers have a dollar that they earned the day before
by helping to carry bags at the grocery store.
They were supposed to have a party, chips and penny candy was the plan.
He takes out fifty-cents and hopes his brothers will understand.
The horn blows again; he grabs his coat and starts running,
the van begins to pull off, Avery yells, "Wait, I see him coming."
He gets in the van a big smile on his face,
says, "God bless you" to Mr. Fox and apologizes for being late.
He sits next to Avery, they laugh at each other's ties,
Avery looks up at him with ashamed and expectant eyes.

It is an expression the boy has learned to understand,
he takes one of his quarters and puts it in his best friend's hand.
Avery whispers, 'thank you', the boy says, 'anytime.'
When they arrive at Sunday school everything is just fine
especially when they sing the boy's favorite song of all time:
This lil' light of mine ... I'm gonna let it shine ...
I stand here before you with a humble heart and an open mind.
That little boy— now a man— still determined to shine!!

The Letter

Celine Ross let out a heavy sigh as she parted the thin drapery covering her kitchen window. She pondered the overcast sky that matched her melancholy mood. It was early, Sunday morning, usually her favorite day of the week. Gospel harmonies floated from the clock radio and morning worship service was only an hour away, yet Celine felt a deep sense of despair clinging to her, weighing her down like a metal straightjacket.

Her only child, Travis, sat at the kitchen table devouring a bowl of cereal.

Slurping milk from the spoon, earned him a disapproving look from his mother.

"Travis, honey," she sat down at the table across from him. "I know we agreed that once you turned 16 I wouldn't force you to come to church with me, but it's been three—"

"Aw, come on Mom, not again." Travis cut her off. "We already talked about this."

"I know Travis, but you've only gone twice in the past three months. Your football season is over and you're not doing anything. I don't understand why you won't come and hear the word of God."

"I hear the word of God every day, right here at home. You make sure of that." Travis got up and put his bowl in the sink. "Mom, I can't sit in there and pretend I feel something when I don't."

Celine frowned at him. "God loves you, Travis, you have to feel that," she implored.

"But I don't, Mom. I don't feel anything."

"O taste and see that the Lord is good; Blessed is the man that trusteth in Him," Celine quoted from her favorite Psalm.

"Trust in Him?" Travis asked doubtfully. "Trust in Him how? Dad died in a storm God created." As he spoke, the painful images of the hurricane that changed from a category three to a category five so quickly they were forced to take cover in their basement, seeped into his conscious. He remembered the power going out, the wind waging war on the small windows until they exploded. The water racing in, rising to their knees. The cold; his mother sloshing through dirty water to grab blankets from a box marked Goodwill. His father trying valiantly to keep a candle lit, finally finding success beneath the wooden staircase that led up to the kitchen. The support beam breaking, sounding like a gunshot. The staircase collapsing. His father buried under heavy, jagged wood, bleeding; still alive, but barely. His mother screaming for help into a storm that screamed back at her. And him sitting there in the icy water, too in shock to cry, holding his father's hand, staring at a portion of his father's face through a small gap in the broken and splintered lumber as his father talked to him. Talked until his breath was all gone.

Travis blinked away the images and looked his mother in the eye, "God took Dad when we needed him the most, so you tell me, why I should trust in the Lord."

"I understand you're still angry, son, but when you believe in—"

"Believe in what, Mom?! What should I believe? Hunh? That we're all going to be together again in that magical place called Heaven, and that some—"

"Travis Lamont Ross, that is enough! I don't care how upset you are, you will not speak like that in this house." Celine closed her eyes and took deep breaths, trying her best to hold back her tears.

Travis watched his mother fight to control her emotions. He knew full well how sensitive she was and how she cried at the drop of a hat. Her attempt to stand firm and keep a stiff upper lip impressed him, but eventually that lip trembled and the tears fell.

"I'm sorry, Mom," Travis passed her a clean dish towel. "I really am, but I can't help how I feel."

Celine swiped at her tears with the towel. She reached up and gently cupped her son's face in her hand. "God will help you, honey, but you have to open up your heart and let Him back in," she stroked his face lovingly as she added, "He heals all hurts Travis. Not some of the hurts, all hurts."

"I don't know, Mom," Travis said as he turned away from her touch.

"Yes you do!" she insisted. "What did your father tell you before he passed over?" she asked with a hint of excitement creeping into her voice. "You remember, don't you? Tell me what your father told you?"

Travis eyed his mother sympathetically. She was small and fragile, yet willing to bear the burdens of all mankind on her tiny shoulders. Tragically widowed at age 34, in the two years following her husband's death, Celine never questioned God or complained about her life. A life that Travis imagined as being lonely and unfair.

She stood in front of him shifting her weight from one foot to the other. The lines around her eyes made her look older, but she was still beautiful. She smiled expectantly, waiting for him to recite his father's last words so they could hug, laugh and pretend everything was alright.

"I don't remember," he said slowly.

Celine's face clouded over. She blinked rapidly and swallowed back her disappointment.

"Okay, Travis, you don't have to tell me."

"I don't remember, Mom. I really don't," he lied unconvincingly.

"Yes, you do. If you don't want to talk about it, that's fine, but don't lie to me."

"I SAID I DON'T REMEMBER!" Travis shouted as he banged both hands on the kitchen table and upset the sugar bowl.

"Okay honey, it's okay," she held his hands and tried to pull him into an embrace, but he jerked his hands away to wipe his eyes.

"I miss him, Mom."

"I know honey, I miss him too."

Travis crossed his arms and looked at her skeptically. "Are you sure? Because it doesn't seem like you do. You have good old Jesus to keep you com—"

He wanted to say company, but Celine slapped the last two syllables out of his mouth.

"How dare you?" she hissed. "How dare you question my love for your father and blaspheme at the same time. Yes, I have Jesus and I thank God for the peace, grace and love He fills me with.

"It is His love that provided the foundation for the love your father and I shared. It is God's love that brought you into this world and guided me how to love and raise you. And it is His love that keeps me going, keeps me from crying every morning when I reach for your father … and … he's not there."

"Of course I miss your father. I miss him so, so much. I love your father, but I remember his promise and I believe it. Even if you don't."

Celine collapsed against the sink, fresh tears washing down her face, while Travis sat on the edge of the table trying to rub the sting out of his cheek. The silence stood between them like a living person; some stern adult demanding that they kiss and make up. Neither of them was accustomed to conflict, especially with each other. They didn't know what came next, so they stood there, biting back awkward apologies and stealing sheepish looks at one another.

"Come to church with me, Travis," Celine finally proposed. "I really believe we need to go together. We need to let God order our steps and guide us back into one accord."

Travis chewed on his bottom lip as he stared at his mother. His eyes were wet with disgrace, shame, and anger; mostly anger. His gaze was challenging and defiant. He mumbled something under his breath as he brushed by Celine and grabbed his coat from the rack.

"Travis, wait," Celine pleaded.

He ignored her and eased his 15-speed mountain bike down the back porch steps. As he climbed atop of the narrow seat he looked back at her and said, "I don't think I believe in God anymore. Hell, he sure doesn't believe in us."

He pedaled off without looking back, leaving Celine in the doorway calling him desperately, her voice breaking as she screamed his name. She ran after him, feeling a mother's intuitive urgency to hold him and protect him. It came with a dizziness and a pain that shot from her heart to the center of her womb, stopping her in her tracks and convincing her that if she didn't stop him right then and there, she would never see him again.

"Travis! Travis!" she screamed until her throat went hoarse.

Travis kept going and unfortunately Celine's intuition would prove true.

Dear Mrs Ross

How ar you? I hope you ar well. I am shor this leter will be a sirprise to you and I am sory I took so long to rite it. You mus also forgiv my han ritin and spelen. I don't reed or rite to good and I am ritin from the infermeree and I don't hav my dicshenary. I hav to stay in here for a cupull days but I am fine. My blood presher is just up a bit.

I no it is teribull that I am 78 yeers old and I never lernt to reed and rite until 2 yeers ago. I was rased on the farm and I went to skool only to grade 3. Then I stoped to help my pa wif the feelds.

Did you no that in jail they make us go to skool if we never got a deeploma. It is a rool. Can you emagin that? A old man like me in GED skool. I reely just sit in the back of the clas and reed the scors in the sports page and they leeve me a lone.

One day the GED tooter came to my cell to chek on me. He is a nice kid and all ways speeks to me. He seen yor piccher on my wall. The one from the noospaper. I look at it evry day and I pray for you. The tooter sed that he new you to. He sed wen he was in the county jail you wood come visit wif yor church and you wood sing and bring cookys to them. He sed you wer very nice but you stoped comin and wen he askt one of yor frends if you wer ok yor frend sed she didnt no and that you was not wif the church any mor. I new then that I had to rite you. I askt the tooter to help me lern and even tho I am the worst studen ever he has tawt me a lot.

Mrs Ross I dont want to open up old scars but there ar sum things you need to no bout the nite yor son died. Yes I was drinkin and even if I wasnt leegly drunk I was to old to stil be drivin. My loyer said it was to dark for anyone to see yor son on that bike but I no thats not true. The axsident was my falt. But I did not run away from the seen like they sed. I did not leeve yor son. The docters sed that he died rite away but thats not tru. He was stil alive. Not suferin or in pane but he was cold and sed he couldnt feel nothin. I held him but I was to scared and to week to move him.

He tole me his name and even made a joke bout how he shood of had his helmit on. I tole him not to talk to save his energee. I was cryin caus I could tel he was in bad shape. I sed let me go get help but he sed no sir plees stay wif me. So I held him and rockt him. He was lookin pass me and I gess he could see his pa caus he kep sayin yes dad. I under stan dad. Tears was comin down his face but he was smilin. Then he askt me to tel you sum thing.

I wish I could of tole you in the cort room wen you smiled at me and sed you forgiv me and wood pray for me. But I was confused that you talkt to the juge for me and askt for lenencee. I didnt hav the curage to even say thank you. That is why it was importen that I lern to rite so I could send you this leter. I jus hope you can reed it and even tho it took me 2 yeers I hope its not to late.

On that nite Travis kep saying Jordan and it was weard caus I thawt he new me caus thats my name. Then he sed that you wood be worreed bout him and for me to tel you that he remembers what his pa sed. Travis lookt in my eyes he was reel excited and he laffed and sed my father told me that theres a manchin in heven, a manchin wif many rooms but you hav to cross a few Jordans to get to the promis land. Travis smiled agin and Mrs Ross he lookt jus like a angel. He sed that his pa went to get a room reddy and for me to tel you that he beleevs. He sed, plees tel my mom that Im gone to help dad wif ar room and the las thing he sed was God heals all hurts not sum of the hurts. All hurts. Then he closed his eyes.

I went to git help, but I could not stop cryin and my hans was shakin so I couldnt drive strate I stoped the car and walkt back to yor son. The amulance and police wer there so I jus wached them take him away.

I turnt my self in that nite and you no the ress of the story. I am so sory I didnt tell you this sooner and I pray it dont caus you more pane. I want you to no that yor sons words ekoed in my hed so much that I got saved my firs week in here and God has heald all of my hurts to. I thank you for forgivin me and showin me what ar Lord Jesus Christ died for. So that evry person could have a secon chanc. You are for ever in my prayers.

Yors in Christ, Aaron G. Jordan

Celine folded the letter and held it against her chest. She could feel her heart pounding against the tear-stained pages. She stood at the altar of her church silently thanking God for giving her the strength to share the letter without breaking down.

Over 18 months had passed since she'd last stepped foot in the Nondenominational Church of the Living God—the church that her parents helped establish—the only church she had ever known. She stared out at the crowded congregation; looking into the wet eyes of her dearest friends and couldn't help but feel a stab of guilt and shame.

"I want to thank all of you," she spoke softly into the microphone. "I know you were praying for me. Even though I tried not to, I felt your prayers and your love. I'm here to tell you our God is a wonderful God indeed."

Celine held her hand up to quiet the applause. "This letter!" she yelled out over the praises. "This letter," she repeated in a broken whisper. Her throat closed and tears burned her eyes. She looked away unsure if she could continue.

"Take your time, Sister Ross!" someone shouted.

"Yes, Jesus! It's all-right!" another added.

Celine gazed up at the vaulted ceiling. Sun rays broke through the stained-glass windows and crossed in mid-air, giving the church a celestial glow highlighting the miracle she was about to reveal.

"This letter saved my life," Celine nodded her head emphatically to underscore the truth of her statement. She didn't want them to think she was speaking figuratively or metaphorically.

The congregation applauded unaware and the choir started singing, *'He saved me.'* Celine shook her head in frustration. She grabbed the microphone so tight that her knuckles were white around it. As she leaned in, feedback sent a shrill ring throughout the chapel. Rapt attention followed and Celine spoke into the silence.

"Mr. Jordan died the day after he wrote me this letter." There was a collective gasp, but no one said anything. They all stared at her; a myriad of faces; some surprised, some startled, most confused. They weren't sure what their reaction should be and so they waited for her to continue.

Celine inhaled deeply and gathered her thoughts. She wanted to put her emotions into words. But how could she describe a miracle? She needed a song, a poem or a picture of the sun taken from the surface of the moon.

Her loss of faith was well known. After Travis died she tried for a few months to hold on, but ultimately couldn't understand a God who would take first her husband then her son.

They witnessed how she stopped attending choir practice and Bible study and eventually church altogether. She closed herself off from the rest of the world; her door locked to keep out her worried friends and her curtains drawn tight to keep the darkness in. Loneliness became her religion and suffering, her God.

What they didn't know was how deep her sorrow ran. That she cried all night, afraid of sleep because her dreams tortured her with images of her husband and son; still with her, smiling, happy. Then she'd wake up to the nightmare that was her life.

None of them realized she heard Travis' voice calling to her from other rooms in the house, always saying the same thing, "*I don't think I believe in God anymore. Hell, he sure doesn't believe in us.*"

How could she tell them that only a little more than 24 hours ago she had sat on the edge of her bed with a full bottle of sleeping pills emptied into her hand, ready to say goodnight forever; that she had been contemplating suicide for months and had finally grown the nerve to go through with it.

Could words explain the emotions that crowded around her conscience like marauders in a dark alley egging her on anxiously? How she reached for the glass filled with Jack Daniels to wash down the 25 white caplets that were melting in her sweaty palm. And how the phone rang at that very instant, startling her and causing her to knock over the glass and drop the pills at the same time.

Should she tell them how she cried, not only out of grief and despair, but for her ineptitude in ending it all? Celine shook her head. The details were between her and God.

Rather, she told them about the early morning call from the State Prison. The Warden himself, calling to inform her about the letter. How he mentioned "*unusual circumstances*" and asked if she could pick it up, in person.

She described how the Warden and four doctors were waiting for her when she arrived. They escorted her to an office, gave her the letter and then left so she could read it alone.

"When I finished reading the letter, I couldn't stop crying," Celine admitted to her friends while fresh tears sprang up instantly. "After all that time, I was so afraid Travis was lost to me. I blamed myself and I … I blamed God. I believed Travis had died in sin and ... and I couldn't picture a Heaven without my son.

"When I read this letter, I knew God was holding out His arms to me and saying, 'Come on, it's alright. Come on home.' I fell to my knees right there and praised God. I glorified the mighty name of Jesus. Amen."

Celine explained that after she pulled herself together, the Warden and doctors returned and had a few questions for her, if she didn't mind. She told them how she sat and waited patiently, peacefully, and none of them asked her anything. They simply stared at her as if she was supposed to weigh some evidence and then pass judgment.

"They were observing me like I was some type of experiment, but I didn't care," Celine looked up and stepped away from the mic. Her voice filled the church.

"I just sat there and when I looked at the letter, I got to thinking about God's grace and His mercy. I told them the things Mr. Jordan mentioned in the letter, he could have only heard from my son."

Celine described the dispute that erupted amongst the doctors following her statement. How they screamed out, 'impossible!' and turned red in the face. How one doctor flipped his chair and stormed out in a rage and another eyed her down threateningly as if demanding she change her mind.

"Why are you so upset? I asked them. The doctor leering at me yelled out, 'Because Aaron Jordan is dead and if he wrote that letter, he did so from a vegetative state!" Celine took a deep breath before she went on.

"The Warden escorted them out and begged my forgiveness for their unprofessional behavior. He poured me a cup of coffee. He sat down across from me and said, 'They always fear what they don't understand.'

"The Warden then explained that Mr. Jordan had been in the prison hospital for the past two weeks after suffering a massive stroke in his cell. He sustained a lot of brain damage and was paralyzed from the neck down. He had also been in a coma since the stroke.

"When they found Mr. Jordan dead with the letter and pencil still clutched in his fingers, they assumed someone was playing a cruel joke. However, Mr. Jordan also had dirt on his feet, as if he were pacing the floor as he wrote.

"The tutor Mr. Jordan had been working with confirmed the letter was in Mr. Jordan's handwriting. He also stated that even though they had been working together for almost two years, Mr. Jordan was blind in one eye and his failing memory made his progress very slow. He said that Mr. Jordan had only begun to learn two syllable words and that he had yet to write a complete sentence, let alone an entire letter."

Most of the congregation was in tears again. 'Amens', 'Have mercy' and 'Praise Gods' were cried out in a warm undertone. Celine closed her eyes for a second to remember Mr. Jordan. She recalled his sad eyes almost hidden under a heavy, deeply lined brow, the gray tufts of hair that sprouted behind his ears, and the black mole on his left jaw. She had last seen him at his sentencing. He had stood up as far as his curved back would allow. His County jumpsuit swallowed him and he had handcuffs on his tiny wrists.

When the Judge asked if he had anything to say, he turned and looked at her. His dry lips opened, but he didn't say anything; he couldn't. A single tear squeezed out of one eye and crawled down his wrinkled face. He turned back to the Judge and shook his head slowly from side to side.

Celine opened her eyes and gazed at the letter in her hand. For a second the white paper morphed into the white pills she held the morning before. She shook the image away as she placed the letter back into its envelope. An envelope that read: To C. Ross, A. Jordan. "That's right," she mused, "*To cross a Jordan.*"

Celine held the letter up for the entire church and smiled brightly. "This letter, this beautiful letter written by God through the hand of a dying man saved my life." She kissed the envelope.

"Oh what a mighty God we serve, for I know that there's a mansion in Heaven and my husband and my son are in a room together watching over me and waiting for me to join them. And I believe Mr. Jordan, sweet, sweet Mr. Jordan," Celine lowered her voice as if sharing a secret. "I bet he has a mighty nice room of his own."

Don't Blame Me

In less than eight hours I will die. I'm not on death row nor have I offended anyone to the point where they might feel compelled to take my life as retribution. Maybe I have. I don't know. Lately, I don't know much except, I'm tired. I'm tired of it all.

I'm tired of living in a small cramped, windowless room with three other men, two of whom don't speak English and one who acts as if he is allergic to showering. I'm tired of dreams about swimming pools, amusement parks, homemade sweet rolls and making love. I'm tired of dreaming about fresh air and freedom then waking up to this never-ending nightmare of controlled movements, incessant counts, and meals to vile for human consumption.

I'm tired of being in jail. Tired of being shook-down, strip searched, eyeballed and inspected by tobacco-chewing officers who seem a little to eager in their command for me to bend over and spread them. I'm tired of adapting and adhering to so many different rules: Make your bed by 7 a.m., keep your shirt tucked in, thou shalt not steal, murder, fight, gamble or disobey a direct order. These are the institution rules— universal throughout most prisons and designed to ensure the security and good order of the institution. But there is also a set of unwritten rules; dictated and enforced by the convict majority. These are the complex rules that fluctuate constantly and when ignored, could cost your life: Thou shalt not snitch under any circumstances; thou shalt not lust over another man's wife, daughter, mother or sister, thou shalt not cut line, gamble without money to pay, and never ever violate another man's space. I'm surrounded by burned-out, institutionalized men pretending to be Indian chiefs and to tell you the truth I'm tired of them too.

I'm sick and tired of the TV rooms filled to capacity for soap operas, WWE Wrestling, and idiotic shows like Jerry Springer or Elimi-date. And don't get me started on the rap videos. My God! I've never witnessed such mind-numbing foolishness in all my life. Grown men sit in hard, plastic chairs in a tight closed-in room for hours on end watching the same videos … over and over. They stare at the TV, wide-eyed, slack-jawed, unmoving, as if in a trance. Every now and then they might nod their heads or sing along. The next day, they'll stroll in and set their chairs in the exact same spots for another six hours of hip-hop, bling-blinging. Like brainwashed children gone batty; same Bat-time, same Bat-channel, same damn videos.

I want to tell them to go read a book, but to my surprise, when they're not in front of the TV that's exactly what most of them are doing. Sadly, they've been put on to a bunch of poorly written, unedited, street-tales; appalling publications with the literary merit of cartoon cookbooks. At first, I was impressed to see so many young black men reading. It was a beautiful sight. Nights were peaceful and quiet as inmates climbed into bunks and opened up the book that rested beneath their respective pillows. I caught glimpses of their usually hard faces, softened by the tiny book-lamps clamped to the edges of their beds; eyes straining in concentration and a conspiratorial smile etched across their faces. Brothers were reading, expanding their horizons and stepping into worlds unknown.

Then I noticed the covers: Half-naked women, big guns, flashy cars, piles of money stained with blood. The titles: Hustler's Revenge, Die Shorty Die, Money-Cash-Hoes. And the authors: G. Gangsta, Kocaine, Tim Thug, Dollar Bill and Deep-throat Denise.

What the hell is going on? I thought. Where are the books by Baldwin, Ellison, Wright, Wideman, Walker, Morrison, Mosley, McMillan, Haley, Gates, Himes, or even the great white writers: Hemmingway, Irving, Fitzgerald, Faulkner, Ludlum, Steel, Collins, King, Kellerman, Grisham, Clancy, Patterson, Cook, Sanford, or Sheldon? I gave a book by Mary Higgins Clark to one inmate who asked me if she was related to Mary Poppins.

"I ain't trying to read dat corny stuff, college boy, yanol-I-mean?" Big Moe said when I offered him W.E.B. Dubois' *The Souls of Back Folk*.

"I'm a *skreet* nigga." Yes, he said 'skreet' not street. "And I read skreet books, yanol-I-mean, 'cause I can relate to what the author is sayin'. It's like he's havin' a convo-sation with me, yanol-I-mean? What can Webby Dubose tell me when he been dead a long time ago?"

What should I expect? These same men brag about 15 and 20-year-sentences, like the amount of time they received is a testimony to how big of a killer or dealer they were on the streets. Pardon me, the 'skreets.' I've seen first time offenders with 14-year bids. Their transcripts read like Greek tragedies, yet they won't set foot into the law library. They don't even try to fight the injustice of it all. They don't contest the fairness of their sentences or look for loopholes that could reduce their time. No. They're too busy watching rap videos or reading ungrammatical garbage glorifying the crazy lifestyles that led to them being locked up.

Who am I to talk? I haven't tried too hard either, but that's because I'm tired. I've spent the last 6 years, 10 days, and 21 hours of my life in a Federal Correctional Institution for a crime I didn't commit. Yes, I know, you've heard it all before, but I swear, I'm innocent. I lived the life most people only dream about and this wasn't supposed to be my fate. This isn't my world. I mean, honestly, I did nothing wrong.

Yet, I suffer. I'm living a wasted life and I'm tired. My heart has been tortured and broken beyond relief and I'm tired of ... I'm tired of living.

In less than eight hours I will die. It's crazy. I remember reading a poem in college ending with the lines: "I no longer feel, I can't hear, I can't see. I can only destroy, but don't blame me." I finally understand what those words mean and I realize they apply to me. Yes, I have that notorious, 'Don't Blame Me' attitude, but it's justified. Believe me. If you were in my shoes you'd feel the same and probably would have given up long ago. I sense you're a bit skeptical. Fine, I have a little time to spare. I'll tell you my story and you can decide for yourself. Be warned, it's an ugly tale. Take a deep breath and brace yourself. I'll take you back to the beginning.

***

I was taught early on the world is comprised of 'haves' and 'have nots.' I'm a lifetime member of the 'haves.' I grew up surrounded by wealth and prosperity. My father, Allen Hudson, Esquire, is a corporate attorney and managing partner of one of the most prestigious law firms on the East Coast. He earns seven figures and his investments are worth millions.

My mother, Kimberly Price-Hudson, was born into money. My grandfather, Eugene Price, founded one of the first black-owned Building Societies and amassed a fortune banking and mortgaging for black businesses and homeowners. My mother is a professional socialite who also runs a high-end catering company to indulge her passion for cooking and throwing extravagant parties.

I am the only child and the only grandchild at that. To say I was spoiled is like saying Michael Jordan was an 'okay' basketball player. I was pampered, coddled, and overindulged beyond reason. I attended expensive private schools where the only other blacks were the children of politicians, doctors, entertainers, and athletes. My birthdays were like the happy endings of little-boy fairytales: a pony when I was six, a carousel when I was ten, my own playground when I turned twelve, an arcade at fourteen and a brand new BMW 320 when I was sixteen.

I'm also a second-generation member of the Jack and Jill Society. That wonderful blue-blood organization that introduced me to the self-proclaimed elite and the peculiar ways of the black bourgeoisie.

I summered at Martha's Vineyard, in the Hamptons and Europe. I went white-water rafting and hiking on mountain retreats. I frequented exclusive camps that taught swimming, archery and tennis. My childhood was cotton candy-sweet and more exciting than a three-ring circus. Oh, that reminds me. I had a baby tiger when I was nine years old.

My parents prided themselves on the giving of extraordinary experiences as gifts. When I graduated from high school my they took me on a 12-country tour of Africa. Not to sound ungrateful, but I hated it.

I'm talking four whole weeks of giant bugs and unbearable heat. Not to mention the pestering natives hawking everything from ancient masks (made last week) to the long, lost, toenail clippings of King Tut. Mother couldn't take it and went home early but my dad loved every minute. He purchased beaded jewelry, hand-carved statues, paintings and all kinds of trash from every dirty, little kid who approached us. When we visited the great pyramids, he got all choked up and actually cried.

But that's how my dad is. He doesn't take his success for granted. He grew up poor; raised by a single mother who worked two and three jobs at a time and eventually worked herself into an early, diabetic grave. My father promised her he would finish college and he kept that promise through partial scholarships and by working any and everywhere he could to help pay the remainder of his tuition.

My dad was a free thinker with intelligence to spare. He was an organizer for the Student Non-Violent Coordination Committee and marched a few times with Dr. Martin Luther King Jr. He received his Juris Doctor six months early and clerked for Supreme Court Justice Thurgood Marshall.

"Do everything as if it's the last thing you'll ever do." That was one of my father's favorite quotes and he lived by that adage. Following his clerkship he was vigorously recruited. He wasted no time luring banks and black cosmetic companies to his new firm. He structured the largest, black radio and media conglomerate in the country and rose swiftly amongst the ranks to become his firm's youngest partner. The businesses he brought in put him firmly in charge. Within six years he was managing partner.

"Knowledge is power, Dominic." My dad tapped his index finger against his temple while speaking to me. He was a firm believer in education being the primary tool to overcoming adversity. He constantly urged me to strive for excellence, to be better than everyone, yet never act as if I was better than anyone. Unfortunately, his advice contradicted the lifestyle I enjoyed and the schools I attended. These environments bred in me a capricious contempt for my own kind.

I listened to my father preach on and on about self-love and black pride, but I never felt nor understood what he was saying. Pride in what? Ancient civilizations wiped out long ago with no bearing on today's society? My dad talked about building up our people. *My* people were already built up. *My* people were the elite.

I couldn't relate to those ghetto-blacks I read about in newspapers. We were worlds apart. What could I have in common with third generation welfare recipients or petty drug-dealers who eventually got high on their own supply and became the fiends they once mocked and peddled to? *Those* blacks were thieves, gang-bangers, car-jackers and animals.

I loathed the fact I was part of a race with teenage mothers who give birth to five and six kids to four or five different men. I swear to God it made my blood boil. I saw a 15-year old black girl on the Maury Povich Show. Paternity tests were given to four different men and when the results were read not one of them was her 'baby's daddy.' What a trifling whore! I thought.

They're so pitiful. And it's a shame because I couldn't pinpoint any one thing that sickened me. It was everything. I despised the whole urban, slang-talking, corner-loitering, dice rolling, 40-ounce malt liquor drinking-mentality. And how they thought it was cool to call each other niggers or *niggas*. I couldn't understand them. I couldn't justify the insanity; how they played real-life cops and robbers with real guns; killing each other for sport. I hated them. They were dirty, dangerous and were not my people.

No! My people were the teenage millionaires I went to school with. The guys with names followed by roman numerals who were being primed to run billion dollar companies. My people owned helicopters and yachts. They were legacy members of the Young Republicans and Business Club. They were teenagers with diversified portfolios and an in depth understanding of foreign currencies. My people were the elite and although most of them were white, I wanted to be just like them.

My parents didn't really know me. They viewed me through the rose-colored glasses most parents favor and had no ideal I had become an arrogant, self-righteous snob. That was, until it came time for me to choose a college and all hell broke loose.

"What do you mean you've changed your mind?" My father stood over me; his tone sharp and incredulous. I had been accepted by Harvard, Yale, and Princeton, three of my top five choices, but my father, in his sentimental mind, decided I should follow in his footsteps and attend his alma mater; The magnificent— Ivy-League alternative— Howard University.

"I don't want to go, Dad. Howard is a party school and it's great for turning out entertainers, but be real, Dad, I have the opportunity to go to Harvard or Princeton." My smile was patronizing and my father's eyes became tight slits. He rose from the dining room table and tossed his silk table linen onto his plate, ruining the delicious grilled-salmon my mother prepared.

"Do you actually believe you're too good for Howard?" he asked impatiently. Yes, I did. But I knew better than to answer. "Let me tell you something, Dominic Eugene Hudson." Uh oh, the last time he used my full name was when I stole his Porsche and went joyriding through Pittsburg. "If it weren't for Howard, you wouldn't be here."

My father is a big man and a well-trained litigator. He can manipulate his voice to relax, encourage, or terrify you. I was definitely feeling a little fear. I looked at my mother; my eyes and expression set on full 'Mama's Boy' mode, but Mom, a graduate of Spellman College, was clearly with Dad on this one.

"Nicky, honey, Howard is the crème de la crème of Historical Black Colleges. The faculty is first-rate and I'm sure you'll meet a nice girl you can marry and—"

"Kimberly!" My father cut her off with a smile. "Let's focus on his education first." She returned his smile and waved him on. "Son, Howard University is a wonderful school and—"

"But it isn't the best, Dad." I pouted like I was eight instead of eighteen. "You always say you want the best for me. Well, let me go to the best."

"It is the best!" he shouted with indignation. "But that's not the point. I want you there because you're the best. Are you listening, son?" He placed his hands on my shoulders. "You are my best. You are my greatest accomplishment and I owe them that. I owe them my blood, sweat, and tears; not just the donations I send.

"Don't you see, Dominic? You are my blood, sweat and tears. You are a part of the greatness Howard instilled in me. You go there and you represent me. Go show them what they helped me accomplish." He grinned widely and his voice cracked. "Go as the best and learn from the best. Begin our legacy and I promise you, once you feel that Howard-spirit, you too, will dream of the day your children can attend as well."

I had too much respect for my father to tell him how absurd he sounded. He was treating me like a new car he wanted to show off to the people who cosigned the loan. It wasn't fair and deep down I felt ill. But truth be known; my father, even in his old-school ways was sort of my hero. I couldn't remember him ever telling me no and I knew for certain he had never imposed on me for anything. I could tell by the way he couldn't look at me without shaking his head in disappointment that the whole Howard thing meant a lot to him. I craved his approval and wanted to make him proud. So I gave in.

I figured I would go to Howard for four years then transfer to Harvard Law School for my graduate studies. Howard. Harvard. I'd hang my degrees under a banner that read 'The best of both worlds.' When I finally agreed to go, my father hugged me like I had just awakened from a coma. My mother gave me her patented well done-smile, winked at me and rewarded my selfless decision with a two-week trip to the Bahamas.

In my lifetime I had traveled extensively and seen many different things, but none of it had prepared me for Howard. When I stepped foot on campus, I was completely blown away. It was like nothing I'd ever seen before. It was strange, exotic and beckoned to me like a seedy carnival in town for one night. I stood in front of the Blackburn Center, trying unsuccessfully to take everything in.

There was a plethora of people from different cultures. I saw Africans in dashikis, Middle Eastern Muslims in full garb, and Nation of Islam members in crisp suits and bow ties. I saw Asians, and dread-locked Jamaicans, Ethiopians and Egyptians. There were vendors everywhere hawking their native goods as well as school paraphernalia. My nose, finely tuned to the scent of delicious foods, courtesy of my mother, was accosted by the intoxicating aromas of curry, barbeque, and Caribbean cuisine. Rap music blared, Greeks stepped and everywhere I looked, I saw beautiful women.

Forgive the understatement. I am talking exotic, dazzling women; so attractive you couldn't help but stare. Never in my life had I seen so many gorgeous women in one place. It made my eyes water. I'd lock in on one sister whose bright smile could melt rocks and another sister would saunter pass with a body so sexy, it moved in slow motion. I was surrounded by all flavors of beauty. I was a fat-kid in a candy store with a pocket full of rolled-up quarters, if you know what I mean.

By and by, I'm not a slouch in the looks department myself. Actually, I'm extremely good looking. I'm six feet, four inches tall and built like a track star— lithe but toned. I have a dark brown, polished-mahogany complexion, a small nose, sleepy eyes and fleshy—not too thick— lips. I don't have good hair, but I keep it cut real low and with a little bit of hair grease, my waves be in there, rolling like a river. I'm talking front cover of the Duke box.

I'm pretty much the epitome of tall, dark and handsome and I've never had a problem getting girlfriends. Not only because I'm too sexy for my skin, but because I was schooled by my mother in the fine art of being a gentleman. I learned to hold open doors and pull out chairs by the time I was nine years old. I sat in at my mother's tea parties soaking in the dreams and desires of women whose ages ranged from eighteen to eighty. I listened to the inflection of their voices and I learned to recognize the difference between want and need, passion and performance and most of all I learned to say exactly what they wanted to hear.

Don't misunderstand me. I'm not a player, a mack or whatever it's called these days. Not at all. My success with women stems more from the fact I have money and I'm not ugly. Two plus two equals four... play every time. I had no doubt I would have my way on Howard's playground of plenty.

Now, you can call it the karma of ill intentions or the way of the world, but the first young lady I chose to practice my art of seduction on; became my biggest challenge, my guide to the realm of black pride, my best friend, my first love and the reason I'm locked up today.

Her name was Jasmine Carr and she was even prettier than the flower that shared her name. She was petite, but had curves in all the right places. She had a soft, golden, peaches-and-cream complexion and short stylish hair that framed her doe brown-eyes and deep dimples. She resembled a doll baby someone had wished to life and gotten way more than what they'd bargained for.

Our connection was typical boy-meets-girl. We were in a hallway and saw each other from a short distance. We smiled at the same time. I approached her and asked if I could walk her to class. She said sure, and as it turned out we had the same Afro-American History course. We sat one row apart and the fireworks began.

It was day one and after passing out our syllabus, the professor opened a discussion on the contributions of black Americans to the Republican Party. He asked if any of us were Republicans and I stood up proudly with a few others. We were met with a chorus of friendly boos and Jasmine looked at me like I had leprosy; however, our esteemed professor gave us the opportunity to defend our unpopular choice. When my turn came to expound on my allegiance to what I consider the only real political party alive, I spoke calm and composed; eloquent if you may. I was trying to impress Miss Jasmine and enlighten my peers.

I went back to the great President Lincoln and the origins of the Republican Party compared to the Dixie-Democrats. I followed with today's Democrat who considers the black vote a guarantee and therefore no longer feels obligated to do anything for black people. "There's no accountability," I reasoned. "So why should your vote be promised to a party who no longer cares about your needs."

"They care more than the Republicans who want to do away with anything that helps us," Jasmine quipped smartly and glared as if I had attacked her personally.

"It's not that we want to do away with anything. We simply don't believe in making people dependent on handouts. I'm sure you all know the philosophy. We want to teach you how to fish instead of just giving you fish." My tone was kind and gracious, but my words somehow fanned the fiery flames in Jasmine's eyes.

She stood and delivered a spirited speech dissecting Roosevelt's New Deal and stressed how blacks were given well-deserved benefits only after fighting and dying for this country. She accused Republicans of hoarding money and wondered out loud how any sane black man could associate himself with a party filled with hypocritical conservatives and blatant racists who oppose great programs like: Midnight Basketball, the free-lunch-program and affirmative action. "I'm willing to bet you're probably against affirmative action, too. Aren't you?" she asked snidely.

The room suddenly shrunk and my classmates held their breaths, anticipating my answer. I remembered my dad explaining to me that even in disagreement, honesty breeds respect. "As a matter of fact, yes, I am against affirmative action." There was a collective moan of displeasure, but I continued unfazed. "We don't need it. We wouldn't have survived this long if we weren't strong enough and able enough to make it on our own."

The class gawked as if a tree had just grown out of my face, but I recognized a few looks of interest. Some of them were with me. I decided to swing an uppercut and try to get the rest of them on board. "Let me ask you something. Seriously," I added some bass to my voice to pique their interest. "If a black man and a white man were playing one-on-one basketball, how insulted would you be if the white man offered to spot the black man five points? I mean, come on. Do you need five points? Are you that weak? Or can you win with your own abilities, your own aptitude, your own—"

"You are incredible!" Jasmine cut me off. "You talk about winning the game. It's not a game and if it is; then it's already handicapped. It's their ball. We're playing in their stadium and for everyone who pays to watch the 'game,' the money goes to them."

"Then we should get our own ball."

"How?!" she shouted and I noticed her hands clench into little fists. "There's still racism and sexism and we remain disadvantaged. Whites have more schools, innumerable books, and superior education. Most have both parents and less poverty. Whites don't duck drug-dealers on their way to school or take tests on empty stomachs." She shook her head and sucked in a needed breath. "Affirmative action and similar programs provide a balance.

"You say balance, I say crutch," I winked at her. "We need to stop making excuses for the lazy, bad apples of our race who want to use slavery as an explanation for ineptitude. If you're such a strong black man … or woman, then don't take the points. Play hard, do your best and if you really believe they have an advantage, go get your own ball. They don't cost that much. Trust me, I own a few balls." That earned me some unexpected laughter and the bell rang before Jasmine or anyone else could respond. I reached for my bag and when I looked up she was gone.

After that first day, Jasmine wouldn't say 'boo' to me. A month passed before I finally caught her alone outside the Communications Building. I called her sexy, flashed my winning smile and asked her how she was doing. I had completely forgotten our heated debate and simply wanted to ask her out. Yeah right! I had a better chance of hitchhiking to the moon. She rolled her pretty brown eyes at me and snapped to bite my head off. She called me every name in the book and said she wouldn't go out with me for all the gold in Fort Knox.

I was perplexed. I had done nothing to this feisty little woman and yet, here she was twisting her neck, snapping her fingers and accusing me of being a sell-out. She called me an Oreo. An Oreo cookie. I had the slightest idea what she meant by that. I assumed she was calling me flaky or crumbly. She quickly clarified what she meant. "It means you're black on the outside. But you're white in the middle." She stepped off with a serious, hip-switching stride. An Oreo? Yeah, I liked that one.

I spent my entire first semester pursuing Miss Jasmine. I sent flowers, candy, cards, balloons, concert tickets, even a pair of diamond earrings. All were returned. Being shot down was beyond frustrating. I knew her schedule better than my own and I was beginning to feel like a stalker. She rejected each of my advances and when I'd speak to her she'd outright ignore me. I was ready to throw in the towel. Then, I caught her. Out the corner of my eye, I caught her watching me; her pretty face minus the vicious sneer she usually reserved for me was marked instead with a deep curiosity. Uh huh, I knew it. I was wearing her down. I would bide my time and stay patient.

I spent my free afternoons working out. I jumped rope and lifted weights occasionally, but mostly I swam in the school pool. One of the swim team coaches walked in on me and asked to time me. I had been swimming since I was a kid and we raced a lot at camp, but I never knew I was 'lightening fast' or that I had 'excellent form;' not until Coach Coles told me so and then begged me to join the swim team. I respectfully declined the scholarship he offered me, but permitted him to train me one-on-one. After a month of learning breathing techniques and basic preparation skills, I joined the team and Coach Coles started me as a sprinter in the 100-meter freestyle.

The swimming pool in the basement of Burr Gymnasium became my second home at Howard. I trained hard and learned fast. I was hyped as a freshman phenom and after turning in some impressive times I had my break-out meet in front of a tremendous home crowd that included Miss Jasmine.

It was a late season meet against our rival, George Washington. Our records were tied and the match-up had championship implications. Not to mention, bragging rights were at stake. George Washington boasted a strong diving squad and had Earl Haskins. Earl was a senior sprinter; undefeated in the hundred that year and had never lost to a Howard sprinter.

As fate would have it, the meet would be decided by the winner of the 100-meter freestyle. I was the fastest man on our team and tagged as the 'last hope of Howard.' The atmosphere was electric and the energy from the crowd had me pumped. The whole school was behind me and it felt great.

I was assigned to Lane 5. Earl held the coveted Lane 4. The crowd became incredibly quiet. I pulled my goggles on and stared into crystal-clear water. I took a deep breath. The chlorine in the air stung my nasal passages, but I was focused. The buzzer sounded. I dove in and took off like an eel. I never swam so fast in my life. I kicked with power and my arm strokes were fluidly smooth, but with every glance I took, Earl was right there in front of me. He moved as if he wasn't exerting any energy.

In the final turn my hamstrings cramped up. The pain was unbearable. I couldn't get a full stretch. In my mind there was no way I could win. I dug deeper. I forced my legs through the pain. I kept pushing. Left arm. Right arm. Quick breath. Kick. Kick. Kick. Earl was in my peripheral. We were stroke for stroke. When we touched the wall, the splash was too high for anyone to see who won. There was a quick cheer followed by a nail-biting silence. I could hear water lapping against my burning chest. All eyes turned toward the electronic clock. The red digital dots flashed: Lane 5— 49.6 seconds. Lane 4— 50.2 seconds.

The roar of the crowd was deafening. It was pure pandemonium. The Howard Bisons had beaten the George Washington Colonials and a freshman walk-on had set a new school record. There were smiles everywhere. My teammates and I were hugged and congratulated until Coach Coles ordered us to hit the showers and go celebrate.

After changing clothes, I walked out of the locker room and Jasmine was standing there waiting for me. "I didn't get any flowers this week," she said softly.

"I thought I'd save you the trouble of sending them back." I was feeling like the 'man' so I decided to let her sweat me for a change. She didn't. She simply said, okay and walked away.

"Wait a second, Jasmine."

"Yes?" she titled her head and looked so lovely.

"Were you waiting for me?" I asked.

"I wanted to congratulate you on your race. You did … alright."

"Thank you." I couldn't think of anything to say, so I stared at her, wondering if she had any idea how beautiful she was.

She stepped toward me and sighed, "I don't want your money, Dominic," she threw out of nowhere. "I don't want you buying me gifts or trying to take me to fancy restaurants and stuff."

"Okay," I whispered, silently praying she wanted something. Anything. A bus pass, a Nintendo game, a … kiss. "What do you want?" I ventured.

She pursed her lips and tapped her foot as she thought about it. "Well, I guess I wouldn't mind getting to know you better. I'm curious as to what makes your tall, handsome self tick counter-clockwise."

I maintained my cool, until she reached for my hand and I gave her the cheesiest smile I own. It was my first grade, school-picture smile. She smiled back and we walked out of there hand in hand. No doubt about it, I was a winner.

Our romance was more hurricane than whirlwind. Jasmine and I were the oddest of couples; oil and vinegar, fire and ice. We fought and made up at least twice a week. We argued about everything. Politics, religion, music, race-relations etc … She called me 'bourgeois,' I called her 'ghetto.' We'd curse each other out and vow never to speak again. By evening we'd find ways to bump into each other, both of us too stubborn to apologize. We'd link arms and go on as if nothing had happened.

I cooked for her often. I used the culinary skills I picked up from my mother and made her all the succulent dishes she saw in the last pages of Ebony Magazine. Now and then, just to antagonize me, she'd eat with her hands and lick her fingers, gushing over how delicious everything was. I feigned disgust and embarrassment. In truth, her little hood antics were sexy to me.

She burnt incense and wore men's boxer shorts to bed. She had a way of looking at me that was so sensual it sent chills through me. I was addicted to everything about her; the way she poked her finger into my chest to make a point, how she stuck her tongue out at me when she caught me staring at her, the hot-oil massages she gave me after my meets and especially our lovemaking. My God, the sex was out of this world.

Jasmine lit scented candles and played classic R&B or soft jazz. We danced together slowly, stealing quick kisses and staring into each others eyes until our longing overwhelmed us. She'd undress me slowly, tracing her fingers over every inch of my body. I'd pull her shirt over her head and plant soft kisses on her neck, shoulders, the well of her breasts and her stomach. I'd tease her belly button with my tongue while rolling her panties past her hips.

She'd lay me back and kiss me deep and passionately, her tongue darting in and out of my mouth, tasting, teasing, exploring. She'd climb on me and straddle me. She'd rock so slowly I'd see flashes of light every time I closed my eyes. I'd cup her soft breasts and rise up to taste them. I'd grip her hips to control the rhythm and she'd roll her hips wildly and ride me faster. When she felt my legs stiffen and saw my stomach muscles contract she'd stop moving. She'd hold me inside of her, place her hands on my chest and while gazing deep into my eyes, she'd recite poetry.

Often her own, sometimes a verse from Maya Angelou, Gwendolyn Brooks, Audrey Lorde, or Sonia Sanchez. Her sultry voice breathed words of apology along with a plea for understanding. She'd end her poem and kiss me deeply. "I know I don't say it enough, Dominic, but you are the love of my life." Then she'd bite her bottom lip mischievously and without raising up the rocking ensued. Side to side, slow at first and then she'd throw her head back, dig her nails into my chest, and buck wildly until I couldn't bear it. I'd roll her over, pin her hands above her head, and stroke us into an explosive orgasm.

We'd lay together, sweaty and exhausted. Jasmine settled her head on my chest and she'd talk until I fell asleep. She talked about her dreams of producing TV shows with strong black families and positive messages. She talked about her growing responsibilities as vice president of the student union. And some nights, she talked about her forfeited childhood: Her older brother gunned down in the streets before he turned sixteen; her crack addicted mother turning tricks in a one bedroom apartment; and how at seven-years-old she pretended to sleep while Mommy moaned and groaned with different men, then cursed and cried about what was owed to her.

"I close my eyes and I can still hear it all," Jasmine spoke into my ear as I held her tight one night. "I used to think the men would ask if they could do me next. And what hurts the most is I'm not sure if my mom would have said no."

Her tears left her cheeks and raced down my neck. I rocked her like a baby and reminded her how special she was and how much I loved her, until she cried herself to sleep. I would sit up for hours, watching her sleep and wishing I could wipe away the pain of her past. She had been through so much and even though the things she had to endure were alien to me. I was grateful she was still whole. She had overcome the odds and survived. She loved and could be loved. And that's what I was going to do; love her until her past faded into the smoke of an unrecalled dream. Jasmine deserved to be happy and I would spend my life making that happen.

By spring of our senior year, I was seriously considering marriage. There was no doubt Jasmine and I had something unique. Our views were different, but our love was undeniable. We also learned to compromise. Howard University and Jasmine Carr helped me become more open-minded. Together, they introduced me to music and literature that instilled pride in my blackness. I wasn't a complete convert, but I was beginning to see the potential in my people, which is how I became a mentor at the youth center Jasmine volunteered at in Southeast DC.

I remember driving to the center and how it felt to look true poverty in its face. I stared out the window, captivated by the destitution: The boarded up abandoned houses; The houses with sagging roofs, no front steps and screen doors hanging askew that should have been boarded up. The dirty children; barely able to walk, playing in the street, wearing nothing except dingy diapers. The crack heads on every corner, their wide eyes alert, stopping traffic, scouting customers for the drug dealers who leaned against corner stores, beepers clipped to the front pockets of their baggy jeans. They had their fitted baseball caps cocked at arrogant angles, laughing, slapping hands and shooting the breeze like it was just another day at the office. Which, I imagine, it probably was.

We drove past a playground with no swing sets and a half a see-saw, littered with broken bottles and used syringes. We slowed and looked on a pick-up basketball game being played by shirtless brothers who didn't mind the rusted, bent, net-less rims, as long as they could live out their NBA fantasies for an hour or two. We passed a front yard cook-out where the smell of barbecue pushed its way into the car through the AC vents and made my stomach growl. An elderly lady, sitting in a rocking chair on her flower-packed porch waved as we drove by slowly, trying not to hit any of the kids who laughed gleefully as they chased each other with water guns.

A bewildered expression hung on my face as we pulled up to the center. "Welcome to the Ghetto," Jasmine grinned.

Sonny Daniels and Tysean Reeves were the teens I was assigned to mentor. Both were on probation for stealing cars and although they weren't related they were closer than brothers. They came from broken homes and were much more mature than the average 16-year-old. I admit they had me a little intimidated at first. They never smiled and they were too quiet. They seemed sneaky and their distrust for college-educated strangers was evident in the coded grunts they used when I was in ear-shot. Not to mention the condescending, 'you can't be serious' scowls they wore when I tried in vain to speak their language.

Sonny and Ty were also very intelligent and quickly recognized I had something to offer. Once we got past them sizing me up and teasing me about how I talked (they said I used too many dictionary words), we established a respectful rapport. They excelled in the finance class I taught at the center and caught on quickly to the whimsical ways of the stock market, which they called the 'Wall Street dice game.' I taught them how to fill out job applications and carry themselves at job interviews. We visited museums and art exhibits. I took them to their first baseball game and to the theatre to see their first play. I explained to them the benefits of proper decision making and building relationships. I taught them how to order at restaurants, politely instead of saying, "Yo, Joe, get me mine!" I enlightened them to the art of sartorial splendor or what they called, 'dressing fly.'

In turn, they introduced me to new slang terms I slipped into my conversations with Jasmine to elicit that big, dimpled smile I loved so much. I started calling her 'Boo' and letting her know that she was a 'dime' who had me so 'sprung' I would, uh uhm, Lord forbid, 'drink her bath water.' Only hesitating because Jasmine might hold me to it.

Sonny and Ty tutored me on loyalty and friendship. I took Sonny out to eat while Tysean baby-sat his younger sisters. We went to a steakhouse and 'got our grub on.' Sonny ate only half his food. When I asked him if he was sick— because he and Ty could eat like horses—

he said no, he just wanted to save some for later. Of course, I was totally embarrassed when the waiter offered us a doggie bag and Sonny accepted. "Do we look like doggies?" I mumbled under my breath. I paid the check and left double the tip required.

We rode home in silence. I glanced over at Sonny holding his plastic bag filled with potato wedges and half of a two inch Porterhouse and gritted my teeth. We pulled up in front of Tysean's house and Sonny looked over at me with disappointed eyes. "I'm sorry I embarrassed you Big D." He didn't sound sorry at all. "But yo, you have to think about how much food you be wastin'. See, I ain't no baller like you and I can't eat all good when I know my main man might be starving. I could spend twenty dollars and feed me, Ty, my little brother and his two little sisters instead of spending it on one steak. So yeah, I asked for a doggie bag and I fought the urge to tell the waiter to throw in the baked potato and onion rings you barely touched. And I know you all in your feelings right now, but hey, I'm gonna do what I have to do to take care of family."

I looked at him and sighed. If he wanted to buy Ty and his siblings something to eat he could have just said so. I reached for my wallet and started to take out a few twenties. Sonny opened the door and stepped out.

"I don't want your money," he said through the window. "I just want you to understand." He walked away. Tysean was sitting on his stoop fussing at his youngest sister about keeping her shoes on. Sonny handed him the bag and after Ty looked in he gave Sonny a pound and sent his sisters inside to wash their hands and get ready to eat. I pulled off, shaking my head; vexed at myself because I still didn't quite understand.

Sonny and Tysean were my proof there was a wealth of potential trapped behind poor school systems and drug infested neighborhoods. They showed me how one's environment plays a big part in one's future. I learned that given the chance and the opportunity, many of them would make it. Sonny and Ty for certain.

I watched proudly as their grades improved. They finished probation early after getting part-time jobs and paying off their restitutions. What really impacted me, was how despite another year of high school to finish, they were both giving college serious thought. We talked about the future often now. Not as before when they hemmed and hawed and avoided my 'what do you want to be' interrogations. Now there was deep thought and questions as to how they could become more, achieve more, and why they should believe they were better than the miscreants society expected them to be.

I pointed to Jasmine and her accomplishments as evidence of what could be obtained with hard work. And working they were. They started dressing better and eating fast food every day. I used to give them money under any pretense I could think of. For example I would tell them I have twenty dollars for whoever knows the first verse to Biggie Smalls' song 'Juicy.'

"It was all a dream!" they'd shout in unison then rap the entire verse, word for word, while reaching for the two tens I placed in front of them. These days when I offered them some pocket cash they declined and said they were 'aight.' They even treated me and Jasmine to a dinner at Red Lobster where they presented us with gifts; a leather briefcase for Jasmine and a pair of monogrammed cufflinks for me. It was their way of saying thanks for us making a difference in their lives.

I can't tell you how elated I was. My life of luxury had been handed to me on a silver platter, but now I could relate to the hard luck stories my father told. I had been to the other side, survived and left my mark on two boys destined to be great men. Those were my thoughts, but Biggie Smalls said, *It was all a dream*, it was about to become a nightmare.

It was the summer after I graduated with a BA in Business. I had taken the LSAT's the year before and scored in the 95th percentile. I was two months away from starting Law School. Harvard of course. Jasmine and I were deep in love with each other and couldn't stand to be apart for more than a few days. Her birthday was coming and I planned on giving her a 5 ½ carat, yellow-diamond engagement ring and asking her to be my wife.

I was interning at my father's firm. I worked hard to avoid the appearance of nepotism. I did the mailroom, document production and all menial tasks put before me. I didn't mind. I was ready for the real world. I wanted my father to see that and be proud of me. And I can honestly say that he was. My father and I discovered a respect for each other that not only drew us closer but helped us become friends instead of just father and son. We were sitting in his office smoking Maduro cigars and debating which sorority had the finest sisters, when we were interrupted by my father's secretary, Mrs. Davis. The nervousness in her voice was evident even through the intercom.

"Uh, Mr. Hudson, there's a Special-Agent Webber here. He says he's looking for Dominic."

My father and I strode into the lobby and met Agent Webber along with three Federal marshals with a warrant for my arrest. We thought it was a practical joke and as one of the marshals read my rights, my father and I laughed and nudged each other. "They're good," my father whispered.

It wasn't a joke. I was being arrested. The charge was conspiracy to possess and distribute in excess of 500 grams of crack cocaine. It had to be a mistake. I had never even smoked a joint and streaking across campus as a Kappa pledge was the closest thing to a crime I had ever committed. My father read the warrant and could barely contain his outrage.

"You've got to be kidding me," he scoffed. "How dare you come into this firm with these trumped-up, frivolous charges? My son is not a drug dealer!"

I stared at the warrant, dumbfounded. The words swam across the page and my eyes burned as I read them. Eventually, the words paused long enough to tell a story my heart could not take. Sonny and Tysean had been pulled over by state troopers while driving on the New Jersey Turnpike. A subsequent search of the vehicle turned up a half a kilogram of crack in the trunk. The car was a Nissan Altima, leased in my name and charged to my American Express card.

I had rented a car for them a few months before, so that they could attend their Junior Prom in style. It was my gift to them for doing so well in school. Then after they started working; at least I *thought* they were working, I would use my credit card to rent them a car every other weekend. They would pay for the car and any extra mileage with their own money, my credit card was used as a security deposit, which I always got back. I thought I was doing them a favor; helping them to escape their dismal, depressing neighborhoods. I thought I could trust them.

But no, these two ingrates were cruising to New York City to meet their supplier and then selling drugs in D.C., Maryland, and

Virginia. One of their out-of-state rivals wanted them out of the way and tipped the police off about their trip. The car was in my name, so I was added to the conspiracy and since Sonny and Ty were underage and were overheard referring to me as Big D, I was tagged as the leader. Unbelievable.

I was escorted out of the building with my suit jacket draped over my cuffed hands. My father walked beside me, barking orders to his staff and ordering the onlookers to return to work. "Don't worry, son," he encouraged as he punched the numbers on his cell phone. "Kurt? Yes, this is Allen, I have a situation and I need you to meet me at the Federal Building right now. Thanks, I'll see you there." My father hung up and smiled at me with the assurance of the cat that ate the canary.

Mr. Kurt Beasly, Esquire was my father's friend. He was also one of the best criminal defense lawyers money could buy. After being photographed and finger-printed I was ushered into a small courtroom where Mr. Beasly and my father stood at one table while Agent Webber, accompanied by Anthony Persico— a stocky Italian who was U.S. Attorney for the Western District of Pennsylvania— stood at the other.

"Remove those handcuffs from my client," Mr. Beasly ordered then shook my hand after the marshal removed the iron bracelets from my wrists. "Don't say anything," he whispered as he guided me to the defendant's table. He didn't have to worry about that. I couldn't think straight, let alone say anything. I was weak-kneed and disoriented. I didn't know if I should punch a wall or lie down and have a tantrum.

Everything went quickly. I barely remember rising for the Judge's entrance; the reading of those ridiculous charges or Mr. Beasly and Mr. Persico arguing over how high my bail should be.

Two hours later, I was released on a fifty-thousand dollar cash bond. I emerged from the courthouse with a brand new appreciation for sky, fresh air, and sunshine. My father and Mr. Beasly shook hands and laughed at how they were going to sue the government. Their audacious talk reassured me and reminded me who I was. I sat in the passenger seat of my father's Jag headed for home. Mark Morrison was on the radio singing, "It's the Return of the Mack." I nodded my head to the music, confident everything would be all right.

But everything wasn't all right and after each court hearing things got worse. I was sick and tired of being scheduled to appear on such and such date at so and so time and waiting hours, only to be told a continuance was ordered and I'd receive notice of the new date. The notices were traumatic in and of themselves. I felt my heartbeat catch each time I received a letter that read: *The United States of America vs. Dominic E. Hudson.* My God! It was the whole damn country against me. How could I not be scared? The U. S. government was coming after me with both guns blazing.

They labeled me the worst kind of drug-dealer. One without any motive except the thrill of corrupting two innocent young men who never had the advantages I had. Ah, come on. Innocent my behind. Sonny and Ty were professional drug-lords in training and had played me like a piano. To top things off, they were sitting in the county jail not saying anything to clear my name. Mr. Beasly advised me they were more than likely keeping quiet to protect themselves. Of course they were, but how was that fair to me. My life was at an upside-down stand-still and I hadn't done anything wrong.

After about six months had passed, U.S. Attorney Persico offered me a plea bargain that promised a sixty-month sentence if I admitted guilt, accepted responsibility for my crime and agreed to cooperate with the government in future investigations. We all got a good laugh at that. Five years and be a rat. It was funny alright, but deep down I was panicking. These people offered me five years and made it sound like they were doing me a favor. Hell, I was waiting for a dismissal of all charges and a public apology or a note that said, "Oops, our bad!"

Three months later, the deal was down to 36 months. Mr. Beasly was hammering them with the lack of any physical evidence found following a vigorous search of my townhouse, my car, as well as my parent's house. He stressed my clean record and my educational pursuits. He wanted the case thrown out and assured me it was only a matter of time before that would happen. So, imagine my surprise when Jasmine suggested I take the deal.

"Are you crazy? Have you lost your mind?" I asked her as we stood on the balcony of my townhouse. "Why would I do that?"

She didn't answer me right away. She leaned against the doorway with her arms crossed, staring off into space. It was early evening and the smell of rain was in the air.

"Did you know the Feds have a 98 percent conviction rate?" She still wouldn't look at me. "If you're a nonviolent offender you can get good time and early release to a halfway house." She took a quick breath and gave me a heavy lidded glance. "You can still pursue your professional studies. It'll just be after a brief hiatus."

"A brief hiatus? A halfway house for non-violent offenders? I'm not an offender. I didn't do anything, Jasmine!" I screamed at her.

"I know!" she screamed back at me. "I know, Dominic, but this is serious. We're dealing with the Feds and they don't lose!" She wiped her eyes and I noticed for the first time that she was trying not to cry. "It doesn't matter how much money you have or who your father or grandfather is. They don't care about none of that. If they want you they will get you."

I was speechless. Jasmine was still in school, still working; her life was on track. Sure, she was spending every holiday and breaks with me and drove five hours to be at my 20-minute hearings, but she was acting real strange and I would not stand for it.

"The reason the Feds don't lose is because most of the time they're dealing with individuals who are guilty." I shook my head and curled my top lip with disdain. "You know? Like those two crack-peddlers you put me with."

"I ... I said I'm sorry Dominic," the tears fell too quickly for her to wipe away. "I didn't know, baby. Please, don't make me feel like it's my fault."

"But it is your fault, Jas. 'Give back, Dominic.' 'Share what you have learned.' 'They're good kids; they just need someone like you to bring out the best in them?' Oh, and remember this one, 'they've been dealt a bad hand from the same deck I had to play from, please, do it for me, Dominic.' Those were your words, Jasmine—"

"I know, but—"

"And you have the gall to stand here and suggest I plead guilty to something I didn't do. My God, Jas. Is this your way of easing me out of your life? Cause if you don't want to be with—"

"That's not true," she cried harder. "I love you, Dominic. Please don't say that."

"Why not? What am I supposed to think? How could you even ask me to do that?"

"Because I'm pregnant!" She sank into the deck chair and buried her face in her hands. "I'm having your child, Dominic and I'd rather know you'd be home by the time our baby turned three than risk losing you for ten years of his life."

What? Wow! Pregnant! With my baby. I was going to be a father. I sat down beside her; overcome. My feelings were a mix of joy and uncertainty. "Are you all right?" I asked as I placed my hand on her still flat stomach.

"Yes, I'm fine," she put her hand on mine.

"Can you make the baby kick?" I asked seriously.

She laughed. "No, crazy. I'm only six weeks. The baby probably doesn't have feet yet." We were silent for a moment or two, and then she asked, "Are you mad at me?"

"Of course not. I'm relieved. At least now I know why you've been acting so strange. I've heard about how those pregnancy hormones can make a woman go cuckoo."

"Shut up!" She punched my arm. "I'm just scared, baby. I can't do this alone. I lived that life and it wasn't fun. I want better for our child."

"I know, Jas. I promise you everything is going to be okay. But you have to understand, you being pregnant is even more reason for me to fight. It doesn't matter if it's three years or ten years, I won't miss one day of our baby's life. I have to fight. Not just for me, but for us. All three of us, Jasmine." I caressed her face and slowly kissed away her tears. "I can't do it by myself either. I need you, Boo. Are you with me?"

She gazed into my eyes, as tough as she was; I knew she had been praying I'd be willing and ready to do whatever it took to stay free. She wrapped her arms around my neck and hugged me tight.

"Of course I'm with you. Always." We spent the night making love and picking out baby-names: Dominic Allen Hudson or Dominique Kimberly Hudson.

I was ecstatic about being a father. A powerful surge of pride flowed through me and I was determined to be a great father just like my dad. I prayed for a boy so I could teach him the things my dad taught me; like how to tie my shoe, ride a bike, and how to look a word up in the dictionary; all little things I took for granted. I also looked forward to watching Jasmine become a mother and sharing the whole parenting experience with her. She was excellent with children and I loved the way her face lit up whenever she was around kids. I could just imagine her with our son, teaching him about Malcolm X and reading him poems by Paul Laurence Dunbar.

There would be some rough spots, especially since Jasmine and I weren't married; at least, not yet. I had postponed my proposal until after my acquittal. In the meantime we enjoyed a wonderful support system. My parents loved Jasmine and treated her like family. They were excited about becoming grandparents and willing to help in any way they could. I was afraid they would be disappointed in me, but as usual, they surprised me with their tenderness, understanding and graciousness. My father explained I, too, was born before he finished Law School and that my birth ignited his ambition and provided a sense of urgency in handling his business.

My mother, in a rare display of impropriety, related to Jasmine the infamous tale of her twelve-hour labor with me and warned her to be prepared to ask for lots of medication. "Look at Dominic's head," she spoke in a dramatic undertone. "Look at it, Jasmine. I'm quite sure it was that same size when he was born." Jasmine gasped and almost spilled her tea. My mother patted her knee and smiled good-naturedly.

We were going to be fine, I was sure of it. We owned a blue-print for success passed down from my parents. Marriage, school, work and happiness. It was simple, but first I had this frivolous case to beat.

On the day of my trial, Mr. Beasly walked in with a concerned frown on his ordinarily smug face. "Daniels and Reeves are in a holding cell waiting to testify," he groaned as he sat next to me.

He was referring to Sonny and Tysean, but I couldn't understand his distress. I considered their presence a good thing since they would clear everything up by telling the truth. But that wasn't going to happen. Sadly, the truth would be held hostage. Tied with thick ropes, braided by the 30-year-threats to Sonny and Ty if they didn't say exactly what the government expected them to say.

I almost threw up when Tysean took the stand, poised with confidence and lied through his teeth.

"Yes, Mr. Hudson rented the car for us … Yes, he knew where we were going … Yes, Mr. Hudson gave us money. He taught us about stocks and how to invest our money. You know, so we could make it clean … Yes, Mr. Hudson is a drug dealer."

Then Sonny took the stand in his loose-fitting county jumpsuit. He tried to stay true to the script, but faltered during the cross-examination. Beasly drilled him with yes-or-no questions challenging his testimony by contrasting it to the statement he made following his arrest. Sonny wasn't a good liar. He was getting flustered, but I refused to feel sorry for him. If we were allowed to beat the truth out of him I would have gladly swung the first blow.

He swallowed hard when Beasly asked him if he had ever seen me with drugs in my possession. He ignored Beasly's query and instead looked at me.

"Why didn't you just take the deal, Big D?" He frowned and blinked back tears. "I can't do no 30 years," he mumbled into his chest.

"What's that? Please, speak up Mr. Daniels!" my lawyer demanded.

"I said I can't do 30 years."

"Ah, so you admit you're lying under oath in order to avoid a lengthy sentence. Isn't that true, Mr. Daniels?

Sonny kept his eyes trained on me, but said nothing.

"That's right, Mr. Daniels. Look at him. Look at the man who tutored you in Algebra and helped you study for your final exams. Look at the man who took you to theatres and museums. Yes, look at him. Look at the man who donated computers to your youth center and who attended your little brother's PTA meeting when your mother was ill. Look at him! This man who fed you, not only food, but knowledge. This man, who referred to you and Mr. Reeves as his little brothers. Look at him and tell us, Mr. Daniels, is this good man really a drug dealer?"

Sonny closed his eyes and said nothing. The courtroom was a still photograph. Beasly approached the stand and spoke softly, his voice, reassuring; a father promising no punishment in exchange for a truthful answer.

"Tell us, Mr. Daniels. Is this man, who loved you like a brother, a drug-dealer?" Sonny looked away and Mr. Beasly raised his voice. "Answer the question, Sonny. Is Dominic Hudson a drug-dealer?"

Sonny sat up straight and jutted out his chin. "Yes, he is and ... I'm just saying, no one is worth protecting that much. Not for 30 years. No, I can't do that."

The wind was knocked out of me. I had to force myself to unball my hands. I watched Sonny get down and as he walked away I remembered something he had said to me over a year ago. The words turned in my head over and over like set-dice: *'I'm gonna do what I have to do to take care of family.'* Now I understood.

The twelve strangers who were designated as the 'jury of my peers' took exactly 2 hours and 13 minutes to come back with a verdict; guilty.

The air in the courtroom went thin. My ears clogged like I was in a free-fall. The sound became muffled then swirled as if a large seashell was held to my ear. I couldn't hear nor see the commotion that exploded in the courtroom, but in an eerie, psychosomatic sense, I felt everything.

I could feel my mother and Jasmine hugging each other and crying, their mascara running, turning their tears into tiny black rivers staining their broken faces. I could feel my father, his face pinched in anger and confusion, speaking loudly with Mr. Beasly about an appeal. I could feel Sonny and Tysean being led out a side door, Sonny fighting hard not to cry and Tysean, maintaining his shackled-swagger, telling him not to worry because "Homey has enough money to stay out of jail and fight for years."

My ears popped as the judge told me to surrender my passport, ordered a Pre-sentence Investigation and scheduled my sentencing for the following month.

My father and grandfather tried in vain to call in some favors. Nothing could be done to influence a federal sentencing hearing. They garnered sketchy promises of low-level security at a facility close to home, but my appeal bond was denied and all efforts to postpone my sentencing were shot down.

My father held on to my shoulders. The pain in his voice flooded the basement of my heart and hurt me more than any prison sentence ever could. He told me he was sorry for letting me down.

"You'll have to go to prison, son, but I promise you not a day will pass without me fighting tooth and nail to get you out. I … I promise you, Dominic. I swear to you, I …" he walked away so I wouldn't see him cry.

My sentencing hearing lasted three and a half hours. It was standing room only and included character testimony from my parents, Jasmine, Coach Coles, two of my professors and a U.S. Senator, who was a good friend of my grandfather's and unbeknown to me, knew me since I was 'knee-high to a grasshopper.'

There were a lot of flowery words and exaggerated descriptions of my great standing in the community, all of which reminded me of a funeral filled with phony eulogies. When all had been said, the judge banged his gavel and without ceremony or fanfare said his hands were tied by sentencing guidelines our guest Senator should be familiar with.

"Dominic Hudson," the judge pronounced my name like one of my professors calling roll. I almost answered, 'present.' "You have been found guilty of conspiracy of possession with the intent to distribute 500 grams of cocaine base or crack. Frankly, that kind of weight outweighs the fact you're a first-time-offender. Excuse the pun. Your leadership role and failure to cooperate with the United States government places you at an offense level 36. Your failure to accept responsibility for your actions keeps you there." The judge took a breath and stared at me as if trying to read my mind. He looked up at the vaulted ceiling then back at me. "I hereby sentence you to one hundred and forty-four months in a Federal Correctional Institution, and believe me, I'm being generous."

Twelve years. Twelve years for helping some hoodlums rent a car. I cast a final glance at my family and friends. Most of them shook their heads in disbelief and couldn't bear to meet my eyes. My parents and Jasmine sobbed, wailed, rocked and moaned as if watching my casket being lowered into the ground.

Two federal marshals appeared at my side like genies and ordered me to place my hands behind my back. I wanted to fight them, bang their heads together and throw them to the floor. I wanted to run, grab Jasmine by the hand and make a mad dash to the streets where they would send helicopters and dogs after us. I wanted to scream. I did nothing. As the cold steel clicked around my wrists, pinching some of my skin in the process, I simply winced, hung my head and walked between my escorts through the ominous side door.

I spent three weeks in the county jail and two weeks in transit before reaching my designated institution in southern Pennsylvania. I was less than two hours from home and a little over three hours away from Jasmine. It took another two weeks to get my visiting list approved and Jasmine came to visit me that very weekend.

We sat side by side like statues in the overly-air-conditioned visiting room. I was happy to see her, especially after the two months I had just spent with hundreds of loud, belligerent, foul-smelling men. Neither one of us knew what to say. We sat and observed the other visitors like students studying for a psychology final. I watched one inmate play with his three-year-old son, picking him up and holding him out so he could pretend like he was flying. "Again, Daddy!" the little boy cried each time the man tried to put him down. The whole scene tugged at my heart, but I couldn't muster even half a smile.

"My parents will help you with the baby," I assured her as we stared straight ahead. "My trust fund is open to you and the baby and you won't want for anything. I promised you and I can keep that promise. I don't expect you to wait for me. I mean, even though I'll more than likely be released once my appeal is heard, that might take a few years and well, you don't have to wait. Please, all I ask is that you let me be a part of our child's life."

I went on like that for 20 minutes or so until I finally looked over at Jasmine and noticed she was crying. Not just tears, but breath-catching sobs that can't hide the sorrow that lies beneath. I reached for her hand, not sure if it was against the rules to do so. She squeezed my hand painfully.

"What's wrong, baby?" I asked. "Stop crying, please. I'm not mad at you. I don't blame you; please tell me what's wrong."

It took her a few minutes to stop shaking and even after I wiped her eyes, she refused to look at me. She stared at our hands and rubbed her thumb over the small impressions her nails had made on my skin. Then she spoke the four words that pushed me over the edge and into the abyss of hopelessness.

"I lost the baby."

She had a miscarriage a week after my sentencing. The stress was too much for her 115 pound body to handle. That was her story. Honestly, I didn't know what to think. Again, we sat. We may have spoken two or three more words for the remainder of the visit. When visiting hours ended we stood up. She gave me a long, forceful, and poignant hug. The embrace emptied her suffering into my soul. She walked out slowly, fighting hard not to look back. She didn't. Five years would pass before I'd see her again ...

I warned you. My story is ugly. And that's only the beginning. The reason I'm about to die in a few hours is truly beyond belief. Yes, there's more and it gets better as it gets worse. See, my story is also a love story. Not a typical love story; I mean, how many men fall in love while in prison? It's a love story none the less. I have some time. I should probably finish what I started, but I'll need a little help to tell it, that way, when all is said and done I'll know for sure you … don't blame me.

--To be continued--

My Forever

So afraid of love, an unconscious fear to feel, an overwhelming
passion, a heart still trying to heal.
A desperate dream to save everyone I loved,
I lost sight of the Angel who loved me.
Blinded by disbelief, suffering from acute amnesia, unable to
recognize my own rib,
I walked away from Forever ...

A real life nightmare, my soul lost and lonely
Lashing out until I finally fell, a prisoner, a cell.
Caged in physically—emotionally locked down as well.
A sincere prayer, a promise to God, A desperate wish for a tiny sign.
A loud and crowded room, the perfect time,
A visit from a Queen with tears in her eyes.
A divine plan, a path ordained, two hearts, two souls—their genesis
the same, their destiny regained,
I fell in love with Forever ... again ...

A candle-lit suite with a rose petal path, love music low, a romantic bath.
Beautiful bare bodies touching timidly at first,
Longing ... desire ... hunger ... thirst.
Tasting and teasing, slow riding waves of ecstasy, hot, sweaty,
thrusting deep, making love relentlessly.
Breath taking climax, perfect connection remembered, our past ...
our present ... our future surrendered.
On both knees, gazing into the bright eyes of paradise, a radiant
diamond reflecting brilliant rays of light.
My entire essence anxious, but at peace, everything is blessed,
I proposed to Forever ... and Forever said ... Yes!

Acknowledgments

First and foremost, Father God. I thank you so much for loving me, protecting me, guiding me, and using me. You saved me and you continue to bless me abundantly. My faith in you is unshakable, for I know the plans you have for me. I promise to edify and glorify you with this gift you have given me. I pray that I make you proud. Amen!

When I was in the 3rd grade I won second place in a Dr. Martin Luther King Jr. Poetry and Essay Contest. I didn't realize I was a writer. At the age of 12, I started rapping (one love to Ace/Duce). I used a creative story-telling style or rhymed witty metaphors while battling other M.C.s, who were 4 and 5 years older than me. I won most of those battles. I didn't know I was a writer. I wrote and directed a play when I was 18. I performed original poetry at local readings when I was 20, and at the age of 22 ran an independent record label (one love to DownLow Ent.), where I wrote raps and R&B songs for different artists, still, I had no idea I was a writer.

I would like to acknowledge and thank the following people for not only knowing and believing that I am a great writer, but for convincing me of the same.

My mother, Doreen Queen. I watched you laugh, cry, and curse as you read so many books (I won't tell anyone that they were mostly Harlequin romances). I remember being amazed at how words could stir up so many different emotions. You blessed me (and cursed me) with your sensitivity and you inspired me to want to create those words (emotions). Thank you, Mommy!

Aunt Gert. You have been a second mother (sometimes first) to me and many others. You have taught me a lot and I promise you your labor was not in vain. Thank you for being there for me every single time I needed you.

Aunt Bone (Donna Queen). Your love courage, and resilience along with your afro-centric advice have always made me proud of the Queen name. Your spirit shines bright. Thank you!

Aunt Marva. You have also been there for me throughout my life and you'll never know how many dark days you helped me get through with your old-school photos, crazy cards, and stick-figure drawings. I am so grateful for you. Thank you!

My children: Traymayne, thank you for opening up and being honest with me, your sacrifices are my motivation. Jonathan, thank you for still looking up to me, your respect is my strength. Jonee, thank you for reminding me of how far I still have to go, your dreams are my determination. Jazmine, thank you for staying Daddy's girl, your love is my confidence. Frankie, thank you for becoming a good man in spite of my absence, your accomplishment is my pride. Cheyenne, thank you for letting me into your life with open arms, your love is my music. Mekhi, thank you for sharing your world with me, your love is my joy. I love you all and while many parents try to live out their dreams through their children, I only want to help make all of your dreams come true.

Lenia Queen, Victoria Jenkins and Denitta King-Williams. Thank you for doing such a wonderful job with our children.

My brothers, Jahsun (J.J.), Caron, James, and Jeron. Each of you in your own way have inspired me and made me proud. As the oldest brother I set a negative example for many years. I only pray that you notice the example I set now.

My sister Damali. No matter what, I have always felt and known how much you believe in me. That alone means the world to me.

My baby brother Jaalil and my baby sister Janelle. I've been gone for over 80% of your lives, but I assure you we will make the most of everyday we are blessed to share.

My cousin, Shawn Queen. You are a true soulja indeed. You brag so much about what you learned from me, yet you fail to recognize all that I have learned from you. You held me down like a brother and I could never thank you with words. Just know in your soul I got you.

I have a very large family, most of whom have followed, supported and encouraged me in my endeavors. I would love to name all of you because in some way you all have contributed to the man I am, and trying to become, but time and space does not permit. So a big thank you to the following families: Queen, Bates, Wheatherly, Anthony, Cooksey, Mason, Johnson, Howling, Roberts and Whitehead.

Also, my gratitude is extended to Mr. Doug Smallwood and Mrs. Yvette Smallwood and the entire Smallwood family. Thank you for not judging me by my past and welcoming me into the fam.

I must also thank a few people for being in my corner throughout my incarceration and holding true to the Word which states: Remember the prisoners as if chained with them (Heb.13:3). Ms. Brenda (Mom), Jubair, Kirk T., Tracy (3X), Mitch, and Shawna F.

And for the convicts. I've been incarcerated for over nine years. I've done time in 3 county jails, 2 state prisons, and 5 Federal Institutions. I've met some strong, talented, and intelligent brothers, who have inspired and encouraged me to build and become better. I pray that I have done the same for you.

Big Pooh Hudson, Suny Barmore, A. Knowledge Ransom, Gee Jivens, Dre Butler, J. Lee, Jamal A, 'Slug' Singleton, 'Son-Son' Robinson, Marc Lawrence, R. 'Big' Chambers, Robert 'Boom' Manning, T. Traynham, D. Thompson, R. Blackwell, Murphy, 'Moe' Burton-El, Rich, Abdullah, Kev Rutledge, Carlo Malone, Brothers –B, Jesse, Joe-Joe, Brad, Luke V., Elisha, Trini, Wade, Preacher, J. Logan, Dre Rice, Q, Nino, Big B, Giant, Rell, Culp, Juice, Katt, Black, Yaziz, Twin, Motif, Uti, Joey, Frizz, Bones, Keith, Franks, Jose C., Keith, Al, Big Bamma, Tino, S. Carter, F. Carter, D., Mike, Earl, J. Rusnak, D. Burry, Nutt Jones, Hawk, Vic, Big Shorty, Kumah, Six-Nine, Shaw, K., Bill, Mack, Dunn-El, Dirty, H.Scott, X.Scott, O, Cee, Esco Atkins, BK, BX, J-Rod, John X, Reg, Trae, Corey A., Shawn O, Daliyl, R. Carew, Chi-Town, Detroit, Jamaica, Dread Jay, VA, LA, Tex, Joker, Fats, Man. Special Thanks to Tisdale, Fab, Bill & The Old Mill, J. Feaster, L. Abrams, Nigel, J. Cooper, M. Ross, Class 105 & the RDAP Community, (my typers) Keith H., Earl, Aki, R. Ward, (my editors)J. O'Donnell, T. Coles, S. Kaiser (you're input was priceless) C. 'Universe' Culp, Naji, and all the other incarcerated authors (keep pushing that pencil) And to those I may have forgotten, please charge it to my mind

(I'm a little burnt out!) and not to my heart. Hold your head Souljas. We're doing life until God grants parole.

And my Baby, Lenia. My wife, my rib, my Queen! You believe in me more than I believe in myself and although you've convinced me that I am a great writer, I still fail to find words to describe how my love for you expands infinitely like the universe itself. I want to create a new language with words you have to chase down meanings to, so you can feel what I feel when my heart and soul have a conversation about you, and although I have no idea what they're saying I know it's beautiful. Thank you for supporting our dream. I love you, Forever and this is only the beginning. "Not an Option"

JZQ 11/05

In loving Memory of:
Dorothy L. Queen (Gramps)
Jonathan J. Johnson (Dad)
I know you got me.

Where the Word is mightier than the pen and the sword

PRESENTS

Diesel Therapy

(The Convict Chronicles Volume II)

Edited By: Jonathan Z Queen

Coming Fall 2008

ASKARI Publishing

Where the Word is mightier than the pen and the sword

PRESENTS

Are You S.A.N.E.

(SETTING A NEW EXAMPLE)

Changing Who You Are

By

Changing How You Think

BY: JONATHAN Z. QUEEN

Coming Fall 2008